CELESTE

NORMA ERICKSON NELSON

Norma Erickson Nelson

Bloomington, IN   authorHOUSE™   Milton Keynes, UK

AuthorHouse™
1663 Liberty Drive, Suite 200
Bloomington, IN 47403
www.authorhouse.com
Phone: 1-800-839-8640

AuthorHouse™ UK Ltd.
500 Avebury Boulevard
Central Milton Keynes, MK9 2BE
www.authorhouse.co.uk
Phone: 08001974150

First published by AuthorHouse 5/5/2006

ISBN: 1-4259-0893-4 (sc)

Library of Congress Control Number: 2005910883

Printed in the United States of America
Bloomington, Indiana

This book is printed on acid-free paper.

Dedicated to my husband,
Joe Nelson, my best friend and fan!

ACKNOWLEDGEMENT

A special thanks to those who were such an encouragement and to my readers who kept asking for the next chapter until "The End." Also a special thanks to those who were so sure the story would be published and requested a copy.

Beverly Brophy, Luelen Brown, Ruth and Dale Carpenter, Betty and Goldman Cothren, Heather Gluba , Irene Harrison, Judy Jones ,Kathy Mickleson, Dee Palrang, Dorothy Erickson Smith, Marilyn Teague, Ralph and Ruth Wheeler

Sisters.....Marian Darlington, Pat Walker

Brother......Bob Erickson

Aunts........Esther Johnson, Pearl Lovel, Evelyn Penoyer, Dot Phillips

My dear friend.....Ann Hogan

I cannot mention or remember all of you, so thanks to those I did not mention.

A special thanks to my niece Kim Brandt, my own special editor!

And thanks to my new friend, Sharon Jensen, who read the final story for me.

FORWARD

The story of Celeste takes place in the mid eighteen hundreds. Covered wagons, pulled by horses or oxen were used for long journeys. Despite the many hardships, the settlers loved the freedom the new land offered. The Lorells were one of the families who lived, loved and struggled to survive through a desperate and seemingly hopeless tragedy.

LIST OF CHARACTERS

1. Jonathon and Dolores Morgan ... Parents of Louise Morgan Lorell
2. Louise Morgan Lorell .... Wife of Aaron Lorell, Mother of Michael and Celeste.
3. Eliza .... Louise's Nanny from England
4. Aaron Lorell .... Husband to Louise and father of Michael and Celeste.
5. Michael Lorell .... Son of Aaron and Louise
6. Celeste Lorell .... Daughter of Aaron and Louise
7. Sydney .... Louise's best friend from childhood
8. Dan and Sarah Rivers .... Husband and Wife, Hired hand of Aaron and Louise
9. Frank and Ann Dubois .... Husband and wife. Louise's neighbors at one time.
10. Red Feather .... Apache Indian
11. Cochay .... Red Feather's squaw
12. Sharon Thompson .... Friend of Louise in Shreve Town
13. Richard Jenner .... Lawyer and Politician
14. Bob and Linda Edwards .... Brother and sister. Owners of Mitzi.

CHAPTER ONE

Louise 1851

Louise Lorell pulled angrily at the stubborn weeds in her garden. Her long auburn hair had curled into ringlets from perspiration and bounced in spirals as she moved about. Lovely green eyes reflected the exhaustion she felt. It was out of character for Louise to be angry and she mulled this over in her mind. Memories of the past pulsed painfully through her heart. She tried to brush the pain aside as she usually did; but this time the scalding tears assaulted her eyes, washing a lone teardrop over her lower lid. Now the pain persisted. She was inundated with the memories she had tried so hard to forget, and now the tears came in a steady stream. Her heart and chest felt unbearably heavy. She lifted her apron to her face and for the first time since her husband's death, allowed the tears to fall. She cried until there were no more tears and was surprised when she realized the heaviness and acute pain had subsided as the last of her tears fell. She rose to her feet, aware that her bereaved heart had been liberated. It was like rain after a drought.

Louise left the garden and hurried to the pump. She pulled the handle up and down until the cold water was gushing out and quickly splashed it over her face. She sat down on the bench swing and rocked gently back and forth. Thoughts and memories of the past filled her brain. At last, she could relive the past and revel in the wonderful love she and her husband Aaron had shared.

Louise had no way of knowing she had regained her strength just in time for a misadventure that would change everything about her life and touch every person that played a part in the intrigue. If she had known, her heart would have been filled with terror.

Reminiscing

It had never been easy for Louise to express her feelings; especially to those she loved the most. She recalled the first time Aaron held her in his arms and proclaimed his love for her. Her heart demanded a release as it overflowed with love. "I love you so much that my heart aches." Words, perhaps easy for some people to say, not grandiose; but they came from the depths of her heart. Even so, she knew his love surpassed hers. Often, he had looked at her with soft wonder in his eyes and a look of love caressing his face. Once he had said, "You never ask for anything Louise, tell me something I can do to make you happier." She had laughed and said, "I have everything I want. We were quite poor when we lived in England and had all we could want in America. Poor or with plenty, I was happy. Now, I am happy just to be with you." Life had been like that until she lost him. She allowed her mind to wander into places she had not been for a long time.

England, Louise's Heritage

Louise had not always lived in America. She was born in England as were all of her forefathers. Her grandfather Charles was a mineworker. The work was hard, dangerous and the income from this type of labor put them in a lower class. Charles did not want his son Jonathon to work in the mines, so he asked his best friend and Cousin LeRoy, to give Jonathon a job in his factory. LeRoy was a duke, rich and influential. In no time Jonathon was an apprentice and learning to upholster carriage seats. This was considered skilled labor and quite respectable. Jonathon did not enjoy upholstering but was thrilled he was not a miner and could now afford a better lifestyle.

Leroy's son Travis was one of Jonathon's best friends. Travis introduced Jonathan to Dolores Sinclair. Unlike Jonathan, she came from an upper class family. Dolores was a very vain person and was enamored by Jonathan's good looks. She thought he was the most handsome man she had ever met and loved to be seen with the handsome Jonathon. Dolores had always taken it for granted that she would marry a rich man with a title. She would have never let Jonathon call on her that first time, if she had thought there was even a remote chance that she would fall in love with him.

Jonathon was young and impressed by lovely Dolores's attention. He was a very intelligent man of great character but he was not a blue blood and certainly not rich. Titles were not given to a man because he was noble and upright. Jonathan realized Dolores was vain, but he was a man who needed someone in his life to love and protect. She would always fill that need and in his heart he knew that Dolores would be faithful, as well as a compliment to his lifestyle.

When Jonathon asked Dolores to be his wife, he explained to her that he planned to eventually leave England and settle in America. Dolores agreed, thinking she would deal with that later.

Jonathon and Dolores had a very beautiful wedding. If Dolores had any qualms about marrying a man without a title, she hid it on their wedding day and ever after. After the wedding, Dolores's father handed Jonathon a set of keys, He explained, "We do not use our summer home anymore, so it is yours until you leave for America."

The lovely Dolores soon began her plan of talking Jonathon out of going to America, but when she heard of so many becoming rich there, she decided it might be a good idea.

They were only married a short time when Dolores became pregnant. Instead of feeling happy, she was very disappointed. Dolores did not want the responsibility of motherhood. Nothing about the pregnancy pleased her. She couldn't bring herself to tell Jonathon how she felt. She did share her feelings with her mother. So when Louise was born on January 02, 1822 on a cold wintry night, Dolores's mother had already hired a nanny for her. She promised the woman her wages as long as she took good care of her new granddaughter Louise. At first Jonathon was angry that a nanny had been hired without his consent but it did not take him long to realize that Dolores did not enjoy caring for the baby and actually found little joy in being a mother. Jonathon apologized to his mother-in-law, but insisted he would pay Nanny Eliza's wages, even though it was difficult to manage.

Several years passed before Dolores could bring herself to leave England and set sail for America. Nanny Eliza asked to go with them. She explained, "I have taken care of Louise since she was born. I love all of you and I want to see Louise grow up. You are my only family. I will pay my fare."

Jonathon assured her, "You will do nothing of the kind. There would be no happiness in this adventure if we did not have our Eliza with us."

Louise was nine years old and ready to start fourth grade when they boarded the ship for America. The grandparents shed tears and promised they would come to see them when they were settled.

At the last moment, Dolores's mother handed her an envelope and hugged her one more time. When Dolores opened the envelope, she found an abundance of money, enough to help them buy a great deal of land and perhaps have some left over.

CHAPTER TWO

America-March 1831

Dolores was thrilled to arrive in America, mostly because she was off the rocking ship, on dry land again and rid of the forced confinement. Jonathon was thrilled for a different reason. He could not wait to explore and start a new life in this country of freedom. It was not long before he found a plantation for sale. It was in Louisiana, near a town named Natchitoches. A wealthy man and his wife wanted to return to their beloved England so much that they were almost ready to give their land away. Dolores was impressed with the lovely home and Jonathan was impressed with the price as well as the land.

Jonathan asked the man what he intended to do with his colored servants. "The man answered, "I feel like you are a man of character and would treat the slaves well, if you will give me your word that you will deal kindly with them, I will sign them all over to you. We have no family here and our greatest desire is to return to England." Jonathan gave his word, they shook hands and it was settled.

School in America

Louise was anxious to start her new school and was happy when Nanny Eliza informed her, "I think you will be excited to know that you will be starting school tomorrow." Louise turned to her mother, "Are you coming with me to meet the teacher?" Mrs. Morgan was busy writing a note. She laid her pen down and in an annoyed voice answered, "No, I will not be taking you to school. It isn't as if you were starting first grade. Nanny will take you."

Louise was secretly glad because she wanted to go alone. When her mother left the room, she begged her nanny to let her ride her horse to school, as many of the children did. Nanny said, "Your mother told me to accompany you. You wouldn't want your mother to be angry with me, would you?" Louise laughed at the thought and said, "You are the only one I know, other than daddy who can get away with going against her wishes. If I dared to question Mama, I would be in very serious trouble. Besides Nanny, you know I don't like to be treated like a baby. This isn't England. I want some freedom and I want to learn how to do things on my own."

Nanny held her hand up to signal her to stop talking. She said, "Your mother expects me to take you and I shall do what she says." Louise threw her arms around her nanny and begged, "Oh please Nanny, you know Mama will never even think about it again. Daddy told me where the school is and it's not far." Louise watched as Nanny's face softened and she said, "Since it means so much to you, I guess it would be alright for you to ride your horse, but I will follow in the carriage to see for myself that you arrive safely. There will be no talking me out of that." Louise was elated and said, "You are the best nanny in the whole wide world."

Louise was up early the next morning. She had butterflies in her stomach but was determined she could start school without any grownups helping. Nanny promised she would keep the carriage at a distance so no one would realize she was being escorted.

Louise's dad had explained to her that the school had two floors. First through fourth grade was on the first floor and fifth through eighth was on the upper floor. Each teacher taught four grades.

It didn't take Louise long to ride the four miles and she could see the school. It was a rather ugly looking building standing alone in the countryside. It looked as if it had been put up in a hurry. It was square and two storied, painted white with no other color or offsets to give it some style. Several steps in front led to a rather large wooden porch and to the front door.

When Louise was closer, she saw a large grassy area. On one side there were several bare spots. She imagined the bare spots were the bases for baseball games. This brought a smile to her face as she had heard girls played baseball in America. In England a very similar game was called Rounders.. She had always loved to watch when the boys played Rounders and now she hoped she would get to play baseball. Several large trees were around the perimeter of the schoolyard. Horses were tied to hitching posts under a shelter.

The children stopped playing and watched as Louise tied her horse to one of the hitching posts and walked up the steps to the school door. She hoped she would meet someone to direct her. She stepped inside and was met only by a deserted hallway. She tried another door and found herself staring into a broom closet. Before she could close that door, a girl with short dark hair and a cute little pixie face, entered the hallway. She had a smug look on her face as she said, "Do you want the broom or the mop?"

Louise felt her face redden and answered, "Neither, this is my first day and I am trying to find the fourth grade room."

The dark haired girl said, "Well shut the door and try that one." She pointed to a door further down the hall. She warned, "You can go in if you want, but you may be in trouble because the teachers ring the bell when it is time for us to come back

7

to our classroom." She started outside and then turned and said, "My name is Sydney, what's yours?" The girl sounded bored as if she really didn't care if Louise answered or not. Louise considered not answering. She relented and said, "Louise Morgan." Louise watched the girl until she closed the door. She thought to herself, "I hope she isn't in my room."

Louise suddenly felt alone and a little sad. Just then a lady stepped out of the very door that Louise had been shown. Seeing Louise, she asked, "Are you Louise Morgan?" Louise wondered how she knew as she responded, "Yes, I am."

The teacher smiled and said, "Your father stopped to tell us that we would have a new student today."

Louise smiled to herself and thought, "Thank you daddy!"

The teacher continued," My name is Miss Mainey and I will be your teacher." She put her hands on Louise's shoulders and guided her into the room. She showed Louise her seat and left to ring the bell. Louise was only too glad to sit down.

The children were laughing and talking as they came in. When they spotted Louise, the room was suddenly silent and all eyes turned to stare at her. One of the bigger boys in the back of the room stood to his feet and exclaimed, "Well what is her name? All we know is she has big green eyes and red hair." Louise was shocked. Such actions would never have been tolerated in England.

"Well Wayne," said Miss Mainey, "Let's introduce ourselves. Since you are being so vocal, you can start. We will let our new student be last."

The boy responded immediately, "Wayne Carpenter." Each student announced his or her name. Louise wished she could memorize each name with the correct face. She felt a slight twinge of disappointment when she saw that Sydney was in the same row of seats as she was. When it was Sydney's turn, she stood and said, "We've already met." She sat down and then stood to her feet again. "I didn't tell her my last name, it's Mayfield."

Louise disliked Sydney even more. She sounded so matter-of-fact and outspoken.

It was Louise's turn and she tried to sound sure of herself like Sydney. "Louise Morgan," she said quickly and sat down.

The teacher clapped her hands and said, "We are glad to have you Louise and now we will begin our first lesson of the day."

The teacher explained, "Because we have a new student, I will start with her class and then do the first grade." She stopped at Louise's seat and said, "That way you will have an assignment to be working on. Sure enough Sydney was in her class. When the teacher moved on to the first grade, Louise finished her study lesson in a hurry and then listened to the teacher as she taught the other grades.

The time went so fast that Louise was surprised when Miss Mainey informed them that it was recess time. The children hurried outside and some of the girls in her room sat on the steps. When Louise came outside, one of them called, "Sit here!" Louise sat down and it seemed each one had a question and they all talked at the same time. She answered the best she could and then at least three of them were asking, "Will you play with me?" Louise felt confused. She finally blurted out, "Why can't we all play together?" No one responded and now someone from behind her was covering Louise's eyes with her hands. A girl's voice called out, "Guess who?" This irritated Louise as she thought, "How silly, I was hoping I could remember their names and now someone wants me to guess who she is by her voice."

At that moment, Louise did hear a familiar voice. It was Sydney skipping by. She stopped and called out, "You are such a bunch of silly gooses! How do you expect her to remember all of your names? Leave her alone!"

The girl quickly withdrew her hands and looked embarrassed as she said softly, "My name is Ardyce." Louise was glad Sydney had interfered but she felt sorry for Ardyce and said to her, "I'll remember your name next time." Louise had a smile on her face as she turned to call out to Sydney; but only Sydney's back was in view. She was skipping away as if she had already forgotten the incident.

Just before school was over, it started to rain. Louise stood in the doorway with some of the other children and watched for her Nanny to arrive. She did not want to ride her horse home in the rain.

Louise was surprised when Sydney came up to her and said, "Why don't you ride home with me? We go right past your house."

Louise answered, "I rode my horse this morning but since it is raining, my nanny will bring our carriage."

Sydney laughed and said, "Don't you think you could have more fun with me than your nanny?" She grabbed Louise's arm and said, "Come on!" Louise relented and climbed into the Mayfield carriage. When Nanny arrived, she gave Louise permission and the Mayfield carriage sped away.

On the way home, Sydney bombarded her with questions, "When did you come to America? Do you like living here more than in England? Do you have any brothers and sisters? What do you like to do?" Before Louise could answer, she added, "Maybe we will like to do the same things. Maybe we can be the best friends in the whole wide world!"

All of a sudden, Louise wanted Sydney to be her best friend more than anything. Her best friend now and her best friend forever!

Louise revealed all of her dreams and desires to Sydney. She confided that her most favorite thing was to ride her horse, "Horizon," and her biggest dream was to ride in competition. She said she and her dad often raced and her own horse could outrun his. She confessed, "I try all kinds of tricks on my horse when no one is around to watch. I can stand on Horizon and ride her bareback, even when she goes fast."

Sydney was visibly impressed and exclaimed, "I love to ride too, but I never thought of riding in shows or other competitions. What a great idea! I will ask my daddy this very night if he will set up a practice field for us. I know he will. I have never tried trick riding though. Will you help me learn some of the tricks you know?" Louise would have promised to try and help her fly to the moon if she had asked at that moment.

By the time they were ready to say goodbye, they had made plans for Louise to come to the Mayfield's on Saturday and spend the day.

It was the beginning of one of those 'once in a lifetime' friendships. The two of them shared all their dreams together. Neither had any brothers or sisters, nor a really special friend before. Each filled a need neither knew had existed. They practiced riding for hours and entered every competition they could find. Both soon excelled and became known to horse lovers near and far. Both were very well liked and won many ribbons and awards. Best of all they loved competing with each other which of course gave them a plus over other riders. Their fathers never let them miss a meet if they could help it and stood side-by-side as they cheered for both of them.

Sydney's mother, Mrs. Mayfield often came to watch. Louise's mother came once and although she seemed quite proud of Louise, she never came again.

Louise loved and adored her father. She loved her mother but as much as she wanted to adore her, she could not. Through the years she had come to realize that her mother's first concern was for herself. This was heavy on her heart and when Louise was about thirteen, she bared these feeling to her father. She tried to explain, "Mama doesn't treat me the way I see other mothers treat their children. She is always nice to me but she expects Nanny to answer my questions and take care of me. I know Nanny loves me but I want mamma to love me best. She talks to me in the same way she talks to the servants. She doesn't seem to ever care or feel what anyone else wants, except maybe you. The funny part is that everyone tries to please her, including me. We all love it when she praises us for something we did for her, even her snobby friends!"

Jonathon tousled her hair and pulled her on his lap. He hugged her and then tried to explain, "My little Louise, the first thing I want you to understand is that your mother does love you, but for some reason she does not know how to relate to babies or children. I am sure you will be much closer to your mother when you are older. She often confides in me that she is very glad that you have Nanny Eliza to care for you and teach you the things that you need to know. As for people wanting to please her, you must realize she was raised in a wealthy family with rather severe social demands, which is expected when you are of a noble class in England. She is used to being treated with respect and actually takes it for granted. The esteem your mama enjoys comes from centuries of an established and undisputed place of wealth and English class. She expects and accepts it. This makes others want to please and gain her approval. The most important thing for you to realize is that although she is not perfect, she does love you. Does that help you to understand, Louise?"

Louise nodded her head, hugged her daddy and said, "Well I do love Mama, no matter what her faults are and I am glad I have a wonderful daddy and nanny too."

The Invitation

Louise was seventeen when she graduated from high school. She was surprised when her mother said she would like to see her attend college. This pleased Louise and she planned to ask her father what he thought. It was about this time that her mother decided to have another of her many parties. Louise would have to wait to discuss her future at a later date. Louise never dreamed the invitations would change her course in life.

CHAPTER THREE

Aaron Lorell

In 1835, Aaron Lorell turned sixteen. That was the year his family left England and came to America. They settled in Baton Rouge, Louisiana. He and his two older brothers loved the excitement of moving and the challenges awaiting them. Aaron fell in love with Louisiana, the miles of lush greenery, acres of lakes and bayous. His dream was to own some of this beautiful land.

When Aaron was eighteen, he was determined to find his own place in life. His parents soon realized Aaron could not be talked out of leaving, so his father took him aside and said, "Aaron, you have been a wonderful son and have always worked hard. Your mother and I would like you to have this money. We feel you have earned it. More important than that is the fact that we both know your mother will worry less if you have some money to back you up. Take this and may the Lord be with you!"

Aaron's heart was sad as he embraced each of his family in farewell. His heart was heavy as he swung himself into his horse's saddle. When he was almost out of sight, he turned to give his family a final wave. They returned his wave and Aaron prodded his horse to move on. As Aaron traveled, eagerness replaced his melancholy mood. He guided his horse expertly through the heavily wooded area, wondering where his venture would take him.

Traveling north, he searched Louisiana for land that he would be proud to call his own. So many areas were breathtaking. Beautiful magnolias with white blossoms, almost as big as his mother's dinner plates. Vast areas of forest laden with greenery, areas where leaves from creeping vines covered every tree and bush. Dogwoods were abundant and their delicate pink, white or red petals accented the beauty of the trees around them. He never tired of the ancient oaks, spreading their limbs with green majesty; clumps of gray moss hanging from their branches in long streamers. Such pleasure he derived from the eerie appearance of the cypress trees, looking naked, as if they had somehow forgotten to cover themselves with bark.

Aaron found the land he wanted near a growing settlement called Shreves Landing, (later named Shreveport). Because it was not yet a city, he bought the land for a nominal sum.

Aaron hired two local men to help him build his one bedroom cabin. By the time the cabin was finished, it was springtime and time to plant his crops. Aaron did not believe in owning slaves, so he hired two men to help with the crops. It did not take Aaron long to realize that he did not have enough manpower to plant and care for much acreage.

It wasn't that Aaron wanted to be rich, but someday he hoped to marry and have a family. He was constantly wondering what he could do to increase his income. He would catch himself thinking, "I should have gone to college like my father wanted me to," yet he knew he would never go home until he was successful. Worst of all, in his heart, he knew he was not a farmer.

Aaron did not like the rough-hewn table and chairs that he had in the cabin. He decided to build nicer ones. He was impressed with the final results, so tried his hand at making other pieces of furniture. They also turned out very well. What really surprised Aaron was the enjoyment and pleasure he felt while building. He gradually replaced all of his furniture. He worked late into the nights and enjoyed every minute of it.

Aaron's grandfather had been a craftsman in England and owned his own company. His work was not as well known as Chippendale although the quality of work and beauty were comparable. Aaron had often watched his grandfather building and finishing furniture, never dreaming he would ever want to do it himself. He realized now he was happiest when designing or building. Aaron thought about it for a long time before he finally realized, "This is what I would like to do. I will never be happy unless I see if I can make this my livelihood." It did not take Aaron long to master the technique of wood finishing. He purchased the tools he would need and put in his first order of raw wood. The Red River was nearby, making shipping and traveling readily accessible and less costly.

Aaron's friends were amazed when they saw his handiwork and brought their wives to see the furniture. Each of their wives ordered at least one piece of furniture. Soon it seemed every lady in the area was placing orders. He was a perfectionist and each piece was beautiful. Before long he had to hire several men to help him.

An English lady came to visit her daughter and when she saw his work placed a large order. After she received her furniture, orders from England poured in. His reputation and business soared. He was shipping to England as well as neighboring states. Price didn't seem to be of importance and no amount was too much. He heard exclamations such as, "I don't care what it cost, my dear, just make it for me." Eventually Aaron had to construct a larger building to house his new business. He was doing something he loved and what's more, he was becoming wealthy doing it.

Aaron had promised his mother a visit as soon as possible. He was happy with his work, contented with his life and anxious to see all of his family. He also wanted them to see that he was happy and well. Aaron closed his shop temporarily and went to visit his family.

After their initial greeting, his mother asked, "Have you met a special girl?" Aaron laughed and said, "I have met them all and they are all special." His mother didn't find this humorous. His father and brothers did and laughed heartily.

Not giving up easily, she asked, "Are you going to visit Martha Ann while you are here? I think she is the sweetest little thing." Aaron retorted, "Oh Mom, she is as sweet as honey, but I don't believe she has ever had an original thought in her entire life."

Mrs. Lorell did not relent, "Well, what about all those lovely southern belles you thought were so darling when you spent those weekends in New Orleans? I just can't stand the idea of you living alone in a strange place so far from your family!" Aaron hugged his mother and reassured her, "Mother, I am as happy as can be and I am not alone. I have many wonderful friends, not to mention my work that I love. One of these days, I will meet the girl for me. You will come to my wedding and say, 'Son, I can see that you know how to pick a wife,' then I will tell you, 'I got that knack from my father!'" This time she joined in the laughter.

It was true that he had never met anyone he wanted to spend the rest of his life with. Not until he met Louise Morgan.

CHAPTER FOUR

You Are Invited!

Joshua and Hallie Evans, friends of the Morgans since their days in England had also settled in Shreves Landing. When they received a party invitation from Dolores Morgan, Hallie was thrilled. Unfortunately, Joshua had injured his hand and knew he could not manage the horse's reins for such a distance. Joshua did not have many servants and felt he could not take any of them from their chores just to drive them to a party.

Hallie Evans racked her brain trying to think of someone who could possibly drive the carriage. Aaron Lorell came to her mind. They had bought much of their furniture from Aaron and had grown very fond of him. He would be perfect. If only he would agree to go.

Joshua did not want to ask Aaron to leave his work and travel so far. After much pleading, Joshua relented and took Hallie to Aaron's. She begged Aaron to take the trip with them. She explained, "Joshua's hand has not had time to heal and he couldn't possibly handle the reins for such a long trip." Trying to make the trip more appealing, she mentioned twice, "They have a precious daughter, Louise that I know you would love to meet."

Aaron knew how much the trip meant to her. He thought it over. He had been working too many hours lately. At this point, business was right on schedule. A change might be the thing for him. He couldn't bear to stifle the anticipation he saw in Hallie's eyes. He laughed, pretended to bow and said, "At your service, Mrs. Evans. Why I couldn't bear to think of you missing a party. It would be my pleasure to drive you there." Hallie and her husband thanked him over and over. They made arrangements to leave in three days. Aaron never once thought of the girl named Louise that Hallie Evans mentioned until the night he met her. Friends often thought they had found someone Aaron would really like, however he had never been impressed by any of them.

Aaron and Louise

When Aaron, Joshua and Hallie arrived at the entrance of the Morgans, a servant was waiting to park their carriage along the lane with the many other carriages. They were directed to one of the outbuildings. The sounds of a piano, guitar and violins floated through the air. Aaron recognized the *Strauss Waltz*. The musicians were laying their instruments down and the dancers were leaving the floor when they stepped inside. Jonathon and Dolores Morgan greeted them and Hallie introduced Aaron. Hallie spotted Louise across the dance floor and exclaimed, "Oh there is Louise. I promised Aaron I would introduce him." She hooked her arm in the crook of his and guided him across the dance floor.

Louise had her back turned and was laughing with some of her friends. When she turned to face Aaron, his heart beat so rapidly that he found it difficult to catch his breath. Louise stood there in a blue green dress, looking as if she had stepped out of a fairy tale. The straight lines enhanced her tiny waist. The turquoise color and material had a shimmering effect and the sparkle of it all was reflected in her lovely eyes. Eyes as pretty as the blue greens in a sunset. Her dark auburn hair hung in a cascade of ringlets such as he had never seen before. As his eyes met hers, he saw a face that was not beautiful, but pretty, pleasant to look at, and to him, fascinating.

Aaron couldn't wait to dance with her and when he did, he blurted, "You fit perfectly in my arms." His face reddened and he could have slapped himself for acting like a schoolboy. Anticipating laughter, or a look of chastisement, he was relieved to see only twinkling eyes and the hint of a smile. It was love at first sight for Aaron and his world never seemed to stop spinning once he held her in his arms. If it were possible, he would have spent every moment with her.

Aaron loved the aura of shyness about her. He found her interesting to talk with. She was a good listener with deep thoughts and a mind of her own. He loved the way her eyes lit up and sparkled when she was excited. He enjoyed her wonderful sense of humor.

After the party, Mrs. Morgan invited the Evans to spend a few days with them. When Hallie Evans asked Aaron if he could possibly stay longer, he couldn't believe his luck. This was one time, he wouldn't mind letting his customer's wait.

It didn't take Louise long to realize that she was falling in love with Aaron. It wasn't just that he was the most handsome man she had ever met; it was the kindness she saw in his face and actions, the way he looked at her with adoration in his eyes. She liked the intense way he felt about things. She valued his integrity and high standards.

They were married a year later, in 1841. Aaron was twenty-one and Louise had just celebrated her eighteenth birthday. Dolores Morgan planned an elaborate wedding. Louise did not mind, as she did not want to have any words with her mother or regrets when she left for her new life and besides it was a great chance to tell her friends' goodbye.

After the wedding, Aaron's mother hugged him and said, "You were right son, you do know how to pick a wife." In a serious voice, he quipped, "I got that knack from my father!" They laughed together, enjoying their private joke.

It was very difficult for Louise to tell her Nanny Eliza goodbye. She would have taken her to live with them, but Nanny was getting old and traveling was difficult. Nanny Eliza cried when she told Louise, "You know I love you as my own. I will miss you my dear Louise, but it is better if I stay here. I know you will come and see me as often as you can." Louise hugged Nanny Eliza and through her own tears said, "I can't bear to leave you. If only you were going with me, it would be perfect. I promise I will come and see you as often as I can."

Parting was also very hard for Sydney and Louise. Sydney planned to be married in a few months to a local doctor. He had kept his eye on Sydney since grade school and when he graduated, asked her to marry him as soon as he got his degree in Medicine. Sydney had happily agreed. She reminded Louise that she wanted her to stand up with her at her wedding. Louise promised, "I wouldn't miss your wedding! We'll be there.

CHAPTER FIVE

Home

Louise had never asked Aaron what her new home would be like. It just wasn't important to her. She remembered Aaron apologizing, "Louise, this cabin is only temporary, and I haven't had much use for my money until now. I want you to have whatever suits your fancy. Just tell me about your dream home and I'll see that you have it."

Each evening, they would sit on the small porch of the cabin and Louise would add or take something away from the plans for the house, until they were both sure it was just the way she wanted it.

Aaron's many friends spent as much time as they could helping Aaron build their home. Louise promised herself she would not go inside until it was completely finished. She watched it taking shape from a distance. It was like watching the person you love the most wrapping a present for you. A present filled with love, warmth, hope and tranquility.

Louise couldn't believe how quickly the house was finished. She watched as all the men packed up their tools and left. She saw Aaron walking towards her and ran to meet him. Silently, he took her hand and led her to their home. Easily he lifted her over the threshold. Aaron watched and smiled as he took Louise on a tour of the house. When she had seen it all, they walked outside and stood looking at their home. Louise spoke, "It is just as I have dreamed it would be. The windows will let in plenty of light and sun. The red azaleas will soon fill in right up to our porch. The lovely oak trees enhance the beauty of it all. I love the way the lowest branches are huge, yet so close to the ground that I can just walk up and sit on them. I can picture our children playing there. Everything about it is beautiful" Louise was talking so fast she had to pause and take a breath. Aaron wrapped his arms around her and held her close to his heart. They stood that way for a long time.

Aaron was always willing to take Louise to visit her family, Eliza and Sydney. Aaron was content to visit with Jonathon while Louise spent most of her time with Nanny Eliza or Sydney.

Children

Probably the most gratifying and ecstatic moment in Louise's life was when the doctor announced, "It's a boy." He placed her baby son in her arms and she fell in love for the second time in her life. She named him Michael Aaron. She could see that Aaron was elated that he had a son. He told her, "February twenty fifth, Eighteen hundred and forty two, what a special day. Mrs. Lorell, I think you have made me the happiest man in the land!" Aaron kissed her lightly and said, "Now you need to get some rest." Louise wasn't quite ready to sleep, she undressed her son and checked every part of her newborn, making sure he was whole and complete. Satisfied, she sighed as she handed the baby to Aaron. She said, "He is perfect! I am sure he is going to have your beautiful brown eyes and dark hair." She leaned back on her pillow, exhausted, but euphoric.

Their daughter Celeste was born four years and eight months later, on October seventh, Eighteen hundred and forty six. Louise could not believe that they were fortunate enough to have a daughter. As soon as she was placed in her arms, she undressed her and checked to see that she was complete and whole. Louise announced to Aaron, "She is perfect Aaron. I promised you could name the baby if we had a girl. Do you have a name picked out?" He laughed and said, "I have had a name picked out since the day you gave me that promise. I would like her to be named after my grandmother whom I loved with all my heart. Celeste."

The new baby's hair was as black as coal, but gradually came in blonde. Her dark blue eyes turned to greens which changed with the colors she wore. Aaron adored her and often remarked with pride and love in his voice; "It's like getting to see you as a little girl, Louise. She already has so many of your ways."

Yearning

Aaron's business flourished. He now employed several men. He had no time for farming. He had horses and cows; but the land lay idle. Every so often he would say to Louise, "I feel guilty not raising something in this fertile land we own. Perhaps we could have a field of soy beans." Finally Louise said, "You work hours on end in your shop and barely have enough time to take care of the cattle and horses. When you want to see something growing on our land, just take a look at my garden. Let that suffice for now."

Louise thought Aaron had given up his desire to see something growing in his fields until he remarked a few weeks later, "I would love to stand on our back porch and see miles of cotton glistening in the sunlight." Louise looked surprised and asked, "Do you want it badly enough to buy some slaves?" He quickly assured her, "Not even enough to make one single human a slave." Louise, anxious to revive his usual good humor, hugged him and said, "It doesn't seem to bother you that I am your slave." Aaron had laughed, grabbed her arms and pinned her to the wall, "Now, my slave," he said, "You will kiss me so hard, your lips will bruise. If you do not, I will have you thrashed and tied to a hitching post."

CHAPTER SIX

Dan and Sarah

One evening, when Aaron and Louise were sitting on their porch, a stranger approached them. The man removed his hat when he saw Louise and said, " Evening ma'am," then he turned to Aaron, skepticism in his eyes, "I'm looking for work. I've been down on my luck for a long spell. I'm not afraid to work hard. I don't need much to get by on. I've got a wife to take care of and I'd sure be obliged if you would give me a chance."

Aaron sensed the man was desperate. He didn't really need anyone, but he could not bear the look in the man's eyes. He heard himself saying that he might be able to use him in his building trade.

The man lowered his head, methodically kicking the toe of his boot into the red dirt, as if chipping away at it for a reason. When he looked up at Aaron again, he said, "I ain't cut out for nothing but farmin. I'm happy working with the earth, ain't never done much else, but I'll take whatever you've got." He motioned to Aaron to move away from the porch where Louise was sitting. "My name is Dan Rivers," he said. Aaron reached to shake hands with the man, "Aaron Lorell", he said.

They shook hands and the man explained, "I've had trouble getting work, mostly cause my wife ain't, " he paused as if groping for the right words, "well, people call her 'touched,' they don't like her around. She don't take to folks, she won't talk to no one, 'cept me.' Just likes to stay to herself. I don't ever tell this, but I feel I can tell you, she was taken during an Indian raid and they hurt her bad. They had her a long time. I made a trade with the tribe and she has been with me ever since. Sarah has been a good wife, and she wouldn't hurt a flea." Pain constricted his face, "She can't help it, she just doesn't trust anyone but me." Aaron was very touched, "Let me talk it over with my wife," he said, "She would have to agree before I could hire you."

Aaron took a good look at the man. He was tall and very muscular. His eyes were a dark brown with plenty of smile wrinkles around them. His hair was brown and somewhat shaggy. Aaron looked deep into the man's eyes; he could see sorrow and dedication there. Aaron gave Dan a big smile and he smiled back. He saw kindness and warmth in his smile.

Dan stepped aside as Aaron walked back to the porch to discuss it with Louise. She listened intently. "They have been having a rough time. He has not been able to find work. He thinks one of the reasons is people consider his wife strange. "He says she is a good wife and harmless. Would it frighten you to have her around?" Louise turned and looked toward the road. A woman straddled a roan colored horse. A pack mule, evidently carrying all of their worldly possessions stood near by. The woman's hair was dark brown and wavy, almost reaching her waist. She wore britches and a light shawl covered her shoulders. Her head was bent forward and down, her small shoulders drooped, as if someone had just beaten her.

Aaron asked Louise, "Would you be afraid to have them live in our cabin if I hire him?" He says she stays to herself and talks only to him. I won't hire him if you have any negative feelings about my doing so."

Louise did not have to be told that this woman had been terribly abused by someone. Her heart went out to both of them. She turned to Aaron, "It would please me to have you hire him,

I trust your judgment and I have always been an admirer of your kindness." She smiled up at him, looking for the appreciation she knew she would see in his eyes.

Aaron went back to Dan Rivers, "I have often told my wife that I would love to see some crops growing on our land. It has been sad for me to see such good land sitting idle. You could plant some crops for me. It would also give me a little more free time if you cared for the animals. The crops do not have to be big. Do you think you could do the job"?

The man's eyes lit up, his entire countenance changed. He reached out to shake hands with Aaron again. He said, "I will do all of that for you and more if I can. I have never been afraid of working hard. I just can't thank you enough, Mr. Lorell."

The cabin was well furnished and had not been used since they had built their new home. Louise opened the door to let the couple in. The woman never looked up as the man said, "This is my wife Sarah." She held the shawl across her face, only her eyes were visible. Sarah turned her head if they looked her way. Louise gave them a tour of the house. Sarah kept her eyes lowered; but Louise saw her shoulders quiver several times. She had the feeling that the woman wanted to cry. Once, out of the corner of her eye, Louise saw Sarah running her fingers across the fine finish on the wood of one of the chairs. Dusk was settling in, so Louise lit the whale light. Aaron pointed out where Dan could get the water for their drinking and washing. They said "Goodnight," and left.

When they were a short distance away, Louise and Aaron looked back. Through the window, they could see Sarah running from one piece of furniture to another and then back to embrace her husband. Later, they saw them both carrying the large copper tub and knew they were going to be clean, if not very sociable.

On the walk to their house, Louise told Aaron, "Later, I would like to give her some of my things to wear. It's too bad you are such a little man," she teased, "This man could never wear any of your clothes." "Hey!" Aaron said, pretending to be upset, "Since when has a six foot man looked little to you?" He grabbed her and threw her over his shoulder. She laughed, snuggled up around his neck, and whispered, "Only since I saw that man, he must be six foot two and outweigh you by thirty pounds."

In a serious voice, she asked, "Do you think we were wise to hire him? We don't know a thing about them." Aaron took both of her hands into his own, "If there is one thing I am good at Louise, it is reading people. He is a good man, we won't regret it."

Dan knew more about farming than Aaron ever had. He didn't need anyone following him around to tell him what to do. Although Sarah kept to herself, she often helped Dan with the work.

Louise took some of her clothes for Sarah. She was quite sure Sarah was inside, but no one answered her knock. She left the bundle on the porch. It sat there until Dan came home and took it inside. The next day, Sarah had on one of the dresses. The old shawl still covered her shoulders. Louise noticed she never came out without the ugly thing draped across her shoulders. They had been on the farm for a month and none of them had seen her face.

The following day Dan knocked on Louise's door. He broke into a big smile and said, "I wish you could have seen my Sarah when she tried on those clothes. I ain't never seen her so happy since I took her away from that Indian tribe. Oh, I just wish you could have seen her; it would have lifted your heart Miss Louise! She kept askin me to thank you and she kept spinning round and round, making those dresses twirl out till she got dizzy and I had to hold her up." Louise said, "Dan, say no more! I will feel good all day just thinking of Sarah being so happy. Tell her that she made me happy too."

CHAPTER SEVEN

The following winter, a nightmare came into their lives, a nightmare that turned into reality. It started suddenly, gradually covered the house with a black cloud and then carried Aaron away forever. Influenza had been prevalent in the area, but most of the cases had been mild. It struck Aaron with the sharpness of a sword. The local doctor, James Stangland, was one of Aaron's closest friends. He did everything he could, but Aaron's illness never yielded. Louise stayed at Aaron's bedside. The only way she could bring herself to eat was the fear that she might get sick herself and not be able to care for him.

Dan came by every morning and evening to check on Aaron. His eyes were filled with despair. One day he asked Louise if he could talk to Aaron. Louise led him to the bedroom. Dan stood by Aaron's bedside, turning his hat over and over. "Mr. Lorell," he said, "Don't you worry about your family. I won't ever forget how you took Sarah and me in when no one else wanted us. I will take care of your family and land as long as the Lord allows me to."

Aaron was visibly touched and said, "God bless you Dan, your promise gives me much peace of mind." Awkwardly, but lovingly, Dan placed Aaron's hand in his own. He patted it softly as if to reassure him and then replaced it ever so tenderly on the sheet. With tears running down his cheeks, he fled from the room.

Dr. Stangland was with Louise the night Aaron passed away. As usual, Aaron had refused his food. Louise was wiping his face with a cold cloth. Aaron looked up at her, love and pain intermingling in his eyes. She leaned and kissed him softly. With great exertion, he pulled her close and kissed her again. Then, with his hand on the covers and his fingers extended, he moved them back and forth and Louise knew he was waving goodbye. It was November tenth, eighteen hundred and forty eight. He whispered, "My sweet Louise." He smiled for the first time in days. He looked contented and serene. The doctor closed Aaron's eyelids. For some reason, Louise thought of Sarah and how she tried to hide her grief and pain behind a shawl. "No! No" she pleaded, "I have children, and I must be there for them. There is no shawl big enough to hide my grief. How can I go on? Will I live with this unbearable grief until the end of my days?"

Aaron's family came; they were devastated by the loss of their beloved Aaron. Before they left, they begged Louise to let them help her financially or in any way they could. Louise thanked them for their offer, declining softly, yet firmly. Before they left, they asked Louise to promise that she and the children would visit them. Louise gave them her word. She also promised to write them often.

After the funeral, Louise's father pleaded with Louise to let him send some of his servants to help her. "Louise, you know I could spare several of them, please let me do this." Louise hugged him and said, "Daddy, don't worry so. You know I am just like you, strong and independent. Our needs are few. I have Dan and he is a wonderful help. Bless his heart, he refuses to take only a pittance for his wage." She continued, "I know you want to help and I am thankful that I can count on you. Aaron did not believe in slavery and I will respect his wishes." Her parents left when she promised them that she would contact them if she needed help.

Louise fulfilled Aaron's last request when she buried him on the hillside that overlooked their home, his family and the land he had loved with all of his heart.

When Louise's friends and neighbors tried to console her, she would say, " Aaron and I had more happiness and love in our short time together than many people have in an entire lifetime. I am thankful for that." Louise's heart was filled with grief, but she refused to cry. She felt as if an essential part of her had died with him.

It wasn't long before orders for furniture were rare. None of the men who worked for Aaron had the skill or art of designing like Aaron had. Louise was finally forced to close the business. The huge shop now looked empty and forlorn, a grim reminder of a happy past.

After Aaron's death, everything changed for Louise. The fun and excitement they had enjoyed together was gone. The only time she felt any real joy was when she looked into the faces of their little ones. There, she saw a reflection of Aaron and his great love for her.

The children loved hearing anything about their father, especially if it involved them. Louise was sure they knew each little story by heart. If she paused or left out a word, they quickly finished the sentence for her. Each had a favorite.

Michael's went like this:

"When you were about four years old, your daddy came hurrying into the house one day from his workshop. He had a big smile on his face and his eyes were twinkling. He said, "I just had to come to the house and share this with you. I was working on some designs when Michael came in. I looked up and before I could greet him, he asked, "Daddy, Is this today?"

I assured him, "Yes, this is today."

Michael looked quite pleased and said, "Oh there <u>are</u> two todays. Yesterday was 'today' too."

"It was hard not to smile as I explained to him, 'No Michael, it goes like this.' Sunday, Monday, Tuesday, Wednesday, Thursday, Friday and Saturday." Before I could say more, Michael waggled his finger at me and interjected, "You forgot today!"

Celeste's favorite went like this: "Every Saturday afternoon, no matter how busy your daddy was, he saved that afternoon for us. If it was a nice day, I packed a lunch and we would ride into town and shop, go on a picnic or whatever he thought we would enjoy. One Saturday morning, he said to me, ""Let's pack a lunch and take the children fishing. I think Celeste is big enough to hold a little fishing pole."

"Your daddy got busy and made you your very own pole. You were so proud of it. It had rained the night before and the bayou had overflowed in places. This made little puddles and some had tiny fish swimming in them. Your daddy took your hand and showed you the tiny fish swimming around. He explained to you that they were baby fish. You watched the fish for a while and then you knelt beside the puddle and watched them even more closely. Finally you stood up and asked your daddy, "Can fishes walk? I can't see their feet.""

Your daddy explained fish could only swim. He told me later, "Wasn't that just the cutest thing she could have said about the little fish? She must have been trying to see if they had their legs tucked under them as they swam about."

Celeste would always ask, "Did I catch a fish?" She would smile in anticipation as she waited for Louise to answer. Louise would respond, "Your daddy held you on his lap while you held your little pole. You got so tired that you kept falling asleep but you would wake right up. Finally you got a little nibble and when your daddy helped you pull it up, there was a big bunch of algae caught on your hook. You were so excited. Michael called out; "Celeste caught a whale!" Even though it wasn't a real fish, you seemed just as happy because we all laughed so hard. You were so tired that by the time we finished laughing, you had fallen asleep in your daddy's arms."

CHAPTER EIGHT

The Present Time-March 27, 1851

Louise forced her mind back to the present. Michael was eight years old now. He still missed his father and talked about him often. He was a serious little boy, kind and obedient. He rarely needed to be reminded of his chores. Often, on his own, he would help with the dishes. One time Louise told him, "Michael, it isn't necessary that you help with the dishes." He had replied, "I know I don't have to, but I know you appreciate it." Louise had hugged him and said, "Michael, I couldn't even begin to tell you how much I appreciate your help." She was often awed with his compassion and apparent wisdom. It touched her heart and overwhelmed her with love.

Celeste was four and a half. Celeste was about two and a half when her father died and could barely remember him.

Following Aaron's death, Dan kept his promise and ran the farm as if it was his own. They shared the produce, the chickens and eggs, the milk from the cows and the meat when they butchered. Louise tried to give him part of the income from the crops, but Dan rarely accepted it. There was never much and Louise learned how to be frugal. She promised Dan, "If I ever find a way, I will pay your back wages. Of course I will never be able to repay you and Sarah for your loyalty. Aaron told me when he hired you that we would never regret it and he was right."

Dan had replied, "Those words you just said makes me happier than any money could."

Aaron's mother was never well after Aaron's death. She wrote often, yearning to see her grandchildren. Two months after Aaron's death, Louise allowed her father to send one of his servants and a carriage to take her and the children to visit the Lorells.

The grandparents and uncles were ecstatic to have them. Michael and Celeste loved the attention and had a wonderful time. The Lorells told the children everything they could about their father. Mrs. Lorell never knew if Louise was really listening to the stories of Aaron. She sat as if she was off on a lonely reverie of her own.

All too soon, it was time to leave. Parting was very hard for all of them.

Sarah

Louise kept hoping that Sarah would overcome her distrust in people and the two of them could form a friendship. She would have enjoyed having someone to talk with, but Sarah kept her distance. There was no real contact until the day Louise was sitting on the back steps watching Michael and Celeste playing in the back yard. Celeste stopped by one of the flowerbeds and picked a small bouquet of flowers. She walked towards Louise with the flowers. Then Celeste looked up and saw Sarah walking along the path from her cabin. She paused a moment and then turned and ran toward Sarah, offering the flowers to her. Sarah dropped to her knees and carefully took the little bouquet. In doing so, the shawl fell, exposing one side of her face. Even from the distance, Louise was surprised, she thought, "What a lovely face." Michael ran over to join them and as Sarah turned towards him, her entire face came into view. The other side of her face seemed foreign to the rest. It was terribly scarred. Louise was filled with compassion, then anger, as she thought, "The Indians must have tortured her and burned that lovely face."

Michael stood by Celeste now. Sarah was talking to them and when she turned and saw Louise, she snatched the shawl across her face and hurried to the cabin.

When the children came back, Michael said, "No one must have ever given Sarah flowers before, she just kept saying, ""Thank you, Thank you,"" and she knew both of our names Mama." Neither child mentioned the scars on Sarah's face.

It was only a few days later that Celeste woke up with a fever. Louise was hoping she was just overly concerned when she sent Dan to bring the doctor. After he examined her, he told Louise, "I am not certain what is wrong with her. I don't think it is anything serious and I feel she will be better in a short time." He left a tonic for her and promised he would be back in two days to check on her.

Dan came over with a lovely bouquet, "Sarah sent this," he proudly announced, "She is crazy about those two kids." Louise let Dan give the flowers to Celeste. She took the flowers and said, "Tell Sarah, Thank you, Thank you, Thank You!" Dan grinned broadly, "She will like that." Louise knew why Celeste had repeated the words and her heart ached even more.

In the days and weeks that followed, Celeste would seem almost well on some days and then the fever would return. The Dr. told her it would eventually run its course. Celeste played on her 'good' days and laid around on the days when her temperature was elevated. Michael played with her when she felt well and read to her or played nearby when her fever was up. Louise took heart in the fact that her fevers were further apart each time and she was definitely getting stronger. Louise was hoping the Dr. would soon tell her she could start playing outside. She felt the sun would be wonderful for her.

Ann Dubois-April 10, 1851

Two weeks had passed since Louise had cried so hard that day in the garden. She was happy she could think of Aaron and their wonderful days together and yet go on with her life. Even the children noticed how she had changed. They too, were happier and more content now. She was thinking of this as she hung the last of her wash on the clothesline. She was turning the doorknob when she heard someone call her name. It was her closest neighbor, Ann. She and her husband, Frank Dubois lived about a mile up the road. They had not turned out to be Louise's favorite people by any means; but they seemed suited for each other. Both were known to be selfish and mean spirited. For some reason, Ann had wanted to be friends with Louise.

"Oh Louise," Ann called, "I came to tell you goodbye. We are leaving in a few days and this will be my last chance to see you before I leave. Louise invited her in. Ann sat down at the kitchen table. Louise sighed as Ann started talking. She knew everything Ann was going to say, she had heard it often enough. Gold had been discovered in California, Ann and Frank were convinced they were going out west, find gold and become rich. It was just that simple, to hear Ann tell it.

Louise poured Ann and herself a glass of cider. She joined Ann at the table, and then patiently waited for Ann to launch into what Louise knew would be a one-sided conversation. At least she could rest while she sat there, knowing all that would be required of her was to listen and perhaps make a comment now and then. Ann didn't disappoint her. "We will leave early one morning this week. As soon as we get everything packed. Probably in three or four days. We both hate to part with our riding horses, but we will buy more when we get settled." She took a deep breath and said, "Oh, I just know we will find gold right away. So many people have become rich overnight! I know it will be a long hard trip; but every fiber in my body tells me that it will be worth it." Ann paused, took a sip of cider, and waited for Louise to comment. Louise's mind was somewhere else. She had been thinking that she needed to start supper. Ann's silence alerted Louise. Trying to look interested, she said, "It all sounds so exciting." Her response seemed to please Ann, and she continued, "Once we have our gold, I am going shopping. I will buy nothing but the latest fashions. You know Frank came to America from France. Frank says the French women really know how to dress. He loves nice things and he can't wait to see how wonderful I will look. The first thing he wants to buy for himself will be the best carriage that money can buy and a beautiful team of horses to set it off."

Louise wondered to herself, "How can anyone with such a pretty face, lovely blue eyes, high cheekbones, beautiful blonde shoulder length hair, petite and put together so perfectly, make you wish you were anywhere else but with her?" Louise decided it was the look she had in her eyes. "Cold and calculating." She never talked of anything but herself and her own desires.

Ann continued, "We plan to come back here, buy lots of land and build a big, lovely home. We will have oodles of slaves, and parties! We will have gala affairs, everyone will want to attend. We will only invite people who are wealthy and influential." Ann paused again, waiting for a response. Louise had no desire to acknowledge such frivolity. Smiling wryly, she said, "You certainly have everything all planned out." Ann took this as a compliment, and returned to her conversation. "Oh Louise, of course we will invite you to our very first party. If you don't have a dress that is exquisite enough, I will let you use one of mine."

Louise had a hard time with that remark. She decided to let it pass, after all, the poor girl was just dreaming out loud.

Ann rattled on a little longer, and at last announced she had to leave. Louise was relieved the visit was over. They embraced and Louise said in all sincerity, "I hope you and Frank strike gold right away." Ann swung herself up on her horse, jabbed her heels into its sides and rode off. Louise watched as Ann quickly brought the horse to a gallop. She thought, "How gracefully she can ride, what a strong will she has. I wonder if they will come back and if she will be rich."

For some reason Louise felt a cold chill and a strange premonition. The thought came to her mind, "Things are not going to turn out the best for these people." Anxious to be rid of this feeling, she shrugged her shoulders and hurried to check on the children. She found herself hoping the next neighbors would be someone she and the children could enjoy. The children were sitting together on the sofa and Michael and Celeste were engrossed in a game of Checkers.

CHAPTER NINE

The Gold Travelers

True to her word, Ann and her husband Frank left before the week was out. Everything was packed and as soon as they dressed that morning, they climbed onto the seat of their covered wagon. Frank cracked his whip and called "Giddy up!" The horses trotted off. Long before the sun started to peek over the horizon, they were on their way to the West and the anticipated gold

At first, they laughed and talked, but fell silent as the day wore on and tiredness set in. They stopped once to eat their lunch and give the horses a rest. When they climbed back onto their seats and started out again, Ann complained about how miserable she was. Frank put his arm around her waist; "You have to be strong if you want to become a rich, prominent lady." She understood this and sat up straighter, her stamina and determination returning. Ann let her mind wander and found herself thinking of her visit with Louise. She turned to Frank and said, "I have a feeling I will never see Louise again. That makes me feel sad, I want so much to come back and show her how rich we are. Oh well, maybe I will never want to leave California once I get there. Yes, I'm sure that's it. I'll love California so much, I won't ever want to leave."

The Question

Dr. Stangland came to examine Celeste the day after Ann's visit. He felt it was safe to let her play outside for short periods. Celeste couldn't wait for the next morning to come so she could play in the yard. Louise, Michael and Celeste were disappointed when it drizzled the next day. The following day was beautiful and Celeste played outside for an hour or so in the afternoon. The next day Michael and Celeste knocked on Dan and Sarah's door. The couple was thrilled to see them. Sarah brought milk and cookies outside and they all sat on the steps.

Only the paleness in Celeste's face and dark circles around her eyes remained as reminders of how sick she had been. The following day, when they came in after being outside, Michael said, "Celeste didn't play much, she just sat and watched me." Alarmed, Louise pulled Celeste onto her lap, scrutinizing her face. A sigh of relief escaped her lips, Celeste looked better then she had for weeks. Louise sat quietly for a moment, thinking of how sick Celeste had been. One minute she had been hot with a fever and the next shaking with chills. The doctor was unable to diagnose her sickness as her only symptoms seemed to be fever.

The last time Celeste's fever had been high, she had asked, "Am I going to die like my daddy?" Although Michael had been busy drawing a picture for Celeste, he looked up, his beautiful eyes terror stricken. Louise's heart almost burst. She dropped to her knees and embraced them both, "No, No," my darling, you are not going to die. You are going to get better; it is just going to take awhile." Louise had cuddled them both in her arms, trying to think of what to say to ease their worried little minds.

"My dear ones," she began, groping for the right words, "We are all going to die sometime. You both have lost someone you loved very much, so death is very real to you. I feel both of you will be very caring even though you are both very young. You will probably be kinder and more understanding since you know how it feels and you will be able to comfort others and share how sad they feel when they lose someone they love. I must tell you that there are some things worse than dying. Wanting to die and can't is one of them. People who are suffering terribly want to die and even pray to die. None of us can die until our time. Your daddy was so sick that he was ready to die. God is taking care of him now. Celeste honey, you are going to get well, I promise you are going to get well." Instantaneously, she made a silent prayer to God that it was His will that Celeste would mend. Louise could never ask Him to spare her if it was not His will. She took it for granted that His decisions were always the best. As Louise spoke, she watched their eyes changing from despair to resignation. Michael went back to the table and Celeste slid down from her lap and sat next to him.

After supper, Louise lit their whale oil lamp and led the children to their bedroom. She tucked Michael in and sat down in the rocker, pulling Celeste into her arms. Rocking her back and forth, she sang them a quaint little lullaby. Celeste was asleep before she finished the song. Louise kissed Michael goodnight, then carried Celeste to her bed and tenderly kissed her goodnight. She slipped out of the room yearning for her own bed. She hurriedly put on her nightgown, then knelt and said her prayers. She crawled in bed, leaned over and extinguished the lamp. Exhausted, she sank into the softness of the feather mattress and immediately fell into a deep sleep.

In the middle of the night, Celeste awakened. She felt as if she was burning up. All she could think of was getting a drink of water. She crawled out of bed and wandered through the dark house, calling softly, "Mama." Celeste had such a high fever that she did not realize what she was doing. She might as well have been walking in her sleep. She pulled a chair to the back door and worked feverishly to open the latch.

She stepped outside closing the door behind her. Only one picture was burning in her brain, the cold water that flowed from the pump." Confused and disoriented, she wandered into the moonlit night.

CHAPTER TEN

The Disappearance-April 10, 1851

Louise awakened the next morning with Michael pulling on her arm. He was pleading, "Mama, get up, I'm going to be late for school." She jumped out of bed and hurried into the kitchen. Quickly, she fixed his breakfast. She went to the door and started to unlock it. It was not locked. "Michael," she inquired, "Did you unlock the door?" He replied, "No, Mama, I ran to get you as soon as I got up." She knew she had felt exhausted last night, but how could she have allowed herself to forget to lock the door. Anyone could have just walked in. She thought of the Indians who sometimes wandered about. She must never let this happen again. Louise kissed Michael goodbye and hurried to check on Celeste.

Ordinarily Celeste was the first one to get up in the mornings. Since she had been sick, she rarely got up until ten or later. Louise was surprised to find Celeste's bed was empty. She looked through the house, calling her name. Louise became more concerned each second. She ran outside and looked all around. She ran to Dan and Sarah's cabin and knocked on the door. No one answered. She shoved the door open, "Sarah," she called, "Have you seen Celeste? I can't find her anywhere." Sarah could hear the terror in her voice and see the naked fear in her eyes. Not even grabbing her shawl, she shook her head violently, indicating she had not. Louise started to ask where Dan was and realized he would be taking Michael to school as he did every morning. Louise ran to the barn, jumped on one of the horses, and rode bareback to catch them.

Trying not to sound alarmed, she asked Michael, "Did you see Celeste this morning?" Michael thought a moment and replied, "No, mama, is something wrong?" Louise tried to assure him, "I don't think so Michael, she must have gone outside and perhaps she is in the back yard. Louise could see that Dan understood. He assured her, "I'll be back as quick as I can Miss Louise!" He snapped at the horses and they tore away.

Louise raced home, searched the house again, then the yard. Sarah came out of the barn, and shook her head negatively. Louise searched it again anyway. They both searched every out building, the garden and pecan grove. When Dan came back, he told her to ride for help while he continued to look.

Terrified, Louise rode to the nearest neighbors. Frantically, she told them that Celeste was missing. Guilt registered in her eyes as she admitted, "Although I could have sworn that I locked the back door, it was open when I got up this morning. It's all my fault." She sobbed uncontrollably, wringing her hands in desperation. The neighbor touched her shoulder gently and asked, "Did Celeste know how to unlock the door?" Louise had never thought of this. "Yes," she replied, "She can, and has done so, but she would never go out at night alone."

Immediately the neighbor saddled his horse. He told his wife he would ride back with Louise. His wife was already on her horse, setting out to notify the rest of the neighbors.

When the neighbors arrived, they spread out in a long line. They searched the woods and fields. They even went as far as the nearest house, which had belonged to Frank and Ann. It was about a mile south of the Lorell farm. They searched the empty house and its' surroundings, all to no avail. They took turns calling her name until every person was hoarse.

One of the older ladies, Mrs. Everson, stayed behind with Louise while the others searched. Glancing out the window, Mrs. Everson saw four of the men carrying a dugout and long poles. She quickly moved to block this view from Louise; but Louise had already seen them. She knew they were on their way to search the bayou. She could picture them poking and prodding. Louise was very aware of the danger of the slithering alligators that made their home in the bayou. This picture in her mind was too much, she fell over in a faint.

When Louise came to, Mrs. Everson was on the floor cradling her in her arms and rocking her back and forth as if she was a baby. She helped Louise to a chair. When Louise was feeling stronger, she started talking, desperation in her voice. She had to keep the picture of the men searching the bayou out of her mind. She went over everything that had taken place the day before and that evening. She sobbed, blaming herself because she had slept so hard. "If only I hadn't slept so hard," she lamented, "I might have heard something." Mrs. Everson begged her not to blame herself. "When we work hard, we sleep hard," she told her, "You must not blame yourself." They both tried to imagine what had happened to Celeste. Each avoided mentioning anything that might leave Louise without any hope. At last they were out of words and Louise sat still, shoulders slumped, a prayer on her lips, her eyes darting every which way, hoping to see her dear Celeste. The warmth of the house was gone, replaced with gloom and a strange chill.

Darkness came too soon for Louise and the searchers. Looking defeated and depressed, the neighbors had to give up the search until daylight. When they left, Louise's closest friend Sharon stayed. The next morning the neighbors returned to search again. It was as if she had vanished. Sharon stayed for several nights. At last, Louise insisted that Sharon go home to her own family.

Michael secretly blamed himself for Celeste being gone. He tried to think of how he could have prevented it. He had trouble sleeping now. The burden was heavy for his little shoulders.

Everyone had different versions of what may have happened to Celeste. Those who knew Celeste had been ill were convinced that she had wandered out in the night and some wild animal had attacked her, or the alligators had swallowed her up, or she had died from the elements. Then there were those that thought that Indians had crept in the house and carried her off. Many of them defended this accusation by saying, "Indians are fascinated by anyone with blonde hair. We have all seen Indians roving about in the forests." Of course, there were those who insisted, "You can be sure that 'crazy' woman who lives in their cabin could tell you exactly where she is!"

Louise did everything she could think of to aid in the return of her little girl. For weeks, she had the newspaper print about her disappearance. She sent pamphlets to all the surrounding towns and passed them out to people on the streets. When she had to describe her little girl, it almost broke her heart. Many people wrote sympathetic letters. No one provided a single clue. Eventually, people stopped looking and even asking about Celeste.

Faith and Hope

Louise's love for Michael and the hope that Celeste would be found were the only things that kept her going. Then one night she had a dream. It was so real she had trouble believing that it did not happen. In her dream, Celeste had crawled in bed with her, touched Louise's face and said, "Mama, I am going to come home." Aaron was also in the dream; he had smiled at her as if to say, "Everything will be all right, have faith." It may have been just a dream; but it gave her strength and hope.

Louise realized that Michael might be blaming himself for Celeste's disappearance. She knew he was suffering and wanted to assure him that it was not his fault. "Michael," she began, "There is nothing we could have done to prevent whatever happened to Celeste. I had a dream last night, so vivid, that I had to convince myself it wasn't real. I am certain that someday we will have our Celeste back. In the dream, your daddy and Celeste both promised me that. Just think of the happiness we will all feel on that day." Michael looked directly at his mother and saw the conviction in her eyes. Relief permeated his own eyes, and for the first time since his sister had disappeared, the guilt and sorrow turned into hope.

Louise's parents had been begging her to bring Michael and stay with them for a while. After the dream, she felt that she could. The Morgan plantation was approximately fifty miles southeast of Louise's farm. Dan assured her he would watch out for her house as well as the rest of the farm. Louise left a note on the door telling exactly where she could be found. Dan promised he would ride and tell her if anything was learned of Celeste.

At the gate, Louise turned and looked back at their home. She couldn't bear to live in it now. Still, she made a silent promise to herself that someday all three of them would return.

CHAPTER ELEVEN

Unwanted

Meanwhile, Frank and Ann had been traveling for two days and had stopped for the night. Both were tired and not in the mood for conversation. The horses were quietly grazing. There had been a soft breeze all day but now the wind was picking up and the temperature dropping. Ann suddenly shivered, and then called to Frank, "Get the blanket in the back of the wagon. It's draped over the chest. I think we will need an extra one tonight."

Wearily Frank walked to the wagon. He pulled the canvas aside but there was no blanket on any of the chests. Just as he was ready to complain, he noticed one lying on the wagon floor. He pulled it toward him, and as he did so, stopped in complete astonishment. Though her cheeks had large red areas and her hair was matted, he recognized the little person.

It was Celeste Lorell!

Frank was astounded. He could tell she was very ill. He picked her up and shoved her in front of Ann. They stared in amazement and disbelief. Both were dumbfounded.

Ann recovered and pushed Frank's trophy away. She exclaimed, "I never saw anyone so sick. Frank, we can't have a sick child with us, this trip is bad enough already." Frank muttered, "Surely, you don't think we should take her back home." Ann thought a moment and said, "No way, Frank, We are not adding any extra time to our trip. When we pass close to a house or town, we will just drop her off and they can worry about her." Frank thought this was a good idea. As if to make it all right, he said, "She looks so sick, she would probably die before we got her home anyway."

Celeste's lips were swollen and crusted; but she managed to whisper, "Water." This was to be the last spoken word that Frank and Ann would hear from Celeste.

Frank put some water to her lips. She managed to take a few sips. It was enough to save her life. She had been unconscious for two days, but now she slept. Frank carried her back to the wagon and tossed the pouch of water beside her.

In the days that followed, Celeste wondered how she got with Frank and Ann. Eventually she remembered a dog snarling at her. She was standing by a wagon and she climbed into it for protection. Though she tried very hard, she couldn't remember why she was by the wagon. Now, all she wanted was to go home and be with her mother and Michael.

In the days following, Ann kept asking her, "Why were you in our wagon?" When Celeste didn't respond, Ann would say, "I bet your mother put you in there, even your own mother doesn't want you." Sometimes they would slap her when she didn't respond and other times were not even aware that she was not answering them.

Frank and Ann wouldn't allow Celeste to cry when they were anywhere around her. One or the other would take her by the shoulders and shake her severely. They complained bitterly that she was in the way. She was allowed only small amounts of food and she was always hungry.

When they came to a lake or river, Frank and Ann would bathe and wash their clothes. Celeste longed for a bath and clean clothes. Once, she timidly stepped one foot into the water hoping they would let her bathe also. Ann had screamed,

"Get back in the wagon, do you think we want your filth in our water?"

At last, Frank complained to Ann, "Can't you find something else for that kid to wear? She smells so bad that I can't stand her." Ann took out one of her blouses and told Celeste to bathe in the nearby stream. "Wash out your clothes," she ordered, "When you finish, put this blouse on until your clothes dry. You better take care of my blouse, or you won't eat again today."

Celeste ran to do as she was told. The water felt wonderful. She had watched Ann washing clothes in the rivers and streams, and she did her best to copy her. Up and down she dipped her nightie and underpants. She even tried getting the stains out by rubbing them on the sand, as she had seen Ann do. Any person with an iota of feelings would have been touched by her efforts. It only irritated Frank and Ann.

Celeste hoped they were stopping long enough for her to spread her things over rocks like she had seen Ann do. She knew they would dry faster. She hated wearing Ann's blouse and wanted to put her own clothes back on. This wasn't to be. She no sooner came out of the water and put the dreaded blouse on, when they started screaming that it was time to go. Quickly, she grabbed her wet clothes and climbed back into the wagon. Though the blouse draped over her little shoulders, at least it covered her. She felt all the more vulnerable sitting in the back in Ann's hateful blouse. She hoped her clothes would dry in a hurry. Then she came up with a thought. She would hold her clothes out the back of the wagon as they rode along. In no time, they were dry enough to put on. She took off the blouse, laid it carefully on top of some of the crates, and painstakingly put her worn nightie and panties back on.

At first, Celeste cried a lot when she was alone in the back of the wagon. The tears finally stopped. It seemed as if her eyes had stopped making tears. At least, Frank and Ann could no longer see tear lines running through the dust and grime on her face, and stopped calling her "Cry Baby.' The aching in her heart stayed. She desperately clung to the picture in her mind of her mother and brother. Deep in her heart, she was afraid that if she forgot how they looked, she would forget them and who she was. She never looked Frank or Ann in the eyes. Partly because she feared them and partly because she didn't like the meanness she saw. Most of all because she was afraid they would erase the image she carried in her heart of her mother. Picturing her mother's face gave her hope and helped her through the terrible times.

The shock of all that had happened to her, the terrible sickness and the fear of these people seemed to have snatched her voice away. Gradually, she became aware that she could not speak. Instead of being frightened, she was actually content with her silence, glad that she didn't have to talk to these people or answer any of their questions.

Frank and Ann hated that she wouldn't look at them, or speak. Often, they would grab her by her shoulders, their fingers pressing and bruising, and shake her, yelling, "Look at me when I am speaking to you," Sometimes, they would slap her sharply across the face. This crushed her to her very core, but she refused to allow herself to cry. Celeste cringed every time one of them made remarks, such as, "What a dumb one she is, can't even talk, no wonder her own mother didn't want her." They took her blanket away. She shivered through the chilly nights. Finally she got up the nerve to open one of the trunks, inside she found the articles and trinkets Frank had brought to barter with the Indians. There were beads, plumed hats, eyeglasses, red and gold brocaded jackets, and best of all, a lovely multi-colored shawl. Each night, she would cover herself with the shawl. As soon as she awakened, she would hurry to put it back. Worrying about getting caught with the shawl made her sleep fitfully, but it was better than suffering in the cold. Nothing they did crushed her spirit of hope. She focused on her mother's kind and gentle face whenever they hurt her. Lucky for Celeste, much of the time they ignored her.

In spite of the hardships and loneliness, Celeste was finally well again. Whenever they stopped, and Celeste was given her small ration of food, she would find a pleasant place to sit while she ate. She knew she could wander as far as she wanted. She realized Frank and Ann would be only too happy to go off without her, so she always kept the wagon within her sight. She made friends with the horses and often they would lower their heads so she could stroke them. Sometimes they would nuzzle at her neck and she loved that. She looked for pretty stones and kept the prettiest ones in her corner of the wagon. She planned on giving them to her mother. She picked wild flowers, and each time would think, "Today might be the day my mother will come and get me and I will surprise her with the flowers." She would imagine her mother telling her how beautiful they were. Sometimes, she would find wild berries and poke them into her hungry little mouth as fast as she could. What a wonderful feeling it was to climb back into the wagon and know she could ride along without the usual hunger pangs. During the horrible bumpy rides, she thought of the fun she and Michael used to have together. She remembered her mother telling her that she would be five on her next birthday. She wondered if her birthday had passed or if she was still four. She hoped she was still four, so she could have her birthday with her mom and Michael.

The Overnight

Frank and Ann had been traveling for about two weeks when Ann called out, "Look Frank, I think I see houses in the distance." As they got closer, they saw that it was a fairly large town. This really pleased Ann. She couldn't wait. At last she would have someone new to talk to. Perhaps they would invite them for a meal. Maybe invite them to sleep in a real bed.

Suddenly, Ann had an idea. She turned to Frank and said, "This is our chance to get rid of her. We'll just drop her off on the outer edge of the town. Frank was all for it; but reminded her, "If we stop to visit, we can't leave her. They might figure out it was us, so take your choice, visit or get rid of her." Ann chose visiting.

Before they were close to any of the houses, Frank stopped the wagon and went to the back. He told Celeste, "We are going to be stopping up the road. You stay in the wagon and don't you make a peep. We will put some food and water in here for you and you better not cause us any trouble. If you do, we will leave you in the middle of the deepest woods. And the last thing I will give you is a whipping that you won't forget."

They never made it into the town before some of the people were waving and encouraging them to stop. Several of the neighbors had gotten together for a picnic that day and the guests were getting ready to leave the home of the couple that had invited them. Frank pulled the horses to a stop, and he and Ann climbed down from the wagon. Now, the people were in no hurry to leave. They loved it when someone came along to tell them news from other places.

Celeste watched through a small opening in the canvas as all the people gathered around Frank and Ann. Ann sounded like a different person, her voice now, soft and sweet. She chattered on and on. When Ann told everyone they lived in Shreves Landing, Louisiana, no one seemed impressed. Ann paused momentarily when the grown-ups heard a child crying and had their attention elsewhere. She hated when she was not the center of attention, so when they focused on her again, she quickly decided to change her locality from Shreves Town to New Orleans. She mentioned New Orleans and could see the ladies were now all ears. Ann had only been there once but what she didn't know, she guessed. She told how the ladies dressed and what glorious times she had on her many visits. She found it easy to exaggerate and add exciting things that were not true. The ladies 'oohed and ahhed.' Ann loved being the center of attention.

As Celeste watched, she noticed two people in particular. One was a man about Frank's age. For some reason, she felt drawn to him. When one of the little girls fell down, he lifted her onto his lap, and ever so gently dried the tears from her eyes with his handkerchief. Celeste longed to be held like that. The other person that caught her eye was a boy who looked a lot like her brother Michael. She hadn't cried for days, but now tears ran down her cheeks.

The couple that lived there invited Frank and Ann to spend the night with them. They accepted eagerly. Ann crawled into the back of the wagon and filled a satchel with things they would need for the night. Celeste crammed herself into a corner, anxious to stay as far from Ann as she could. Talking quietly through clenched teeth, Ann warned Celeste, "You stay in this wagon and don't you make any noise. Do you hear me?" Celeste, eyes riveted to her feet, nodded just enough to satisfy Ann. Celeste watched as the man opened the door to let Frank and Ann into his home. It was the man that she had watched and wished was holding her. Oh, how she would have loved to be going inside too.

As they were walking to the house, Celeste heard the woman say, "We just ate at the picnic, but I will fix some supper for you and your husband. I know you must be hungry for a home cooked meal." Celeste reached for the left over mush that Ann left for her. She tried not to think of the good food Frank and Ann were probably enjoying.

Celeste finally fell asleep. She awakened in the middle of the night. She needed to go to the toilet. As the minutes passed, she became more and more miserable. She peeked out the slit in the canvas. The moon was shining brightly. No one was in sight. Urgency gave her the courage to climb out. She jumped to the ground, and immediately sensed that she wasn't alone. Celeste cringed, her body paralyzed by fear. Then she saw a dog. Her fear eased as she saw the dog was wagging its tail. This dog wasn't like the mean one that had forced her to hide in Frank and Ann's wagon that fateful night so long ago. It was a lovely collie. She patted the dog's head, thrilled to have someone that made her feel welcome and wanted. The dog followed her into a grove of trees and waited. Celeste had the feeling that the dog was guarding her, suddenly she felt safe. Now, the dog took the lead and Celeste followed. The collie walked to her doghouse, turned and looked at Celeste. She wagged her tail, inviting her in. As if it was perfectly natural, Celeste dropped to her knees and crawled in. She sat by the dog, patting and petting her. She knew she should get back in the wagon, but she felt so wonderful sitting there. She would stay just a little longer. Celeste leaned her head against the dog. It was the softest thing she had felt for a long time. The dog licked her face and Celeste knew that it was a promise of friendship and loyalty. For the first time in weeks, she felt safe and secure. She basked in the feeling. Before she knew it, she was sleeping.

The next morning Frank threw their overnight satchel in the front of the wagon. They also had several packages of food and supplies that the nice people had given them for their trip. They called, "Thank You," and waved as they rode away.

Ann was so excited that she talked non-stop. She asked Frank, "Do you think I impressed those ladies?" Frank laughed, "They had to be impressed, you told so many lies that I almost got impressed myself."

After an hour or so, Frank said, "We better check on the brat." When he found that Celeste wasn't in the wagon, he hurried back to his seat. "She isn't there," he announced. "We better drive fast and furious before those people try and bring her back to us." He cracked the horses with his whip and they bolted off.

By nightfall no one had caught up with them. They felt safe now. After talking it over, they decided it had worked out perfectly. They laughed about the peoples' reactions when they found her. "Well," said Ann, "At least she can't talk, so they won't be able to find out much, if anything." "Maybe," Frank mused, "they will never find out she was with us. We won't take a chance, when we come this way again, we will skip that town." Ann was disappointed. She did want those people to see her when she was rich and traveling in style.

CHAPTER TWELVE

Bob and Linda Edwards

After telling Frank and Ann goodbye, Bob and Linda Edwards walked back into the house. Linda had really enjoyed the company and loved listening to all the exciting things Ann had told her. She was surprised when Bob said; "I didn't like either one of them." When Linda pressed him as to why, he answered, "Did you notice that they didn't have one bit of interesting news to tell us? The woman did all of the talking. Silly, frivolous talk. They both seemed very shallow and false to me." Linda laughed, "Oh Bob, you just don't appreciate 'woman' talk."

Bob and Linda were brother and sister. They moved to Dallas, Texas when their parents died and had lived their ten years. Bob was not a bachelor because he chose to be one. If the truth were known, it was his sister who did her best to keep him one.

Bob was a very disciplined person and not afraid to work. He had always wanted to have his own business. He opened a small store in Dallas and it had steadily grown. The people enjoyed doing business with him. He was honest and fair. Though he was not the type to stand out in a crowd, men and women did not forget him once they knew him. He had very dark wavy hair, brown eyes, and a suntanned, clear flawless complexion. His features fit his face nicely. He carried himself well, tall and erect with an athletic trimness. He was someone a woman did not consider especially handsome, until he smiled. Since he had a tendency to see things more seriously, he did not smile a lot. When he did, he eyes lit up and changed his entire demeanor. More than one woman's heart had been broken because of that smile.

Linda on the other hand had always been spoiled and selfish. She expected everything to revolve around her. She was a very pretty girl, capable and industrious. She also had wavy dark hair, dark eyes and a flawless complexion. Many men had tried to court her, all to no avail. Linda turned away every suitor that came her way. One by one they had all married someone else.

Whenever Bob became interested in any of the available ladies, she pouted and did her best to break up the relationship. She felt life had been very unfair to her and often told her brother, "You are responsible for my unhappiness, you shouldn't have insisted on moving here. I'm going to end up an old maid. My greatest dream was to get married and have a home of my own."

Bob wished she would do just that. He would probably have to care for her the rest of his life. Lucky for Linda, her brother was a very kind and caring person. He felt she was one of his responsibilities and he would honor that. "At least," he would tell himself, "I have my store to run and a good excuse to be away most of the time."

Mitzi

The sun was forming a little arch inside the doghouse entry when Celeste awakened. Realizing she had slept through the night, her little body shook with fright. She saw her new friend lying peacefully in front of the doghouse. The dog heard her stirring, and wagged its tail. Celeste moved as far back into the doghouse as she could. She was terrified that she might hear Frank or Ann calling for her. Surely they would be glad to be rid of her and just hurry off. She relaxed a little with that thought until she wondered, "What will happen to me now?"

Celeste hadn't been sitting there long, when she heard a man's voice, "Here Mitzi." He called, "here's your breakfast." Celeste could see the man's shoes as he walked past the doghouse to set the food down. As soon as the man had gone back inside the house, Mitzi nudged the bowl with her nose until it was in front of the doghouse door. She wagged her tail and looked at Celeste. "She wants me to have some," thought Celeste. She reached out and grabbed some of the scraps. It was leftovers from the meal that Linda had prepared for Frank and Ann. Celeste was starved. She quickly ate the handful of food. The dog still waited. "He wants me to take more," she thought. It was the first time she felt full from anything but berries. She sat back, nauseous, but contented. Only then did Mitzi start eating.

Celeste was thrilled that she had found out her new friend's name. Now Celeste was thirsty. She could see the bowl of water within her reach. She grabbed the bowl, pulling it inside. She drank as much as she wanted and then pushed the bowl back. Now, she had a real problem, she had to go to the toilet. She remembered the nearby woods. Celeste crawled to the entry and peered outside. The only windows in the back of the house had shades that were drawn. She slipped out of the doghouse and ran towards the woods. Mitzi followed her. They stayed in the woods all day. It had been a long time since Celeste had felt so happy and carefree.

Dusk found Celeste sitting by the edge of the woods watching the house. She saw the man arrive home in his carriage. She watched him unhitch the team and walk them to the barn. Celeste could tell that Mitzi wanted to run and greet him.

Celeste didn't move to follow and the dog remained by her side.

Celeste was afraid to go back to the doghouse until it was dark. She imagined all sorts of things that might happen if someone saw her. She wondered what they did with children that were found wandering about. What would happen if someone saw her? Perhaps they would take her back to Frank and Ann. This terrified her, she remembered the beating he had promised her.

It wasn't long before the man came out with a bowl of food and called, "Here Mitzi." The dog wagged her tail and made as if to go. When Celeste didn't move, Mitzi stayed by her side. She didn't budge though the man kept calling her name. At last, he went back into the house. When darkness covered everything, Celeste ran for the doghouse. Instead of crawling inside, she crept to the lighted window. A lamp shone from the middle of the table. She could see the couple eating their evening meal. It brought back memories of her mother, Michael and herself, sitting at their table. With a heavy heart, she slipped away.

The dog's food was still sitting where the man had left it. Mitzi did not touch the food. Celeste picked up the bowl of dog food and took it in the doghouse. She knew Mitzi was hungry and her heart overflowed with love. The dog waited until Celeste pushed the bowl back to her. She patted Mitzi until they both fell asleep.

The next morning, it was Linda who brought Mitzi her food. She petted Mitzi and then walked to the doghouse to set the food down. When she came close, Mitzi moved between her and the entry, a deep growl rumbling in her throat. Linda stepped back, surprised and a little frightened. She tried approaching the entry several times and each time, the dog growled. At last, she went back into the house.

That night, the man called Mitzi several times again. He looked perplexed as he reentered the house. He told Linda that

Mitzi hadn't come when he called her. "I can't understand where she has been for the last two nights. She is always here to greet me when I come home. She doesn't even come when I call her to eat."

Linda looked up, "Oh Bob," she said, "I meant to tell you that she actually growled at me several times today. I hate to admit that I was rather frightened. Do you think she has some kind of sickness? Linda, looking quite alarmed said, "Maybe she has rabies!" Now, it was Bob's turn to look worried. "I will look her over good in the morning, she certainly isn't herself, something has to be wrong."

CHAPTER THIRTEEN

Louise

The first thing Louise did when she arrived home was to run to one of the cabins on her father's plantation. Inside was a wisp of a woman sitting in a rocking chair in front of a window. The woman's hair was silver gray, her face engraved with the wrinkles of time. Louise cried out, "Nanny!" She had always gone to her nanny, when she had a problem. Right now, she needed her nanny very much.

No one knew Nanny's real age, only that she was very old. Nanny could no longer care for herself. Louise's father had a cabin built for her and picked a servant named Olivia, as her caretaker. Olivia's sole responsibility was to take care of Nanny.

Olivia watched as Louise ran to her nanny. She shook her head sadly, "She done lost her mind, Miss Louise, she don't know nobody or nothin no more."

Louise dropped on the floor beside the rocker. She put her head on her Nanny's lap. Nanny continued staring into space. Tears ran down Louise's face. Then, slowly, Nanny's gnarled fingers came to rest on Louise's head. She stroked her hair as she had done so many times in years past. To Louise's surprise and joy, Nanny spoke, "Now, now, my sweet Louise, tell Nanny all about it." Louise told her about Celeste When Nanny spoke again, it was her wise Nanny of old. "Pray for strength while you are waiting for your little one to return. Do what you can to help others. Laugh and cry with them. One day your baby will come home." As if the words had been too much for her, Nanny sighed, and her hands dropped to her side. Louise, full of gratitude, hugged her nanny and promised her she would do just as she said. She didn't know if Nanny heard her, it was like she had slipped out of her own little world long enough to help Louise and back in again. .

It seemed that Louise missed Celeste more each day. She did not want to get up in the mornings and she did not want to go to bed at night. She could think of nothing she wanted to do. Each night Louise prayed that God would help her find someone who needed her. She hoped it would keep her so busy that she would not have time to dwell on where Celeste might be. It was Michael who gave her the idea. One day he was telling her about the wonderful story the teacher was reading them. "Every day, after lunch, she reads us another chapter, and every day we can't wait to hear the next part."

Louise loved to read and thought this was an excellent idea. She knew Michael's teacher had several grade levels in her room and wondered what book the teacher had chosen that would hold all of the children's interest. "What is the name of the book?" she asked. Michael responded, " *The Governess.*" He asked, "Have you ever read it Mama?" Louise laughed and replied, "No, I have not read it but I planned to get it for Celeste when she was older." Michael spoke again, "I complained to the teacher that it sounded like a story for girls. All the other boys in the room agreed so our teacher explained that it was mainly for girls but she was sure we would enjoy it and the next book she will read will be a book more for boys, *The Adventures of David Simple.* Sarah Fielding wrote both of these books. The teacher always appoints someone in the upper grade to tell about the author. The report was almost as interesting as the story.

Her name is Sarah Fielding. She was born in England in 1710 and she had a sad life. Her mother died when she was little and later when her daddy remarried, her grandmother took her away from them. The courts let her do it. She wrote many books but was very poor when she died."

Michael admitted, "I do like the story though. In the first part, the girls get into a big fight. They pull each other's hair and pinch and scratch! One girl, Miss Jennie Peace always tries to get them to be friends again. Mrs. Teachum lets each of these girls tell a story. They all have funny names and they speak a little differently than we do. Louise smiled and said, "You must have a wonderful teacher. What a good idea to discuss the author of the book."

Michael proceeded to tell her, "Do you know who else can't wait to hear more about Mrs. Teachum, Miss Jenny Peace and the other girls?" Without so much as waiting for a response, he went on, "The colored twins, Marty and Mattie! They wait every day by the back porch so I can tell them what the last chapter was about. Mattie says if she could read, she wouldn't stop until she read the whole book, no matter how long it took!"

Michael had another question, "Mama, why can't colored people read and why do they talk different?" Louise thought for a moment and then answered, "The colored people were brought here from another country." She found herself too ashamed to tell him that they were forced to come. She continued, "They had a language of their own. A language very different from ours. I guess when they came to this country; they wanted their own way of speaking. Perhaps some of our words were hard for them to say. Since they aren't allowed to go to school, they haven't been taught to speak like us." She ended up saying, "Actually, they probably prefer to speak differently then we do."

Michael looked perplexed and said, "It doesn't seem fair that Marty and Mattie don't get to read when they want to so much."

Louise put her arm around Michael and pulled him close, "Michael, I am sure that you have already found out life isn't always fair but I do like your thinking and I do agree with you. Every child should be allowed to read." As she said this, she knew what she was going to do. She would teach the children of her father's coloreds how to read, write and do figures. It would be a frightening and possibly dangerous undertaking. She was willing to chance it.

Louise recalled one of the plantation ladies, Esther Clemens, who decided she would teach her house servant, Washington, to read and do figures. She thought it would save her from the boredom and time it took overseeing the purchasing of groceries and supplies. The slave learned quickly and Esther used that time to browse, try on the latest fashions, and shop for yard goods. All of her friends were envious and some were toying with the idea of doing the same. The husbands and shopkeepers were chagrined by the very thought of it. All of the husbands forbid their wives to let any of their servants learn to read.

Meanwhile, Washington was busy reading every book and newspaper he could get his hands on. It was easy to sneak the reading material into his cabin late at night and return them early in the morning. He read in the newspaper that there was talk of not allowing outsiders to bring any more slaves into the country because the slaves were about to outnumber the white population. That could prove disastrous if they ever started an uprising. He also found out that some states protected certain rights of the slaves. They certainly had no rights in Louisiana. And best of all, he read in the newspaper that there was danger of a war between the North and South because the North wanted to abolish slavery. Whenever Washington got a chance, he whispered these things to the other coloreds on the plantation and those he met in town. He didn't think there was much they could do, but he wanted his people to know that there was hope for their future.

Eventually, the slave owners started to notice a difference in their slaves. They obeyed, but the "Yes Mastah," was missing and many had developed a sullen attitude. One of the plantation owners, Eli Stone, who was known to be especially cruel, beat one of his slaves until he told him what had been going on. He immediately called for a town meeting. Every slave owner, except Louise's father, had attended. Her father treated his slaves with kindness and they had a genuine respect for him.

The cruel taskmaster, Eli Stone told them Washington was at the base of all the trouble. He explained how Esther Clemens had taught him to read. An angry stir ran through the crowd. One of them called out, "How dare a mere slave try to disrupt our way of life! Slavery is the very essence of our economy. Without slaves, our large farms and plantations cannot exist. None of us could afford to hire enough help to own and produce like we do now." Another shouted, "We must teach them all a lesson and keep them in their place."

The men put together a plan. Each went home and grabbed his gun, hitched a wagon, picked out some of their smartest and best slaves and rode to the Clemens plantation. All of these colored and those on the Clemens's plantation were forced to watch as poor Washington was hung from a huge tree in front of the slaves' quarters. His body hung there for days before they were allowed to cut him down and give him a proper burial.

Esther Clemens was mortified at what she had caused. Her husband felt so sorry for her that he couldn't bring himself to reprimand her. The other husbands made sure all of their wives knew what had happened. Louise shuddered as she thought about it.

In spite of all the obstacles, Louise was determined to teach the coloreds. She tried her best to come up with a plan, but couldn't think of anything that made sense. Then she thought of her best friend Sydney. Sydney was one of the reasons she was willing to leave her own home and spend such a length of time at her parents. Sydney was one of the few people Louise could be totally comfortable with, especially since so much sadness had become a part of her life. If anyone could scheme and plot for something good, it was Sydney. And if there was anyone she could trust, it was Sydney. She had one of the servant's saddle her horse and then galloped off to her friend's home.

When the house girl told Sydney a guest was waiting in the parlor, she was thrilled to see that it was Louise. They embraced and Sydney was pleased to notice that for the first time, since Celeste had disappeared, Louise had a little color in her cheeks and a light in her eyes. "I want to talk to you, alone," Louise whispered. Sydney took Louise in the kitchen and sent the servant girl to another part of the house. Sydney prepared the tea herself. She filled their cups, and then sat across the table from Louise. Sydney had barely sat down, when she blurted, "Whatever is it Louise? I am dying to know."

Sydney listened in silence as Louise told of her intentions and why she needed her help. The reflection on Sydney's face was a mirror image of what she was thinking. She looked appalled as Louise's plan unfolded. Louise was not surprised at her friend's reaction. Even so, she knew Sydney would do her best to help her. She wondered what kind of a scheme Sydney would dream up.

Sydney took a deep breath and leaned back in her chair. Louise could see she was deep in thought weighing each word she would say to her. Before Sydney spoke, she looked all around the room, as if expecting to catch someone eavesdropping. She reached across the table and grasped Louise's hands in her own. "Louise," she began, "I do not want to sound like I am lecturing you. I know you are aware that this could be a very heart rending, if not dangerous mission you are about to initiate. If the wrong people find out, it could affect not only you but your parents as well. Your mother takes her social status very seriously. Your father's crops could be burned, even the house.

There might be displays of such violence that death could be the result."

Sydney paused to let her words sink in. She watched Louise's face intently as she said, "I see you have your mind made up. I can understand your desire to do this and because I admire you for it, I will help in any way I can."

She sat back again, thought awhile and finally spoke, "As I see it, the first problem is where and when to teach the children. You and I both know that your father and mother would do just about anything to see some happiness in your life. Your mother is too busy with her social life to interfere. So your father is the one you will be dealing with. He would never knowingly allow you to become involved in anything that might cause you more pain. I know it will be very hard for you to deceive him, and I know you will keep it as honest as you can. You do love to paint, so why not start painting again? Everyone knows you have a talent for it. Perhaps you might ask your father to fix you a private area where you could do some oil painting. Now that we have kerosene lamps, you could even do some writing in the evenings. Your parents might think it strange, but they will be happy to see you taking a real interest in just about anything. You can be sure they won't interfere."

Louise laughed and ran around the table to hug Sydney. "It's perfect," she exclaimed, "I knew you wouldn't fail me."

That evening at the dinner table, Louise told her parents she would like to do some painting and perhaps write a little. Her mother looked shocked, started to speak, and then changed her mind. She had always thought Louise a little strange. She would never understand why Louise wasn't interested in the same things she was. "Oh well," she decided, "I simply don't have the time to discuss this now"

Dolores Morgan's mind wandered to the tea she was planning. She wanted to introduce a young man she had recently met who had aspirations of being their next senator. His name was

Richard Jenner and she was going to do her best to see that he was elected. She became absorbed in her thoughts. She recalled how she had met him at one of the socials she and her husband had attended. When she found out he was running for a seat on the Senate, she suggested a tea for him. She would invite all of her lady friends and make sure they would influence their husbands to vote for him. Mr. Jenner thanked her profusely and said he would make it his business to be available. "Well," she thought, "I will show him how much influence I have. I will do everything in my power to help him become our new Senator."

Louise felt more than a little guilty when she saw the happiness in her father's face. He was so pleased to see she was excited about something. She had always been his pride and joy. It had taken a great toll on him, seeing her day after day, with nothing but sadness in her eyes. He had also loved his granddaughter Celeste dearly and had tried every avenue he could think of to find her.

Louise glanced at her mother. She could see she was off in her own little world and had no interest in the conversation. Louise was relieved her mother would not be asking her a lot of questions.

The following morning, Jonathon showed Louise the cabin she could use. It was weather beaten and in need of a new coat of paint. It was quite small with one large room and a small storage area. Not too close to the master house or too close to the slave's cabins. Louise decided it would be perfect. After Jonathon found Louise was satisfied with the cabin, he left and sent one of his most trusted colored men to help her. His name was Calvin and though he was up in years, he was still very good at working and building. The first thing Louise had him do was to paint the cabin white. When Calvin finished painting, he made three different sized tables, each with a wide drawer and an attached bench. The benches were long enough to seat two children.

Louise scrubbed and cleaned the cabin herself. The hard work was good for her. She loved every minute of it and was almost sorry to see it finished. She put colorful pictures on the wall. She went shopping in Natchitoches and purchased the books and tablets she would need. Lastly, she bought her paints and easel. Louise really did love to paint. She decided to start painting a picture and keep it on the easel in case someone happened in. When Louise had everything in order, she set out to find some children to teach.

Louise visited each little cabin in the hopes she would find a mother willing to allow Louise to teach her children to read. She was unprepared for the reactions she found. The colored mothers pretended they did not understand her. Their eyes widened in fear and most just mumbled, "Ize sorry Miss, but I don know what you talking bout." Louise was crushed. How could she teach with no students? She was at a loss until she remembered the twins, Marty and Mattie, who waited for Michael to tell them more of the story, "*The Governess*" each night after school. Louise hurried home to look by the back porch. Just as Michael had said, they were waiting for him. The twins were probably about six years old, but looked much younger because they were so small. Everyone on the plantation adored Mattie and Marty. The attention never seemed to affect them. They had a smile for everyone. Each had one dimple. Mattie had a cute little turned up nose. Marty's mother kept his tight curls cut very short. Mattie's hair was always in tiny little braids and Louise wondered if her hair was as curly as Marty's.

Louise sat down on the porch steps. She called the twins over and said, "Michael tells me you would like to learn how to read." Suspicion and fear replaced their previously shy demeanor. Louise smiled warmly and said, "I know how you feel, I couldn't wait to read when I was a child." Feeling more comfortable now, Marty blurted, "Michael is the one who told us about reading. I would love to read more than anything in the world. My mammy says to forget about school! She says reading is only for white folks and it is pure silliness for us to even think bout reading, cause we ain't never goin to be lowed to do that!"

Louise motioned them both closer and in a low voice asked, "Do you think you could keep it a secret if I taught you how to read?" Their eyes widened and they both nodded. Louise continued, "All of us could be in trouble if anyone found out. You must promise you won't tell a soul, not even your daddy and mama." As young as they were, Louise sensed they were aware this was a very serious promise that she was exacting from them. They both nodded their heads vigorously. Then Mattie said, "Can we start right now?" Louise laughed and said, "I will have to get some things ready first but don't worry, I will let you know when." The children's eyes glistened. Louise went back into the house. Before closing the door, she put her finger across her lips and said, "Not even Michael!" Once again they nodded.

Louise was disappointed she only had two students. Still, it was a start. She thought of Sydney and knew she would be anxious to hear if she had made any progress. "Perhaps, I will take a ride to Sydney's and tell her what is happening so far.

Henry

The young colored stable boy was grooming one of the horses when Louise stepped inside. She asked him to saddle her horse. Louise had noticed at other times that he was very adept with the horses and conducted himself with unusual confidence and dignity for a stable boy. He was always very proper but he had a way with horses and he fairly strutted when he walked about the stable. It was as if this was his very own territory. The boy was quite light complexioned, slim and small boned. Because of his manner, Louise thought he was probably a little older than he looked, perhaps around thirteen. She appreciated his skill because she was such a horse lover herself. This time she watched him with special interest. She thought to herself, "I have a feeling this boy would just love to learn to read!"

Before Louise mounted the horse, she asked him his name. He responded and she said, "Henry, how would you like to learn to read?" He looked her straight in the eyes and said, "You know, Miss, we ain't 'lowed' to learn to read."

Louise explained, "Henry, would you be able to keep it a secret if I taught you how to read?" His face had a strange look, as if she had asked him if he had ever seen the ghost that lived in the loft above." Henry backed away from her and turned, as if to walk away. He took a few steps, then turned and looked at her, his voice filled with awe as he said, "You mean I could really read one of those pretty books with the pictures that I see when I help pick up the cornmeal that my Pappy buys in the tradin post?" Louise said, "I am sure if you work hard and do as I say, you will be able to read."

Louise could see the fear in his eyes. She sensed it emanating from every pore as he realized that his desire to read was greater than his fear. She was sure that every servant in the area remembered or had been told what happened to Washington when he learned to read. Louise showed him which cabin he should come to. She said, "In two nights, as soon as you finish your supper, come to the cabin. Also, Henry, I want you to bring Marty and Mattie with you. They will be learning to read also." Henry was relieved that he wasn't going to be the only one taking such a chance. From that moment on, his main thought was, "I gwine to learn how to read!" Henry wanted to shout it to the world but the only time he spoke aloud of it was when he knew he was completely alone.

Louise was lost in thought as she rode away. She realized that her parents were quite influential but knew it could be a very volatile and potentiality dangerous venture. Her mother would be mainly concerned with what her friends thought. Her dad would be proud of her, though he would certainly never have allowed her to do this, if he knew. She pushed her worries aside and turned the horse toward Sydney's. She thought, "I don't think it will be that much of a problem if someone does find out." I will protect the colored children first and foremost. I know I will be able to handle anything that comes up." Still, Louise was overwhelmed when the trouble started.

CHAPTER FOURTEEN

Red Feather

Red Feather was not an Indian Chief and had no special title in his tribe but was considered brave and very dangerous and therefore was treated with fear as well as respect. Many of the settlers had also heard of Red Feather's crimes against the white people and greatly feared him.

Red Feather and two other braves had been traveling through the heavily wooded areas for several days. They were looking for excitement but were taking care to stay out of sight of the hated pale faces. When confronted by white men, they wanted to be in a position to annihilate them.

Life was becoming more and more unbearable since the white people had started invading the Indian's land. Concern had passed from one tribe to another that the white people wanted to be rid of all the natives. The Indians had always roamed wherever they pleased until the pale faces came. Red Feather warned his people that all of the tribes must come together in one spirit and force the white man across the land until the only ones left would be pushed into the very waters that had brought them there.

At first, most of the settlers had stayed close to the great waters they had crossed to come to the Indian's country. Now, they were going deeper and deeper into their lands, claiming it as their own. The white people were taking their land and using up their wildlife. Many white men dressed like the Indians and were learning how to be as stealthy and crafty as his own people. Indian villages were under constant vigilance. When the Indians lay their heads down at night, every noise they heard, even animal and bird noises could be a sign that the white men were attacking.

Many of the weaker Indians were trading with them, accepting their trinkets and baubles and falling for their talks of peace and brotherhood. He was glad his tribe, the Apaches, wanted no part of the white man and did not believe their lies of wanting to be brothers.

Red Feather had a special reason for hating the white people. Just as he was ready to go through the ritual of becoming a brave and accepted by his tribe as a man, he had been captured by a group of white men who had attacked their camp.

He was put on the slave block with a young Indian girl and several colored men and women. He was chained and his indignation knew no limits. Whenever the slave buyers approached him, he was filled with hate. The worst was when they tried to check the muscles in his arms or legs. He would tense and try to strike them. However, after a couple of days, everyone else had been sold and he noticed the slaves who were most submissive, were not chained when they were led away. He could see no hope of escaping while he was chained on the block, so decided he would pretend to be docile and perhaps someone would buy him and he would escape. So, Red Feather stood still while the white men examined him and even flexed his muscles for them. Soon, several wanted to buy him, and Red Feather could tell the slave traders were happy with the price they received for him. The man who bought him immediately put new chains on his ankles before leading him away. He had him climb into the back of the wagon and to Red Feather's horror was chained to it. " He consoled himself by thinking,

"The white man can't chain me forever, I will escape and find my people."

Red Feather still shook with indignation and anger when he remembered those days of humiliation and loss of desire to live. He had always learned quickly and though he acted deaf and dumb, he learned many words of the white man's language, only because he thought learning their language might help him to escape. "They think I am just a boy," he mused, "I am a man!" He had been beaten many times because he refused to obey their orders or had tried to escape. When complete hope of freedom was gone, he refused to eat.

By now, the white man considered him more trouble then he was worth, so when he passed out in the fields, the overseer ordered, "Take him to the barn and tie him there. See that he gets no food or water. He is far more trouble than he is worth and deserves to die."

Red Feather always softened when he remembered what had taken place later that afternoon. He had come to, sorry that he hadn't yet died. He heard a noise in the horse stalls behind him. One of the servants was leading a pony to its stall. Sitting on the horse was a little girl. Red Feather had often seen her at a distance and knew she was the daughter of the man who had bought him. She climbed down from the saddle and waited while the servant who was escorting her, removed the saddle. For some reason, Red Feather had cried out. All of his anger and humiliation echoed forth in his cry. The little girl jumped in alarm. To Red Feather's surprise, she climbed up on the feeding trough and peered over at Red Feather. There was not enough light for him to see the expression on her face. She stared for a while and then disappeared. He heard the barn door close as they left.

Red Feather leaned back, exhausted, silently begging the Great Spirit Ussen to let him die. He had given his final voice to a little pale face in order to show his hatred and agony.

When Red Feather came to again, the same little girl was standing in front of him. A colored girl was with her balancing a tray of water and food with her left hand. She held a lantern in her other hand. She set the tray down and then held the lantern above Red Feather and the little girl. He thought he had never seen any child so lovely and enchanting. Her hair was yellow like a pale moon, it was naturally curly and her eyes a mixture of greens. She had a sweet smile and her eyes were sparkling with apparent happiness. If he had known about angels, he would have sworn that she was one. There was something about her that softened his heart. The little girl pointed to the ropes that bound Red Feather. Obediently, the girl set the lantern down and unfastened the ropes that bound him. The servant knew the father idolized his daughter and never chastised her for anything she did, but she said, "Your father is going to be mighty mad about this." She smiled as she spoke, as she too adored her.

When the ropes were loosened, the colored girl brought the tray of food and water and sat it in front of Red Feather. The little girl picked up the glass of water and held it to his lips. Red Feather drank. She pointed to the food and Red Feather found himself reaching for a piece of the bread. Why was he obeying a tiny white child? Surely the Great Spirit Ussen had sent her!

After Red Feather ate the bread, she pointed her finger at him and then spread her arms in a wide arch as if showing him freedom. She pointed to the stall of horses. The servant girl said, "She wants you to take a horse and go to your home." Just before she closed the door, the little girl turned to face him and waved "Goodbye." Then she once again formed a wide arch with her hands.

Red Feather felt a smile spreading across his homely face. He raised his hand in a farewell gesture. He did not know that although he would never see her again, she would forever influence his choices in life. He only knew his heart was filled with renewed hope at the thought of freedom. When he was certain he was alone, Red Feather slowly ate and drank a small amount of the food. He hoped he could retain the food and not become sick. As hungry as he was, he put most of the food in the deerskin pouch that hung from his side. When it was completely dark, he used the last of his strength to open the barn door, climb onto one of the horses and flee.

When Red Feather finally found the remnants of his tribe, he never told them what had happened. He was obsessed with the thought of making a white man his slave and often bragged that someday he would own a white slave. From then on his hatred for the whites increased though his heart always softened whenever he thought of the little golden spirit that Ussen had sent to give him back his freedom.

Plotting

Now, Red Feather stood near the edge of the forest, chewing on a piece of deer jerky. It was years later and he certainly was not thinking of any little angel who had once freed him. Red Feather was not much taller than he was those many years ago. He was the shortest man in his tribe and he hated that. His black hair was long and secured in the back by a strip of leather. His large nose made his eyes appear even smaller than they were, and lost in his wide forehead. He rarely smiled, unless some atrocity or meanness was taking place. Several scalps hung from his waist as proof that he had become a great brave, in spite of the white mans' efforts to kill his spirit. His piercing eyes scanned the countryside. He knew the entire area as well as the back of his hand. In the distance, he saw wafts of smoke curling up and disappearing into the skyline. He knew exactly the place the smoke was coming from. It was an area the new settlers traveled and often camped when making their way into his country, claiming more of the Indians' land

and taking more of their freedom away. He walked back to his companions and told them he had found something that would entertain them that night. They sat quietly waiting for darkness, each anticipating what they would find at the unsuspecting campsite.

The Attack

Frank and Ann had made especially good time this particular day and both were in good moods. They were happy to be rid of Celeste and now referred to her as the 'Intruder.' The trail they were on was well packed down from all the people heading for gold country and therefore much smoother to travel on. There had been other days when it had rained and the trail turned into mud, making traveling difficult and sometimes impossible.

Frank had chosen this trail because it would eliminate going through the mountains, taking days off their trip. The negative part was that it would take them close, if not through the Apache country. The Apaches and Creek Indians were the most feared Indians of all. One settler warned them, "There is one band of Apaches you especially need to watch out for in these parts. They are the Chiricahuas Apaches. They have a reputation of being the fiercest of all Apaches. These Apaches do not live in tepees, they live in wickiups." Ann asked, "What is a wickiup?" The man explained, "A wickiup takes the place of a tepee. It is their dwelling place. It is made of slender poles bent to give the wickiups a rounded or pointed look. They are then covered with brush and grass." Frank wished the man had never mentioned that tribe in front of Ann and was glad when one of the men at the next settlement said, "It has been a long time since there has been any serious trouble with the Indians." They asked Frank, "Did you bring any trinkets and bright things to give the Indians? They love to have bright and gaudy things and are easily appeased." Frank laughed and told them, "We brought plenty of bartering items, we didn't bring much furniture, so we had lots of extra room. We even have plumed hats and brocaded jackets. If all that it takes is beads and trinkets, we won't have a problem." One of the men spoke up, "Just remember to be on your guard at all times and pray you don't run into any of the hostile ones."

Frank had pulled the horses to a stop when he noticed a deserted campsite with a small creek of water running through. He was climbing down from the wagon when he saw a rabbit quietly nibbling away. He reached for his gun, took aim and fired. The rabbit fell to the ground. Fresh meat would be wonderful. He skinned and cleaned the rabbit in the creek. Ann had started the fire and held out the pan for Frank to drop the rabbit pieces. After Frank and Ann finished their supper, they laid back on their blankets, contented and happy. The horses had grazed and drank their fill of water at the creek, and now were silent.

The sun was setting and the moon was getting ready to cast its eerie glow when Frank first started to feel uneasy. He had the feeling that someone was watching them. He pulled his gun closer, hoping Ann wouldn't notice. Maybe it was his imagination because Ann never batted an eye, she just rolled over and fell fast asleep. Frank continued to stare into the darkness, sleep now far removed from his weary body. He took his gun with him when he stood up to toss more wood on the fire. He was glad he had a good supply of firewood. He would keep the fire going all night if he had to.

Frank did not hear or see any movement. The three figures that stood before him seemed to evolve from nowhere. They were Indians and they all had a smug look on their faces. Worst of all, he recognized them as being Apaches, he wondered if they were of the Chiricahuas tribe. The scalps dangling from one of the Indians waists sent shivers through Frank. He raised the gun and pointed it at the one with the scalps, as he appeared to be the leader. To Frank's surprise, the Indian raised his hand, palm facing him and said in quite good English, "We come in peace." Frank knew that even if he shot this one, the other two would jump him. In a no nonsense voice, the same Indian said, "We want Firewater!"

Red Feather was proud that he could speak English so well. It gave the whites a false sense of security. Red Feather suddenly turned and kicked the sleeping Ann. This angered Frank and took him off his guard; the gun no longer had the Indian in its sight. In a flash, Red Feather grabbed the gun, and stood back, pretending to admire it.

Ann sat up, rubbing her bruised hip, ready to complain until she saw the scene around her. She knew that Indians did not like cowardice and she made a resolution that she would not show any fear.

This time when Red Feather spoke, he directed the command to Ann. "Firewater," he said. Ann's eyes reflected no fear, as she said, "No firewater!" Red Feather reached in his pocket, he would have fun with such a daring squaw. He pulled out a large, hard object and threw it on the blanket by Ann. "We pay you gold," he said. He knew the pale-faced people loved gold. The Apache's had plenty in their camp and he always carried some with him in case he wanted to barter for some of their wonderful firewater. Frank barely glanced at the gold. For the first time in his life, he was not interested in gold.

When Ann stood, Red Feather grabbed her arm and forced it behind her back. He pushed it upward to increase the pain. Anger enveloped Frank and he started for Red Feather. The other two Indians grabbed Frank. With his free hand, Red Feather shoved the gun into Frank's belly. Frank grunted and dropped to his knees. In spite of the pain and nausea, Frank struggled to his feet. He too, knew he must not show fear or signs of cowardice.

CHAPTER FIFTEEN

Celeste

Celeste felt safe in the doghouse and had slept all night. Of course she had no idea that Bob and Linda were going to investigate Mitzi's strange behavior. She awakened with a start when the back door slammed. She heard Bob and Linda talking in muted tones This frightened Celeste even more. Mitzi raised her head, ears alert. She eased through the doghouse door but stayed in front of the entry. Celeste was glad the dog would shield her from roving eyes.

Bob set the food down. He instructed Linda, "Set the water next to Mitzi and see if she growls." Mitzi only wagged her tail. Bob tried to nudge Mitzi away from the entry. A growl rumbled in her throat and she held her ground. Bob stepped back, looking shocked. "That does it!" he exclaimed, "She has to have something very precious in there to be growling at me." Excitement rang in Linda's voice as she said, "Oh Bob, I bet she has puppies!" Bob laughed, embarrassed that he hadn't thought of that. "I think you just might be right, I'm about to find out."

Linda wasn't thoroughly convinced. It occurred to her it might be some wild animal that Mitzi was befriending. She ran back to the safety of the porch.

Bob tried to think of a way to get Mitzi away from the doghouse. If there was anything Mitzi loved, it was a ride in the buggy with Bob. He opened the back door and brought out Mitzi's harness. Mitzi knew exactly what this meant. Bob held out the harness and called her. She started forward, and then retreated, resuming guard at the entry. Bob had to coax her before she finally came. Bob put the halter on and then led her to the buggy where he tied her. He brought the horses and harnessed them to the buggy. Only then did he return to the doghouse.

In a determined voice, he said, "Now, we will see what is in that dog house." Hearing this, Celeste's heart thumped so hard, it terrified her. Frantically, she looked for a place to hide, and knew there was none. It was hard now for her to breathe. She lay down on the floor and closed her eyes as tightly as she could. Lying down made breathing next to impossible and she sat up again, her eyes still squeezed shut.

Linda called from the porch, "Be careful Bob, it could be a wild animal!" Bob got down on his haunches and stared into the dimness of the interior. He squinted and almost lost his balance, overwhelmed at what he saw. Two little legs crossed Indian style. He moved closer, his face almost inside the entry. He could make out a tiny form, long blonde hair, hands clasped over her eyes. He moved back a little and called softly, "Please come out, I promise you I won't hurt you."

Linda almost fell over when she realized he was talking to a live person. Celeste didn't move. Bob pleaded, "Please come out, I promise you I won't touch you." Celeste never moved. He tried again, "How about opening your eyes?" He saw her quiver and then her body grew tense. He realized that he had said the wrong thing. His heart ached for the little one inside and now he begged, "You can't stay in there forever. Please come out, I want to help you. Please honey!"

Bob had no way of knowing that "honey" was probably the only word that would have moved Celeste. When she was sick, her mother often called her "Honey." It always made her feel very special. Celeste crawled out and stood, head lowered and her eyes still closed. She was at his mercy, waiting for his sentence. Bob and Linda stared at the little waif that stood before them. She appeared quite healthy, but she was filthy. Her blonde hair was matted and snarled, it must not have been combed for weeks, maybe months. The article of clothing she wore was tattered, stained and grimy. The tiny feet looked as if the dirt was etched into the skin.

Linda, aghast at the sight of the dirty, forlorn little girl, recovered, and came down from the steps. She demanded, "Bob, let me have her, I'm going to give her a bath right now." She hurried toward Celeste. Immediately Celeste dropped to her knees and started to crawl back into the doghouse. Bob grabbed Linda's arm. In a voice that was an order, he said, "Go back in the house Linda, the bath will come later."

Celeste stood up again. This time she opened her eyes and looked around, as if looking for someone. Bob knew she was looking for Mitzi and said, " I think, the first thing we should do is find out if Mitzi will let me be your friend too. Bob turned as if he took it for granted she would follow. Celeste longed to have Mitzi at her side again, so she followed Bob, keeping a safe distance behind him. When Mitzi saw Celeste, she barked and whined, and tried to break free of the harness. Celeste's little legs fairly flew as she ran to the dog. She dropped to the ground beside Mitzi and wrapped her arms tightly around her neck.

Celeste's eyes were not nearly as frightened now, Bob could almost see a look of defiance in her eyes that said, "I don't have to go with you now, and Mitzi won't let you pull me away." Bob knew she was right about that, he couldn't even imagine what ruse he could use next.

Nonchalantly, Bob queried, "Do you know what Mitzi's favorite thing is?" Celeste's expression changed, he could tell she had taken the bait. "She just loves to go for a buggy ride! That is what I promised her when I tied her to the buggy. I realize now that she won't go if you don't. We wouldn't want to spoil her good time, would we? Especially after I promised her. Do you think you are big enough to climb into the buggy so she will follow you?" Celeste got up slowly and scrambled until she was sitting in the buggy. Bob untied Mitzi. The dog immediately jumped up and settled in by Celeste.

While they were cantering along, Bob couldn't keep his eyes off this waif of a girl. Even in her pitiful condition, she was a beautiful child.

Mitzi loved to go fast, so he speeded up the horses, watching Celeste's face, in case it frightened her. Now the wind was ruffling through Mitzi's fur and the lilt of a smile was on the little girl's face. They both kept their faces full to the wind, as if glorying in the excitement of it. Bob himself hadn't felt so excited about anything for a long, long time. When the buggy ride was over, Celeste withdrew again and would not look at him. She pulled back when he tried to help her down from the buggy. Bob tried to think of how he could get Celeste inside the house and hopefully take a bath. He asked, "Do you have a name?" Celeste didn't respond. "Can you talk?" No answer. "We have to call you something, so for now, how about if we call you Honey?" The little positive nod of the head made chill bumps on his flesh. He squatted on the ground beside her, being careful not to get too close, and said, "I must go to work now. I have a store to take care of." He smiled at her and said, "It would be nice if you had a bath while I am gone. The lady in the house is my sister, Linda. She is very nice and she will help you bathe and find something clean for you to wear. Usually, we don't let Mitzi in the house, but this time we will break the rules, and you can bring her inside with you. She will think she is getting a very special treat. Be a good girl and let my sister clean you up and I will bring you some candy when I come home tonight."

Bob held the door open and Celeste grasped Mitzi's collar and nudged her through the door. Linda had heated a tub of water and placed it behind the kitchen stove. She couldn't wait to clean this little girl up and see what she really looked like. Bob took Linda aside and said, "Don't be asking her any questions, let her get used to us." He needn't have worried. Linda didn't want to know who or where this little girl came from. Even in her neglected state, she was a darling. Linda already had great plans for her. She had been thinking it over while she was heating the bath water. "I'll make her some pretty dresses. It will be so much fun to turn the spare bedroom into a frilly little girl's room. I'll teach her lovely manners. She can call Bob, 'Uncle,' and me 'mama.' After all I will be just like a mama to her."

After Bob left, the bath started. Linda shampooed Celeste's hair over and over and rinsed it in vinegar to help untangle it. Her feet were so ingrained with dirt, they turned red from the scrubbing and Linda had to concede, it would take time and several additional scrubbings before they were satisfactory. While she was bathing Celeste, she told her, "Everything is all right now, and you won't ever have to be afraid again. Can you just tell me your name?" Celeste gave no indication that she had even heard. Linda thought for a moment and then inquired, "Can you talk?" Celeste shook her head back and forth. Linda assured her, "Well, that's okay, I will help you learn to talk."

If Linda had stopped there, her relationship with Celeste might have been a good one, but she said the wrong thing in her next words. "I think it would be nice if you would think of me as 'mama'. After all, I will love you just like you are my own little girl. We will keep that a secret."

If ever Celeste had wanted to speak, it was now! She opened her mouth and strained to say "No, No," but not a sound could she make.

When Linda brought one of her blouses for Celeste to put on, Celeste wouldn't touch it. Linda gave her other choices of her clothes, but Celeste still balked. Then Celeste pointed to the rack behind the kitchen door where Mitzi's harness hung. Next to it was an old shirt of Bobs. "Well, my dear," she said, a little jealous that she chose to wear a shirt of Bobs, rather than hers, "we can do better then that." She went to Bobs' closet and picked a bright red shirt. She extended the shirt to Celeste who proudly put it on. The red was a perfect shade for her coloring and blonde hair. She looked so innocent and sweet that Linda yearned to hold her; however she had learned something from her earlier rashness and abandoned that thought. She was careful not to try and caress her, but she by no means gave up her plans. "Sooner or later, she will be mine."

Linda rolled the sleeves up until Celeste's tiny hands were exposed. She couldn't wait for her brother to get home and see her handiwork.

CHAPTER SIXTEEN

Louise

Louise had never before experienced the satisfaction and happiness she now found in teaching her students how to read and do figures. She had to force them to leave each evening. The twins rarely played with the other children. Whenever they saw Louise head for the cabin, they would be there to learn more. Henry spent any free time he had there. Horses were no longer his first love. The children hung on her every word and their love and admiration almost overwhelmed her. She couldn't believe how quickly they learned.

Louise had made little flash cards with the letters of the alphabet. She would hold up a flash card and tell them the sound each one made. She gave them an example of each sound. For instance with the letter "f," she explained, "When a cat is angry, it arches its' back like this letter and says 'fff.' That is what this letter says." The children loved it and quickly learned all of the sounds. She taught them how to put the sounds together. In no time at all they were reading quite well. Pride beamed on their faces. Louise began to include penmanship along with their reading. They begged to take the books home with them. It hurt Louise to refuse, but she knew she had to.

Whenever Sydney got the chance, she visited Louise. She loved to hear how the children were progressing. Louise loved telling her. Sydney never left without cautioning Louise, "Don't get careless. Remind the children over and over, ""Never, never, tell anyone."" Their pride in knowing how to read might be your downfall."

Louise wanted to say, "If you only knew how much I worry about that. I warn them every night, but I am so afraid this will eventually happen." In the end, it was not the children that told.

Dolores Morgan

About the only time Louise saw her mother was at the dinner table. Mrs. Morgan was just too busy going to teas or chairing some ongoing cause. Mrs. Morgan had also set a date for the tea for Mr. Jenner. She could just hear herself saying, "Richard Jenner, the best man to be our next Senator." Mrs. Morgan thought he was one of the most gentle and agreeable men she had ever met. When she had contacted him, he let her pick the date and promised he would be there. She was especially happy with his response when she asked him if his wife could also come. "Mrs. Morgan," he had said, "I am afraid that would be impossible, you see I am not married." That is when she first started thinking of how wonderful it would be to have him for a son-in-law, especially if he became their new Senator. "If Louise will just cooperate," she thought, "She can be so stubborn."

At last, it was the day of the tea. Mrs. Morgan had insisted Louise attend. Louise's only wish was that it wouldn't last long. She was aware that this tea was very important to her mother, but she also knew her mother well enough to know that she just might try to play 'Cupid.' She vowed to herself, "I will meet him and that is all. I will have nothing to do with him again." She imagined that he would be handsome, dashing and a snob.

Mrs. Morgan watched Richard Jenner's face closely when she introduced Louise. She could see right away that he found Louise attractive. Louise was pleasant, but aloof. Mrs. Morgan wasn't worried about that. She could well imagine that time and a little scheming on her part would get the end result that she wanted.

Louise found an empty chair and sat down. She was quite surprised at Richard Jenner's appearance. He wasn't at all as she had pictured him. When the man began his speech, she was even more surprised. He was certainly not the type she imagined would impress her mother. He was rather short, probably no more then five foot nine. His face was plain, his blue eyes melancholy. His hair was sandy. Instead of a great oration, he said very little, and Louise found herself wanting to help him. She was certain every lady there had the same feeling. Celeste came to her mind and her heart felt a deep longing. She had to force her thoughts back to the present. When Richard Jenner finished speaking and sat down, all of the ladies clapped profusely. Louise realized that Mr. Jenner had managed to bring out the 'mother' in all of them. She felt as is he had just told them it would be impossible for him to win a seat in the Senate if they did not help him. "In fact," thought Louise, "That is more or less what he did say." After his speech, they all clamored to his side. Before the ladies left, each had promised Mr. Jenner they would do everything they could do to get him elected.

After the tea, Mrs. Morgan said, "Louise, Mr. Jenner is staying for dinner, would you like to show him our flower garden?" Ordinarily, this would have angered Louise, but for some reason, she felt no anger.

During their walk, Mr. Jenner appeared quite shy. In fact, Louise found herself doing most of the talking. She would hardly finish a sentence before he would ask her something else about herself. When they came back from their walk, Louise was embarrassed that she had talked so much. She would make a point of being quiet at the dinner table. She needn't have worried. Her mother monopolized the conversation. Most of it was directed at Mr. Jenner. After the first question, he asked them to call him Richard.

Mrs. Morgan asked him how he happened to get into politics. He explained, "My father was a politician. In fact, he was a senator when we lived in New Orleans. My mother wanted me to be a doctor. My father almost demanded that I get a degree in law and then go into politics. After getting my law degree, I helped to get the governor of our state elected and met many politicians. It didn't take long for me to realize I had found my niche. I find it interesting as well as challenging, rather like playing a serious game of chess."

Before Richard left, his eyes looking as if someone was about to hurt him, he asked, "Louise, do you think I could call on you sometime?" To Louise's own surprise, she replied, "I think that would be all right." Quickly, she added, "I would like to hear what your political beliefs are." It was Richard's turn to look surprised. He promised, "You tell me when I can come, and I will be here."

Richard Jenner

Louise found herself anticipating Richard's visit. She tried to determine what it was about him that appealed to her. He certainly wasn't handsome, though his features were appealing. She had never cared for sandy colored hair. He wasn't even an enthusiastic or intense person. She came to the conclusion that it was his eyes and smile she liked. "But why?" she wondered, "His eyes are not anything special and his lips only ordinary." Still she realized that she wanted to see him smile at her again, dipping his head as if he dared hope to get a return smile. There was something alluring and seductive about the way he looked at her.

Richard came as often as he could get away and Louise found herself looking forward to his visits.   She never realized until much later that she actually never found out what his political beliefs were. Without really talking about what he believed, he somehow made her feel he felt the same about issues as she did. Usually, he answered her questions, with a question.

For many reasons, Louise no longer believed in slavery. Partly because of Aaron, teaching the children how to read and because she was so fair-minded were enough reasons. She sometimes shared her feelings with Richard about the unfairness of slavery. He lauded her for her humanity. He seemed to sense that Louise was not ready for romance. Their closest contact was to hold hands. This suited Louise. She was content and happy just to be with him.

When Richard gave a campaign speech in Natchitoches, Jonathon decided to attend and Louise asked permission to ride into town with him. Since Richard was speaking from a platform on the main street, her dad reined the horses in nearby so Louise could sit in the carriage and hear his speech. Louise was amazed at the difference in this oratory and the one he had given for the ladies. It was as if he was a different person entirely. He spoke distinctly and with authority. On the way home, she mentioned this to her father. He replied, "Richard has made it his business to know the men across our state. He knows what they want and he makes sure they think he is the man who will get it for them. From my observations, I would say he is a born politician." Louise could not tell if his comment was a sincere compliment or otherwise. For some reason she did not feel inclined to ask him. They talked and laughed about other things and in no time were riding up the lane and home again.

Louise would not have been pleased if she had known Richard discussed their relationship with Mrs. Morgan. She would have been really angry if she knew that her mother was the one who initiated the talks. Richard did not want to make an enemy of Mrs. Morgan and was happy to find she would like nothing better then to have him as her son-in-law. She assured him that she was out to help him win a seat in the senate and also the hand of her daughter.

Election time was getting closer. Richard was gone a lot, often campaigning in other cities and rural areas. Louise found herself missing his visits and looking forward to seeing him again.

Reading and writing

As a surprise to the twins, Louise brought two of Michael's books and told the twins that on the days when she did not have to hurry away, they could sit in the classroom and read them. One was a story of a little girl who was not able to walk. Mattie saw the picture and Louise could tell that Mattie's heart was filled with compassion. Mattie laid it on her worktable and turned the pages ever so carefully, while she and Marty looked at the pictures. Tears came to their eyes when they came to the picture of the little girl. When they had looked at all the pictures, Mattie held the book close to her heart and then handed it to Marty who did the same. The children took turns reading aloud from it. While they were reading, Louise often painted, occasionally having to help them with the difficult words or explain their meaning. She found herself painting the children as they read. Skillfully she showed the look of rapture on their faces and excitement in their eyes.

She kept this picture hidden, replacing it each time with the oil she had been doing of the nearby bayou. She enjoyed painting and loved painting while the children read. No one could say she had lied about what she wanted the cabin for. She just hadn't told them all of the reasons.

Sometimes Louise would visit Nanny. She never responded again. Now Nanny was confined to her bed and Louise could see she was suffering. The real Nanny had been gone for a long time and Louise was thankful when her suffering was over. She was buried in one of the plots set aside for the family.

Just Talking It Over

It was August twentieth, exactly four months since Celeste had disappeared. Louise had been depressed all day. One of those days that it was hard to stay in a positive mode. The colored people were having a revival in their little meetinghouse, so her students wouldn't be coming. Louise was sitting on the front porch with her arm around Michael, which gave her a feeling of consolation. She was thinking of Celeste and how wonderful it would be if she also had her arm around Celeste. She was at her lowest point since Celeste had disappeared and was silently counting her blessings to try to overcome her sadness when Michael turned to her and said, "Mr. Jenner promised me that he would take me fishing again. I like it when he goes fishing with me. I like to go horseback riding with him too. I like being with him but not as much as I like being with Grandpa." Louise's mind was still on Celeste and she nonchalantly replied, "That's nice, I enjoy him also."

Louise came out of her reverie with Michaels next question, "Mama, are you going to marry Mr. Jenner?" She realized that thought had never entered her mind. She pondered a moment and then said, "Why Michael, he has never asked me. I have never even thought of it, whatever made you think of asking me that?"

Quickly Michael replied, "The house servants think you will."

Louise laughed, "Well, I guess if he asks me, I just might say yes. Would you like that?" Michael sat quietly for a moment, and then said, "I like Mr. Jenner, but I don't think I like him that much." Louise hugged Michael and assured him, "Michael, if he can't win you over, then he won't be able to win me either."

Michael sat quietly, remembering what his Grandmother Dolores had said to him one day. Michael had been telling her about Mr. Jenner taking him fishing. She had asked, "Do you like Mr. Jenner?" He had assured her that he did. In a voice that Michael knew was confidential, she had said, "Michael, Mr. Jenner makes your mom smile and I think she really likes him too. If they should decide to get married, I think that would make her even happier. We wouldn't want to say or do anything that would keep her from being happy, would we?" She hadn't waited for his answer.

Michael was afraid he might have made his mother unhappy. He wanted to correct that. "Mama," he said, "I think it would be nice if you would marry Mr. Jenner." Louise looked surprised, and then pulled him close, "Michael, if I ever marry Mr. Jenner, I promise you that Michael Lorell will always be my first love."

Louise and Michael lived in an area of the house that was almost separate from the main house. They had their own porch and private entry. The only access to the main part of the house was a hallway door off the sitting room. It could be locked from either side. The outside porch entrance opened into a small sitting room. Their bedrooms were just off this room.

When Louise was going to be gone for any length of time, Michael had his choice of being with his grandparents or having Cleo watch over him. Cleo was the daughter of the main house servant and she was Michael's favorite of any person outside of his family and Dan and Sarah. She had a lovely singing voice and he loved to hear her sing the beautiful, haunting songs that the coloreds sang. Cleo enjoyed all the things he told her about school and his dreams. Michael knew that her dream was to be free. One of his dreams was to somehow help that happen.

Dolores and Jonathon

While Louise and Michael were having their talk, a similar one was taking place in Mr. and Mrs. Morgan's bedroom. This one was actually more like an argument. Mrs. Morgan was seated on her vanity chair, brushing her hair before retiring for the night, she turned to Jonathon and said, "Richard is going to ask our Louise to be his wife."

This took Jonathon by surprise and he retorted, "My dear Dolores, just how would you know that?" Mrs. Morgan, not catching on that he was on the verge of anger fell right into the trap. "Oh, I know lots. I do believe Richard feels he can confide completely in me."

Mr. Morgan controlled his voice as he said, "And what does our Louise think of his proposing?" Laughing, she replied, "Well, to tell you the truth, I don't think the dear girl has the slightest notion that he intends to marry her."

Mr. Morgan could contain his anger no longer, He retorted, "There is something strange when a mother knows about a man's proposal before the intended victim."

This brought Mrs. Morgan to her feet. Shaking an angry finger at him, she exploded, "What do you mean, victim? He could have just about any woman he wanted. I, myself think he would make a wonderful husband for Louise. Did you ever take the time to notice how good he is with Michael and how much time he spends with him? Have you ever noticed that no one coerced Louise to see him? Have you by any chance noticed she has a little life in her eyes?"

She waited for a reply from her usually mild mannered husband. When he did not respond, she went on. "Of course you didn't notice. You didn't like Richard from the start, and I sincerely believe you can't give one good reason why. Well, you better start liking him, because I have a strong feeling that he is going to be your son- in -law." She turned away from him and sat down again, relieved that the conversation was over.

Mr. Morgan moved directly in front of her and stood his ground. His face was like stone, in quiet even tones he warned her, "Dolores, I have always let you do just as you pleased. I even got a kick out of seeing you manipulate and maneuver your ladies clubs, your friends and even strangers. Up to now it never really hurt anyone. This is one time I will not allow it. We are talking about our daughter. I do not intend for anyone to play games with her life. She wouldn't stand for it, if she had any idea. Right now, she is very vulnerable. If you ever try to influence her in any way, I will tell her how `dear' Richard has confided so much in her mother. You can be sure that will be enough for her. I don't like the man, you are right; I can't tell you why. I keep hoping I am wrong because I can see that Louise does care for him. I'm warning you, stay out of it. Let her make her own decisions. She has always had good judgment. If she does marry him, I will do my best to like him, meanwhile I am telling you I do not like anything about that man." He turned on his heels and left the room.

Mrs. Morgan was in a state of shock. Jonathon had never spoken this way to her before. A shudder went through her. She didn't want him to ever do it again. "Oh well," she thought, "Everything is in motion now. I won't do anything to encourage it anymore. I won't do anything to stop it either."

CHAPTER SEVENTEEN

Firelight and Firewater

Frank watched helplessly as Red Feather twisted Ann's arm behind her. Ann felt as if her arm was coming out of its socket. She didn't know how much longer she could keep the scream of pain locked in her throat. Red Feather could have easily broken her arm, but lucky for Ann, he suddenly threw her to the ground. He muttered something to his companions, and they grabbed Frank. Red Feather and the braves always made certain they brought something along in case they needed to tie someone or something. Long leather strips were dried and stretched and were referred to as thongs. Each of them had several tied around their waist, handy if needed. Taking one of the leather thongs from their waist, they bound Frank's hands behind his back. After tying his feet together, they forced him across his blanket and rolled him in it until he looked like a huge cocoon. Another thong was wrapped around the blanket to prevent him from rolling out of it. No part of him was visible. Ann hoped he could breathe. The Indians didn't care one way or the other.

Ignoring Ann, the Indians climbed into the wagon. They threw every thing on the ground until they found the whiskey. One of them threw more wood on the fire. Red Feather took the first drink. He passed the bottle to his companions. With each drink, they got louder. Every so often, they would point at Ann, saying something in their own tongue. Ann felt as if they were trying to plan what would be a good way to torture her. Red Feather got up once, and Ann was terrified that he was coming for her. Instead he brought one of the chests back. It was one with some of the things they had hoped would be useful in bartering or appeasing Indians. They put on the brocaded jackets and plumed hats. Each pointed at the other one, as they chanted and danced. Ann could see they thought they looked elegant. Her eyes filled with hatred, and she thought, "If they only knew how ridiculous they looked." Then she spied the huge piece of gold. She moved close to it until the folds of her gown covered it. With one hand, she dug stealthily in the earth beside her. When she thought the hole was deep enough and the Indians weren't looking, she smuggled the gold into the hole. Carefully, she packed the dirt over it. If she lived and got the chance, she would claim this gold as her own. She looked around for landmarks so she could one day find the buried gold. She marked it parallel to two unusual trees and perpendicular to a huge rock.

The Indians were on their second bottle when Red Feather grabbed Ann and shoved her into the midst of them. "You dance!" he ordered. He started chanting and clapping his hands in rhythm. The two Indians joined him. Ann, not wanting to incite their wrath knew she must do his bidding. She started out slowly and then the beat and chanting seemed to mesmerize her. It took control of her body and her movements were so graceful and articulate that the Indians were captivated. If she had not been so mesmerized herself, and if she could have seen their eyes, she might have seen they were filled with awe and perhaps even respect. She certainly did not know that she had just saved her life. Each time one of them pointed at her that night, he had a suggestion as to what kind of death they were going to subject her to. After the dance, they were not too drunk to realize they wanted to see her dance again and again.

Suddenly, one of the Indians fell over. Deep snores replaced the chanting. As if this was a signal, Red Feather staggered to his feet. He grabbed Ann, trussed her feet and ankles, then rolled and tied a blanket around her. He took one more drink from the bottle, lurched to his side and slept.

Ann waited until there was complete silence, broken only by the deep snores of the three Indians, before she called out, "Are you all right Frank? Can you breathe?" A muffled, "Yes." came back through the blanket. She knew he didn't have a lot of air, so she only said, "We will get out of this Frank, my head isn't covered, so don't worry about me. We need our strength, so try and sleep." Ann was determined that she would, and in no time she was asleep. Even the horrendous nightmares that slipped in and out of her brain did not fully awaken her.

If Frank ever fell asleep, he wasn't aware of it. Struggling to breathe inside the rolled up blanket and thinking of the different forms of torture he had heard Indians use, kept him awake. Would they burn them at a stake? That might be better then some of the alternatives. He had heard of them cutting off parts of prisoners to cook and eat, starting with their fingers and toes. Or would they tie them to the ground and leave them stretched out in the sun, prey to whatever crawling or creeping predators wanted to do to their body? He wondered how long he would have enough strength to keep his eye lids closed. The thoughts of ants and other crawling things in his eyes was more than he could bear. He had seen the cruelty in Red Feather's eyes and knew it would not be a fast and easy death that he would plan. One thing, for sure, Red Feather would have two new scalps hanging from his side. He wondered why they hadn't already started torturing them. Then it occurred to him that perhaps they wanted to take them to their village so they could let the entire tribe witness their demise. This gave him a little hope, perhaps he could find some way to escape on the way. He tried to hold on to this thought.

Sunshine was filtering through the trees when the Indians awoke from their drunken stupor. Red Feather had not planned on staying the night. He did not want to be seen by any of the white people. Bands of soldiers were also becoming more prevalent these days. He thought, "Must try to remember firewater is powerful spirit."

Red Feather had the braves unroll Frank and Ann. He strutted back and forth, threatening them with his knife every so often. He gloried in the control he had over them. He would have enjoyed adding two more scalps to his belt. That could wait because there was one thing he desired more than that at this moment. The scalps could be added later. Right now he wanted to show his people that he owned two slaves. He must get out of this area as soon as possible and take his prisoners back to show his people. He would have enjoyed making them walk. Now, for the sake of time, they would have to ride two of the team horses. They were not riding horses, but they would serve the purpose.

Ann was untied first. While they were loosening Frank's bindings, he whispered, "Get your shoes on." Ann quickly put her shoes on and threw her dress over her gown. As soon as Frank was untied, he slipped his trousers, shirt and shoes on, while the Indians were picking up whatever they wanted.

Ann looked angrily at all of their possessions on the ground. She spotted her comb nearby and shoved it in her pocket. The only other thing close to her was a large handkerchief of Franks. She also stuffed that in her pocket. She was about to sidle around to look for something she might use as a weapon when Red Feather slapped her across the face. He could see the hatred in her eyes and laughed at her, "What a fiery little squaw in spite of her whiteness and golden hair. She would have to be watched, "What sport that would be!"

Before the Indians tossed them on the horses, they put the remaining brocaded jackets on Frank and Ann, and then tossed all of the beads over their necks. One of the Indians picked up one of Ann's bonnets and placed it on Frank's head. They laughed and pointed at Frank, and called, "Squaw, Squaw." Frank's expression never changed, he was too thankful that he was still alive and breathing easily again. The Indians made sure they took the other bottles of firewater. It was a peculiar looking group that started the trek back to the Indian village.

The Indians chewed on their beef jerky as they rode along. Red Feather knew where springs of water were, and they stopped to drink occasionally. He allowed Ann to drink, but pointed to Frank who still had on one of Ann's bonnets, and said, "Squaw not drink." Ann managed to dip the handkerchief in the water. She hid it in her hands each time and while the Indians were drinking, she would smuggle the sopped handkerchief to Frank. Sometimes she managed to dip it more than once. He sucked what water he could from it until the Indians backed away from the springs. Never had water tasted so good.

When Frank dozed off, sheer fright jolted him awake and kept him from falling off the horse. Lucky for Frank and Ann, Red Feather wanted his slaves to look good when he showed them off. Because of this they were allowed some food and water when they camped for the last night. The closer Red Feather got to his village, the taller he felt. Revenge coursed through his blood, like the firewater that lit his brain. He had not one, but two white slaves. What a sight it would be for his people when they rode into the village.

The Apache camp was far removed from any white settlements. The only white people that had ever been in their camps were fur traders. These men were always heavily bearded and dressed much like the Indians themselves.

Most Apache tribes did not have one man as chief, but for some reason, Red Feather's band, had their own chief. Unlike some Indian Chiefs, 'Gray Wolf,' did not want to be brothers with the white men. He, like Red Feather, would have enjoyed driving them out of their lands. He wanted war, not peace.

When they were a short distance from the village, Red Feather stopped the entourage and took the jackets from Frank and Ann, the beads and the plumed hat she wore. He would give the finest brocaded jacket and the plumed hat to Chief-Gray Wolf. He smirked to himself, imagining the laughter Frank would elicit when he told them the man pale face had a woman's bonnet on his head.

The children from the village were the first to see Red Feather and his group. They stopped playing and stared. As they became braver, they pointed and jeered. Soon the entire village joined them. Frank and Ann both had their minds on something else. They noticed this camp did not have tents, they lived in what Ann and Frank recognized must be Wickiups. This must be the cruel band of Apaches they had been warned of!

When they were inside the camp, Red Feather pointed to Frank and told the people that he had a squaw's bonnet on his head. The Indians laughed and joined the two Indians with Red Feather, calling "Squaw."

Chief Gray Wolf was in his wickiup and knew something special was taking place. He put on his finest eagle feather bonnet. He walked to the group and stood with his arms clasped across his chest. Red Feather slid down from his horse and offered the Chief his gifts. Gray Wolf grunted in approval and immediately put them on.

Red Feather tied Frank and Ann, side by side to a large tree. He wanted the tribe to have a good view of his prizes. He pointed to them and said, "Slaves!" Upon hearing this, Frank and Ann both raised their heads high in defiance. Red Feather slapped them both across the face. As if this was a cue, the children and women picked up stones. A very pretty

Indian woman took handfuls of dirt and rubbed through Ann's blonde hair. (Ann would find out later, the Indian woman was called Cochay and was Red Feather's squaw.) The children and women threw stones and dirt at them. Ann felt and looked like a caged wild animal. The pretty Indian brought a handful of branches and sticks. She placed them under their feet. Frank and Ann were terrified. Frank spoke softly to Ann, "Be brave, she is probably just trying to scare us. Red Feather is too proud of his catch to get rid of us so quickly." They both held their heads high, and the Indians finally left to eat.

When the Indians were through eating, Red Feather brought out the firewater. All of the braves knew about firewater. That was the best thing the traders brought for them. Red Feather gloried in all the praise the braves bestowed upon him for capturing the white people and bringing them firewater. The Indians did not understand what the word 'slaves' meant, but practiced saying the word because they knew it pleased Red Feather.

While the men were drinking, the women and children were busy taunting Frank and Ann. Red Feather's squaw, Cochay, who had thrown dirt in Ann's hair brought some hot coals and placed them on the twigs at Ann's feet. Ann was terrified as she saw the twigs smolder and then break into flames. Her leather shoes became hot and the heat penetrated to her feet. A flame shot up scorching her long gown. Terror and indignation were in her voice when she screamed. Even in her terror, she knew the squaws were not the ones to make such decisions. Red Feather looked up and rushed to put out the flames, anger distorting his face. He slapped his squaw so hard that it sent her reeling to the ground. He pointed to one of the wickiups and the woman started for it, but not before she gave Ann a look of sheer hatred. Ann was so thankful to have the fire out that she barely felt the red burn on her leg. The women and children moved off to their own wickiups. They knew not to incite men who were drinking firewater.

Red Feather wasn't through with his surprises yet. He had one more. He knew it would please the Chief and all the braves. He untied Ann and took her to several of the younger Indian women. He barked some orders to them and shoved Ann into one of the wickiups. He rejoined the Chief and braves who were sitting around the blazing campfire.

Ann fought the Indian women as they set out to do Red Feather's bidding. She was no match for them. When she realized the women were going to undress her, she grabbed the handkerchief and comb and held on to them. They bathed and dressed her. They watched in surprise as Ann combed her hair with the strange tool. She laid the handkerchief and comb on top of her gown and shoes and by gestures, showed them not to touch. When Ann was dressed, the Indian women called to Red Feather.

Red feather grabbed Ann by the wrist and led her to the fire. The Indian men were pleased when they saw the way Ann was now dressed. She had on a deerskin dress that fit her perfectly. Stands of beads hung from her neck. Her naturally wavy, blonde hair was pulled back and cascaded down her back.

The moon was out in all its glory. Yellow flames from the fire seemed to be trying to join the beams from the moon. In this lighting, Ann's hair shimmered in all its beauty. Red Feather shoved her forward and in a gruff voice said, "You dance!"

Ann knew it would be to her advantage if they liked her dancing. The Indians began a soft slow beat on their drums. Ann tilted her head downward, clasped her hands on her chest and stood as if lifeless as she waited for the Indians to begin their chanting. Red Feather started and the others chimed in. Ann took a step forward, slowly raising her head and hands skyward. The Indian's increased the tempo of the drums, but kept the volume soft. Her movements were perfect, graceful and fascinating to the Indians. When the Indians became impassioned with the rhythm and Ann was losing her strength, she stomped her feet faster and faster and the Indians increased their tempo with hers. She gradually lowered herself to the ground, sitting Indian style with her hands clasped over her chest and her head bowed. She sat motionless. The tempo of the chanting and the drums slowed down as Ann decreased her momentum. When she dropped her head, the chanting and drums stopped at the precise moment of the tilt of her head. There was complete silence and then she heard the Indians grunting their approval. She had a feeling that she had just danced the dance 'for' her life. She had used the last of her strength and fell sideways in a faint. The Chief called for his squaw and grunted out some orders. When Ann came out of her faint; she was inside the Chief's wickiup. Chief Gray Wolf's squaw, Blue Cloud, gave her water and a small amount of food. Then she bound her feet and hands and left her alone.

Ann worked in the dark to free herself and finally gave up, realizing she was only causing more burning and bruising. She rolled on her side and fell into a deep sleep.

CHAPTER EIGHTEEN

Celeste/ Honey

Celeste was sitting on the floor petting Mitzi when Bob came home that evening. He had closed the shop early, in anticipation of seeing how Linda and the little girl had fared. He kept wondering, "Where could this child possibly have come from? Had she been kidnapped, perhaps by Indians? Had she ever been capable of speaking?" It was all such a mystery. Bob asked everyone he came in contact with if they had heard of a missing child.

When Bob walked into the house, he exclaimed, "I see an angel sitting on my floor. Did she fly in our window?" Celeste covered her mouth with her hand to hide the smile that was on her lips. Linda stood proudly by. Bob turned to her and said, "You did a great job Linda." Linda beamed. Bob reached into his jacket pocket and gave Celeste a peppermint stick. "I didn't forget," he said. It had been a long time since Celeste had seen candy. She couldn't help but smile again. Linda took the candy from Celeste. "Not before supper," she gasped. Bob responded quickly, "Oh for goodness sake Linda, at least let her hold it." Linda placed the candy on the cupboard, saying, "It will just get her all sticky."

Celeste loved sitting at a table again. When Bob said grace, it stirred something far away and nostalgic in her being. Her father came to her mind. A deep longing went through her. Just then, she noticed Mitzi by her side, looking up in anticipation. She couldn't eat unless she gave Mitzi something first. She took a piece of meat off her plate and gave it to Mitzi. Linda started to stop her. Bob quickly interceded, "Mitzi shared her food with you, didn't she? You don't have enough for both of you. Linda will fix Mitzi a plate and you can take it out for her right now. She can come back in after we have eaten." Linda frowned as she prepared the meal for Mitzi. Celeste happily took it outside. After supper, Bob gave her the peppermint stick. She smiled at Bob and thrust one end in her mouth. Bob could read the delight in her eyes.

Ordinarily Bob overlooked Linda's bossy ways, but he knew immediately he was not going to stand for Linda trying to intimidate and control this little girl. He would do his best to make sure that did not happen.

When Linda told Celeste it was time for bed, Celeste clasped her tiny hands on Mitzi's collar. Bob noticed and said, "Mitzi can sleep by your bed tonight." He could see Linda wanted to disagree and gave her a look that said, "Don't you dare!" When Linda tried to tuck Celeste in, she turned on her side and clamped the covers down with her hands. Just then, Bob stuck his head in the door, "Goodnight Honey," he called. Celeste turned and gave him a smile and as if relenting, smiled at Linda.

When they were back in the kitchen, Linda confronted Bob. "You interfere with everything I do or say. I am the one who will be taking care of her all the time. She needs to know that I am in charge. A woman knows how to handle children, not a man." Bob implored, "Linda, I know you mean well, but right now, she doesn't need discipline, she needs to learn to trust us more than anything." He wanted to cover another matter with her; "You can't just `have' her as your own, Linda. We must make every effort to find out where she belongs. If that fails, then she will be ours." Linda did not voice what she was thinking; "You mean mine!"

Linda loved making things for Celeste. She sewed for hours. The dresses were as cute as could be. She took Celeste to Bob's store and picked out a pair of shoes for her. Celeste loved the new shoes though she did miss going barefoot. Linda explained, "Young ladies do not go barefoot." There were no more carefree days in the woods or running free with Mitzi. Due to pressure from Bob, Linda allowed Mitzi to sleep in Celeste's bedroom each night. She let Celeste color and draw pictures and gave her little things to do in the kitchen, which Celeste enjoyed. She did not try to teach her to read or encourage her to speak. Linda hoped Honey would forget all of her past. She definitely did not want her to learn to read and write! What if she wrote her name and where she had lived? Bob would be sure to take her home. She eased her conscience by thinking, "Perhaps she had a terrible past and it would be best if she did not ever remember it, let alone be returned to it."

Linda realized Celeste loved being outside, so she taught her horseback riding, something that she herself enjoyed. Linda asked Bob to buy a pony for Celeste. He loved the idea and purchased one right away. Celeste loved the pony. Linda was impressed at how quickly she learned to ride. Bob asked her if she had a name for the pony. She shrugged her shoulders but that night, she took Bob's hand and led him outside. She pointed to the sky and then to the barn. The stars were shining brightly and he asked her, "Are you telling me you want to name your pony Star?" Celeste nodded her head. Bob swung her in a circle and said, "Then Star she shall be."

Celeste sensed how eager Linda was to cuddle her but she kept her distance. Once in a while, a brief hug was allowed. Celeste would not hug her back, but she would always smile sweetly at Linda. She wasn't going to take any chances of Linda wanting to be called 'mama.' In time she even became used to her new name, Honey.

Celeste's very best times were when Bob let her sit on his lap while he read to her. It became a nightly ritual; Bob loved it as much as Honey. He still questioned every stranger that came in his store, dreading that someone might actually claim her. Weeks passed and Bob and Linda had almost forgotten that Celeste wasn't theirs. The only times they remembered were on Honeys' days or evenings when she completely withdrew and shut them out. During those times, she would disappear. They might find her under her bed, in a closet, just anywhere she could hide. Her shoes would be off and she would be curled in a little ball. Bob never scolded her and would not allow Linda to. It grieved and frightened him. He would tell Linda, "She is missing her own family or recalling some horrendous things she may have been through." Bob was right, Celeste was afraid she would lose the 'picture' of her mother and brother. The images seemed to be fading and it terrified her. She would roll into a little ball, squeeze her eyes tightly and try to sharpen the image of her mother and brother. Afterwards, she would be drained and nauseous and it would take her a day or so to recover.

Linda insisted that Honey should not be subjected to the stares of the town people, so Celeste had only been to town when she got her new shoes. Of course, the real reason was that she was afraid someone would recognize her. Celeste was allowed to attend church with them and most neighborhood gatherings. Their friends and neighbors eventually seemed to forget that she had ever been anyone other than Honey Edwards.

CHAPTER NINETEEN

Give Me Your Answer

Louise was glad that Michael had asked her if she was going to marry Mr. Jenner. It really had never entered her mind. Now that she thought about it, she realized he acted as if he did have special feelings for her. She remembered things he had said which may have been to test her reaction to a proposal. She wondered, "What should I say if he proposes?" As hard as she tried, she could not bring herself to a positive decision one way or the other. Her heart said, "Yes," her brain said, "No." She talked to Sydney about it, of course she couldn't really help, except it was good to have someone to confide in. Sydney had told her that ordinarily, anyone who had to discuss something so serious with someone else surely needed more time to think it over. Louise laughed, "He hasn't even asked me yet! I feel sure he is going to. I just don't want to be caught off guard and say or do something I will regret. Richard doesn't talk a lot, but I can tell he is easily wounded." Sydney had asked her a few questions about how she felt about him, how did Michael get along with him, did she enjoy being with him, did he have the qualities she wanted in a man and so on. Louise could say, "Yes" to all the right things. She explained to Sydney the best she could, "I just can't give my complete heart to anyone like I did to Aaron. Especially when another part of it is with my Celeste." Sydney responded, "I know you so well Louise. You will be totally honest with him and he will have to decide himself if he wants to marry you under those conditions. The problem is that we never know what a person is really like until we marry him."

The Proposal

The following Friday, Richard came to spend the weekend. On Saturday, Michael spent the afternoon with them. All in all, it had been a lovely day for Louise. After a picnic lunch, Louise watched while Richard and Michael fished. She could see they enjoyed each other. Michael caught a bass that must have weighed at least three pounds. Richard seemed as thrilled as Michael.

That evening Louise and Richard were sitting on Louise's porch. It was dark except for the glow of the moon. Richard had his arm around her waist and he said, "Louise?" He sounded serious and she turned to face him. She knew he was going to propose and she could suddenly feel the beat of her heart. He stood to his feet and walked back and forth in front of her as if trying to get up the nerve and find just the right words to say. She couldn't see his eyes; but knew exactly how they looked. That unsure look, expecting a negative answer and yet the glitter of hope shining through. She knew it was hard for him and she almost wanted to help him through it. Finally, he said, "Louise, Will you marry me? I know you can't love me like I love you and I know I am asking someone with a broken heart to be my wife. I realize you will never be able to be completely happy again until you find your little girl and I am willing to share that pain with you. Every town that I have been in since I met you, I have inquired about any child that might have turned up in that area. I have even told of her disappearance in my political speeches in case someone had any idea of what happened to her. You can see that Michael and I have a very good relationship. Even if I don't become a senator, I have my law office and do well at that." He stopped pacing and continued, "You don't have to tell me your answer right now. Just please don't say `no' tonight. Let me leave with hope in my heart."

Louise was deeply touched. He seemed to have covered everything she had worried about. She wanted to cradle him in her arms. She wanted to feel his arms about her. He was willing to marry her even with her broken heart.

He couldn't see the smile that came across her face as she said, "There is one person who will also have to approve, my father." Richard took Louise's hand and pulled her to his side, "Does that mean you are saying yes?" For an answer, she raised her lips to his. It was their first kiss and she didn't want it to end.

Richard had known all along that Louise would expect him to talk to her father. He had lain awake at nights wondering how Mr. Morgan would react. He had memorized what he would say to him. No matter how nice he had tried to treat Jonathon Morgan, Richard knew Mr. Morgan did not care for him and he could sense his dislike. He wanted to get it over with right then.

Richard found Mr. Morgan in his study. When he told him that he wanted to marry his daughter, the man's eyes seemed to turn to steel. Richard continued in spite of the look. "I am very much in love with Louise. I know you think she could do better and I understand that. The fact remains that Louise is happy when she is with me. I also know that she is suffering over her daughter. Feeling happy is hard for her, she almost feels guilty when she is enjoying herself. I realize all of this and promise you that I will do my best to make her happy. One thing is for sure, I will not marry her unless you approve. Louise needs your blessing to give our marriage any chance at real happiness."

Mr. Morgan asked, "Has Louise agreed to marry you?" Richard replied, "Only if you approve." Louise's father rose to his feet and extended his hand. They shook hands and Mr. Morgan congratulated him.

When Richard left, Jonathon hurried to tell his wife. She was at her secretary looking for a letter she had misplaced. Jonathon said, "I have just given Richard my permission to marry Louise. He said she had agreed to marry him, if I consented to their marriage. Actually I was caught off guard because he seemed so sincere that I feel as if I have perhaps misjudged the man." Dolores was thrilled. She knew better than to say, "I told you so."

Richard returned to Louise and told her all that had taken place. Louise said, "I have one more important question to ask you, "Where will we live?"

"If you would like," he answered, "We can live in your house." I think you may be happier there. If I am elected senator; I won't expect you to be with me all the time, only when you want to join me." Louise knew that her home was the only place she could live. She had to be there when Celeste came home. This put a longing in her heart and suddenly she couldn't wait to get home.

CHAPTER TWENTY

Frank and Ann

Red Feather did not want to kill Frank and Ann until he tired of having them as slaves. Chief Gray Wolf had other ideas. He wanted a big celebration and the death of this man. Red Feather explained to Gray Wolf what a slave was. His eyes lit up and then jealousy flickered in them. He said, "Not right you have two slaves and Chief Gray Wolf has none." This prompted Red Feather to give Frank to the Chief as his slave. He would keep the woman. This pleased the Chief. He liked the idea of having a slave.

Chief Gray Wolf ordered a big celebration so all of the tribe could witness Frank and Ann being made their slaves. Gray Wolf told Red Feather, "They will forever bear cuts that mark them as our slaves."

All day the Indians bustled about. The women were busy cooking. There was an air of excitement throughout the camp. Frank and Ann soon realized the Indians were preparing for a special celebration and each was thinking the same thing. "This is probably the night we will be tortured and probably put to death."

Dusk was setting in when the Indians built a huge bonfire. All of the men and women had painted their faces. The Indians feasted. They chanted and danced. Red Feather crammed some food in Ann's mouth though she was so deep in despair that she could hardly swallow it. Frank was not allowed any food. Red Feather, Chief Gray Wolf and several of the braves untied Frank and Ann and brought them in front of the flames of the fire. The Indians stood erect as Red Feather pointed to Ann, "You my slave." He then pointed to Frank, "You now Chief Gray Wolf slave." Frank raised his head in defiance and shouted, "No! Never!" This is what Red Feather wanted to hear. He muttered orders to the braves. The braves crowded closer, forcing their captives closer to the fire. Ann watched in horror as one shoved Frank into the hot coals. Luckily they did not force him to stay there. Some hit him with sticks, some pounded him with their fists. Frank fell to the ground and the young boys taunted and kicked him. Frank's face and other parts of his body were bleeding and swollen. Ann could stand it no longer. She screamed out, "Say 'Yes' Frank, while you are still alive." Frank didn't answer.

Red Feather squatted before Frank, his sharp hunting knife in his hand. The Indians began their chanting watching intently so as not to miss any of it. Red Feather held the knife at his neck and said, "You be slave for Chief Gray Wolf?"

Frank was on the verge of passing out; but he could feel the sharpness of the knife and knew it had already started to penetrate his skin. If he lived, perhaps he could still escape. With the last of his strength, he muttered, "Yes." Red Feather held Frank by the ear and with one quick unexpected movement sliced Frank's ear from his head. He held it up to show the watching Indians. Shouts of laughter and jeers erupted. He gave Frank's ear to Chief Gray Wolf. Red Feather pointed to Frank and announced, "Name now "One-Ear." Frank never uttered a sound before he passed out. He was covered with blood and Ann wondered if he was still alive. It was all too much for Ann. She also fainted. Red Feather's squaw, Cochay, threw water in her face. The Indians pulled her to her feet and now Red

Feather said, "You be my slave?" Without hesitation, Ann said, "Yes." He took out his knife and Ann knew he was going to cut her ear off also. She fainted again. Lucky for Ann, this gave Red Feather time to think. He remembered how enchanting she looked when she danced for them. He rolled her aside with his foot. He then gave orders for Frank to be carried to his new sleeping quarters. A small wickiup had been erected right next to Gray Wolf's. Each night his feet would be bound and his hands tied, so he would be available if his 'Master' needed him.

CHAPTER TWENTY-ONE

Nathan Clark

One day Bob came home and reported, "Your friend Lucy Black was in the store today. She was buying extra groceries, it seems Lucy's brother is living with them and will share their home until he gets his own place. I think it would be nice if we had them over for dinner. We haven't entertained for a long time."

The idea appealed to Linda. "Perhaps, you could stop on your way home from work and invite them. I have missed seeing Lucy. A Saturday dinner would be nice. Honey' and I will fix a fine dinner, won't we Honey?" Honey gave her a serious nod. So it was that they met Nat Clark.

Honey helped set the table. She was nervous about being around strangers. She was happy about one thing in particular though. She would get to see Lucy and Jacob's son Tim. He was the same little boy she had seen that first day when she was peeking out of Frank and Ann's wagon. He still reminded her of Michael. She had seen him several times, from a distance, but Linda never allowed her to run and play with other children. She wondered how he would treat her. Would he think she was dumb because she couldn't speak? Thinking of the word, 'dumb' made her think of Frank and Ann. She moved closer to Bob, who was reading something. He never looked up, but with his free hand, automatically pulled her over and hugged her. She felt better and went to watch for the company from the front window.

When Honey saw the carriage coming, she ran to Bob and pulled him by the hand. He took her tiny hand in his, ducked down to peer out the window, and called, "Linda, our guests are here." The three of them walked out to meet the carriage.

Tim opened the carriage door and jumped down first, and then turned to help his mother. Tim's dad Jacob, climbed down from the top seat and joined them. Honey stood in the background, not wanting to be noticed. Tim spied her and his face lit up with a big smile. He called out, "Hi Honey." Without waiting for a reply, he picked up a rock and sent it skimming across the road. Honey found it was easy to smile when someone treated you so nonchalantly. It was as if he took it for granted that she had called back, "Hi, I'm glad you are here."

Lucy's brother Nat was still holding the horse's reins. When everyone had greeted each other, he climbed down and walked towards Bob, his hand extended.

Bob was surprised this man was related to Lucy Black. She was petite, had an olive complexion and dark brown hair, her brother was just the opposite. This man's complexion was fair and he had blonde wavy hair, enormous muscular shoulders and arms. He was quite tall and probably weighed about two hundred pounds. He looked strong and in the best of condition. A light beard enhanced the feeling that he was a man who led a rustic life. He wore leather breeches, a blue shirt and a soft leather vest. Lucy had already told them he was thirty-four years old.

Nat greeted each of them in a voice that was articulate and pleasant. He was very jovial and it was contagious. Soon they were all laughing and enjoying themselves as they walked towards the house. Nat spotted Honey and said; "Now here's an angel if I ever saw one. I bet she can fly too." Honey saw that he was looking directly at her. She was always afraid when she met new people. They usually reacted in a way she didn't like when they found out she couldn't speak. She lowered her head to avoid his eyes and any further conversation.

Nat walked over to her and lifted her as if she was a tiny kitten. He tossed her on his shoulders and laughed. Mitzi darted back and forth, barking for Nat to put her down. Honey loved the attention. He placed her feet on the ground and said, " Maybe after dinner, I'll tell you and Tim some of my adventures, things that really happened with wild animals, Indians and the mountains. Would you like that?" Honey nodded her head vigorously, excitement shining in her eyes.

After dinner, Tim asked to be excused, then he added, "Could Honey be excused also? We can take Mitzi and play in the woods." Honey raised her head, eyes pleading for permission. Quickly, Linda said, "I'm sorry Tim, Honey is never allowed to play in the woods unless a grown up is with her. I would worry. Why don't you take Mitzi and play with her? Honey can sit on the steps with you later and listen to some of your Uncle Nat's adventures." Honey was visibly disappointed.

Nat had been watching each face and saw 'Honeys' eyes light up and then resignation and sadness wash over her eyes. He was not one to sit by when there was a simple cure. He rose to his feet and said, "If you will excuse me ma'am, I'll be glad to go with the children." Linda did not like that idea at all. He was the life of her dinner party. She spoke quickly, "That won't be necessary. Perhaps Tim will promise me that he won't take Honey out of our calling distance." Tim wasn't sure just how far that was, but he gave his promise. In a flash, Honey was out of her chair and running across the yard with Mitzi. Tim called out, "Hey, wait up, it was my idea."

Honey stopped long enough to remove her shoes and stockings. She wriggled her toes in the soft grass, feeling happier and freer then she had since Linda had taken control of her life. She and Mitzi had roamed the woods before Bob and Linda had discovered her and she was anxious to show Tim all the wonderful places. She took the lead and Tim and Mitzi followed.

First she took him to the bayou. It was dark and rather eerie. Honey loved being there. It gave her the feeling of being in an enchanted place where anything could happen She sensed Tim felt the same way. She stood quietly looking all around, pointing to places in the trees where vacated bird nests sat nestled in the protection of their limbs. Then she took him to a small meadow, full of lovely flowers. She showed him a pile of broken and dried animal bones. Honey was thirsty, so she took him to the spring that Mitzi had led her to when she wanted a drink. They drank from the cold spring water and then sat under the trees. Tim was visibly impressed and wondered how she knew the woods so well. Tim told her about school, his friends and things that he liked to do. He was careful not to ask her any questions, though he would have liked to. He wished her voice would come back and she could tell him where she came from and who she really was.

Then Tim had an idea. "Let's have a secret code." Honey looked puzzled, so he explained. "Since you don't talk, we will make up a sign language. Would you like to do that?" Tim could see the excitement in her eyes as she nodded in agreement. This spurred him on and he added, "We will make an oath of secrecy. That means we won't ever tell anyone else what our signs mean or what we tell each other!" Honey loved the sound of all this. She nodded her head, eyes glistening. Tim continued, "We will learn some of the signs today and every time we are together, we will add more." He thought a moment and then said, "The thumb of our right hand will stand for Miss Linda, the next finger Mr. Bob, a fist, like this, for Uncle Nat. He added several others. When he was finished, Honey stuck a finger above each ear and pointed to Mitzi. Tim laughed and said, "That's a good one Honey!" "Now," said Tim, "It is time to see how many you remember." Tim said each of the words and each time Honey made the sign for it. He was amazed at how quickly she had learned them. Tim, looking serious and sinister mused aloud, "We must think of a way to seal our secret. We don't have any blood; but we do have the bones you showed me. I am sure they must be wolf bones." They found the bones again. Each picked one up and Tim placed his bone across his heart. Honey did the same. Then he extended the bone he held towards Honey's heart. She extended hers to his. Tim laid his crosswise over hers. His voice was just loud enough for Honey to hear, "We promise this is our secret alone, even if we are tortured, we will not tell our code or the secrets we tell each other." He instructed Honey, "Now cross both your hands over your heart." He did the same.

Tim was enjoying the spell he had cast on Honey. He tried to think of something else to prolong the excitement. "Now, we must bury our bones together. The only way we can ever be free to break our promise is to come back in the moonlight and dig up these bones." They were silent, glorying in the moment.

Both knew it was time to go back. Honey walked slowly. What a thrilling afternoon it had been! Then she remembered she wanted to bring Linda some flowers. She ran for the meadow and they hurriedly picked a bouquet. Honey picked one of the biggest flowers out of the bouquet and handed it to Tim. She pointed to the flower and then held up her little finger. Tim laughed, "I know. You want me to give this flower to my mom." Honey smiled and ran off to put her shoes back on. She just kept thinking of their wonderful secret, "Even if someone tortured me," she thought, "I will never tell!"

The children could see that Linda was happy with the flowers. She told the children, "I will put them in my nicest vase." Tim was ever so pleased at the smile his mom gave him when he handed the flower to her. He was glad Honey had prodded him to do so.

Tim reminded his Uncle Nat that he had promised to tell some of his adventures. The three of them went to the front porch. Nat sat in the rocker and Celeste and Tim on the steps in front of him. Tim had heard most of the stories before, yet never tired of them. Each time Nat finished a story and was ready to bring it to an end, Honey would look disappointed and pull on his sleeve and he would tell another. Finally, Nat said, "This is going to be the last one." He was in the middle of it, (Tim thought this was an especially good story.) when he noticed Honey slide quietly off the step and disappear around the side of the house.

Nat noticed Honey slipping away also and said, "Tim, I'm afraid my last story was one too many for Honey. She has slipped away. I think it is time to call it a day. Let's see if your mom and dad are ready to head for home." Tim thought, "How could she have not wanted to hear the rest of such an exciting adventure?"

Jacob and Lucy were thanking Bob and Linda. As Nat was leaving, he turned and said, "I am afraid I told Honey too many tales, she left before I could say goodbye. Would you please tell her goodbye for me?"

Tim did not want to leave without seeing Honey. He said, "I'll run and find her." Tim's father stopped him, "We have stayed too long now Tim. We need to make it home before dark. Miss Linda will say goodbye for you."

Linda walked outside with the guests. Bob immediately started looking for Honey. Linda came back and joined him. They called. There was no answer. Bob called Mitzi and said, "Find Honey!" Mitzi ran across the back yard and to her doghouse. She looked inside and wagged her tail. Bob looked perplexed as he bent down and held his arms out to Honey. He cuddled her in his arms and she clung to him. He felt tiny shivers as she lay in his arms. Once inside the house, he tried to question her, "Did someone hurt your feelings? Are you sick? Did something scare you in the woods? Are you feeling lonely because the company left? To each of these answers, Celeste gave a negative response.

Next he asked, "Do you like Tim? Did you like Mr. Nat?" To each of these answers, she gave a positive nod to her head. He asked her again, "Do you <u>really</u> like Tim's Uncle Nat?" She gave a very positive nod of the head.

Bob and Linda were both deeply concerned. After Honey was in bed, Bob read to her. Before he left, he asked, "Would you like to sleep with Linda tonight?" She shook her head once more. Honey pointed to Mitzi and patted the sheets next to her. Linda did not approve of the dog getting on the bed, but she said, "Well, just for tonight." Mitzi lay on the covers, next to Honey. The tiny smile on Honey's face assured them that she was all right for the time being.

When they were in the privacy of their parlor, Bob remarked, "Something happened to Honey today. We must find out what it was. I can see it is going to be a real set back for her. She was adjusting so beautifully. I am going to leave early in the morning and talk to Tim. I am going to question him about everything that happened when they were together. He was with her the entire time. He is just a little boy; perhaps he said something about her not really being ours. I also wonder if Nat could have possibly said something to frighten her."

Linda responded, "Warn Tim, I will never allow him to play with her again if he has hurt her feelings." Bob knew Tim would never have intentionally hurt her. He thought, "Poor Linda, I am afraid she will always be insensitive to other people's feelings." Bob just hoped he wouldn't say anything that would hurt Tim's feelings when he did question him or ruin the memory of the good time he and Celeste had enjoyed.

CHAPTER TWENTY-TWO

The Slaves

It seemed to Ann that the braves were always going on raids. If they brought back a wounded brave and he died in the camp, the Apaches were very fearful. Ann soon realized the Apaches were not afraid to kill but had a horror of death and the dead. When the wounded brave died, he was buried as fast as it could be arranged. His wickiup and his possessions were also burned. After the burial and burning, the mourners purged themselves in sagebrush smoke and moved away from the immediate area so the buried man's ghost could not harm them. Ann was glad this did not happen often as she and Frank were forced to be purged by smoke with the rest. She didn't mind the moving because it usually was not far and they would once again be in a clean area

Eventually Ann was allowed to wander about the camp freely. She noticed the Indians did little planting or planning for the future. The braves often left the camp and when they returned had all kinds of foods and items. She realized the food had been stolen from white settlers or other tribes. They would laugh and grunt while they displayed and traded the plunder with each other. She would shiver as she watched them, wondering if the families had been killed or tortured. Sometimes they would return and one or more of their braves would be missing. This would call for a special ritual of mourning that night.

After one of their escapades, Ann watched as they traded. They had knives, small figurines, a tin cup, a large wooden spoon, some rope, a quilt and horse reins. No one wanted one of the items and the brave tossed it aside. It sparkled in the sunlight and Ann wondered what it was. After the braves dispersed, Ann looked for the item. It was a mouth organ. She thought of Frank, who was a lover of music. He could play almost any instrument though he had no formal training. She knew he would get a lot of joy from learning to play this simple instrument. She must give it to him.

Chief Gray Wolf soon tired of having "One-Ear" as his slave. He was used to his squaw waiting on him. One or two men always had to guard Frank and Gray Wolf heard much grumbling about this. They led him around by a long heavy strip of buffalo leather, which was tied to his ankle. The Chief told the men to keep Frank away from his wickiup. "Have One-Ear help squaws, he pretty like a woman anyway." Everyone laughed at this. They loved to try and make Frank's life miserable. Frank didn't seem to mind being laughed at and called a squaw. He actually acted as if he enjoyed working with the women. Worst of all, the Indian women seemed to enjoy Frank and often laughed at his antics. Red Feather's squaw, Cochay, did her best to hang around Frank, whenever Red Feather and the other braves were not around. Even Frank noticed she enjoyed being with him. Sometimes Frank would wink at Ann and then toss a basket or something towards Cochay. She would giggle and do her best to catch it. Ann could see she loved the attention. The saddest part of all this, was that even Frank's guards noticed.

Red Feather, unlike Chief Gray Wolf, was thoroughly enjoying his white slave. He had actually smiled several times. His squaw Cochay and "Move-Like-Willow," (his name for

Ann), clearly despised each other. Sometimes they fought, pulling each other's hair and wrestling like the young braves. This was sheer entertainment for Red Feather. He thought they were fighting over him and he enjoyed it. If his tribe allowed more than one wife he would have taken Move-Like-Willow as his second squaw just to make the fighting more intense.

After a few weeks Red Feather noticed the women must have called a truce. The angry words and fighting had stopped. Red Feather was disappointed. When Chief Gray Wolf told him that it was time to do away with One-Ear, Red Feather became angry. He told the Chief, "It was Red Feather who captured slave, you not want him. I take him back."

So Red Feather had two slaves again. The problem was that Red Feather did not really want Frank around. He picked two fat, lazy braves whom he thought wouldn't mind guarding Frank and would mostly just sit outside the camp with him.

The first time Ann got a chance, she headed outside the camp to try and give the mouth organ to Frank. The fat braves ordered her away. Frank saw the mouth organ and Ann had seen the flicker of excitement that came across his eyes. She must find a way to give it to him.

The next day as Ann was sweeping Red Feather's teepee, she noticed a package Red Feather had offered her after a raid. It was wrapped in a large muslin cloth. She knew it had been stolen from some settlers and she had refused to accept it. Now she wondered what it was. She unwrapped the muslin and was surprised to see food from someone's larder. Flour, molasses and lard. She thought of Frank's fat guards. They would do anything for food. She hurried to the cooking area and started a fire. She mixed some of the flour, lard and molasses together. She dropped small amounts of the batter on an iron skillet. Another item the braves had pilfered and brought to the camp. When one side had browned, she turned it over and browned the other sides. She placed the sweet cakes in a small wicker basket and ran for the mouth organ.

Ann hurried to Frank's private little prison. He was sitting on the ground with his ankles and wrists tied. The fat guards were lounging on the grass, near Frank. She showed the guards the sweet cakes and when they reached for them, she jumped back. She held two of the cakes in one hand and motioned to Frank. The Indians never moved as she handed the mouth organ to Frank. She then gave each Indian a small cake. A look of sheer pleasure came over their faces as the taste of the morsel filled their mouth. They reached for more but Ann waited to make sure they would let Frank play the mouth organ. Surprise showed on their faces as they saw One-Ear place the object inside his lips and then watched in amazement as wonderful musical sounds came out of the small instrument. She could see the music pleased the guards. She gave the guards all of the cakes except one. She handed this one to Frank.

Ann laughed as Frank quickly devoured the cake. He said, "Best food I have had in a long time!" and smiled. Ann returned his smile and turned to go. She had not taken three steps before Frank was playing again. The accordion like music of the mouth organ was really quite lovely. She recognized *Oh Susannah*. Frank did not need to learn to play the mouth organ; he already knew. It was good to see some happiness and pleasure in his eyes again. The sounds of *Oh Susannah* faded as she made her way back to the campsite.

In the next few days Ann's brain was filled with plans. She had often noticed that some of the squaws had lovely singing voices. The squaws often chanted as they moved about the camp and she started paying particular attention to their voices. A few days later, she baked more sweet cakes and picked five of the squaws, one of whom happened to be Red Feathers squaw Cochay. She beckoned for them to follow her and she led them to Frank and his guards. The guards were surprised but kept their eyes on the sweets, of which they had been yearning for since Ann's last visit. She gave them each a sweet cake and asked Frank to play *Old Black Joe*. She now started humming and motioned for the women to do the same. In no time they were humming in the right time and tone. After a couple of times, Ann started to sing the words. She again motioned for the women to keep humming. Their voices blended so well with the mouth organ that *Old Black Joe* had never sounded so haunting and lovely. Even the fat guards were truly impressed. Ann gave Frank another sweet cake and the rest of them to the braves. They knew she was paying them for their silence.

Several days later, the same band of braves who had stolen the mouth organ, came home with one of the braves missing. This meant a ritual would be held that very night. Ann had been waiting for something like this. The entire camp had to attend, so Frank sat between his two guards. After the ceremonies were complete and all were still around the campfire, Ann was expected to dance. She danced for awhile but as she whirled about, she put her arms around one of the five squaws who had sang when Frank played and one by one stood them side by side next to where Frank was sitting. In a plaintive tone, as though calling the deceased, she called out, "*Old Black Joe*."

Ann turned to Frank and he knew she was asking him to play. He took the mouth organ from under the waist of his trousers and began the song. Ann started humming and the women joined in. Frank kept playing, the women kept humming and Ann sang *Old Black Joe* as it had never been sung before. The camp was silent when the song ended and then the Chief motioned for them to do it all over again. When the song was over, the Indian's were still silent. Frank decided he needed to play a happier song. He broke the silence with a new song. It was a happy song with a very good beat. Many of the Indians rose to their feet and moved about to the rhythm.

Ann hoped Frank would be treated better since the Indians had enjoyed his music.

This was not to be.

Frank's guards sometimes wandered about the camp with Frank. They were always hoping to find something extra to eat. They too, became weary of keeping an eye on him and jealous because Cochay and some of the other tribal women smiled and batted their eyes at Frank. Cochay gave him the most attention. The braves agreed, "Red Feather should make One-Ear and Cochay suffer for this." The two Indians told other braves about it and now all of the braves wanted One-Ear to die.

The guards were afraid of what Red Feather might do if they told him about Cochay making eyes at One-Ear, so they went to Chief Gray Wolf. He too worried what Red Feather would do, so he suggested it was time for One-Ear to die. Red Feather became very angry. He argued, "One-Ear belong to me. I decide when he die!"

The Chief motioned for one of Frank's guards to come forward. The Chief ordered him to repeat what he had told the other braves. The fat brave looked around, making sure the Chief and other braves were between him and Red Feather.

The brave told Red Feather, "Your squaw make eyes and smile like she has stars in eyes when she is by One- Ear. Ask other braves, they see too."

The Indians knew Red Feather would fly into a rage. When he pulled his knife from the sheath and went for the brave, several were prepared to stop him. Chief Gray Wolf said, "I let you plan One-Ear's way to die. Maybe you want Move- Like-Willow to die also. Red Feathers' face was alive with fury as he said; "Squaw Cochay and One-Ear will die together. Move-Like-Willow will be my new squaw."

CHAPTER TWENTY-THREE

Louise

Since the most important people in Louise's life seemed to approve of marriage between her and Richard, Louise decided there was no reason to wait very long. She had already learned that happiness could be snatched away at any time and she was no longer sure of what the future held. Also Louise did not want to give her mother time to plan a big affair

Richard had a campaign speech to make in one of the larger towns. He planned on being gone several days, so when he said, 'I have an aunt that I hope to visit while I am campaigning, I would like to invite her to our wedding. Other than my mother and father, she is the only close relative I have. Do you think you could decide the date so I can invite her?"

Louise felt a little uncomfortable at having to decide so quickly, but realized there was no time that would be easy for her. Perhaps it was better that she was forced to come to a decision right away. Celeste's birthday would be October seventh. She had hoped so desperately that Celeste would be home again by then. She had to let that day pass before she married. Of course if Celeste did come home, the wedding would have to be postponed until Celeste was comfortable with Richard. She decided on October twenty second.

When Louise and Richard told her parents of their plans, she was surprised her mother agreed to keep the wedding simple. Actually, Dolores Morgan was too smart to suggest a big wedding. She knew one thing for sure, "There would be a gala reception at a later date." She hoped he could be called "Senator" by then.

The Edge of Terror

Louise had not held classes for her students for three nights and she felt guilty, since she knew how much it disappointed the children. To overcome her guilt, she let them stay an hour longer when she held their next class. It was an especially dark night and she planned to walk the twins to their cabin. They had each been taking turns reading from *The Governess*, when an inexplicable feeling struck her. She looked towards the window facing her. The shade hadn't been pulled all the way down and she could have sworn she saw a movement outside the window. Quickly, trying not to frighten the children, she went to the door and peered into the darkness. No one was in sight. She closed the door and pulled the shade all of the way down. The children were so busy with their story they never even glanced up.

The twins loved it when she walked them home. Before the children went inside, she told them she would be busy for the next few days and she would let them know when they could come for more lessons. Disappointment registered in all their faces; but they did not question her. After the twins were safely inside, she insisted on walking Henry home. Henry wanted to carry on a conversation with her about how happy he was that he was learning so much. Louise was worried and could not concentrate on what he was saying. Henry realized something was wrong and continued the walk in silence. All Louise could think of was that she might have endangered the children. Maybe she just imagined she saw a movement. When Henry was safely inside, she ran as fast as she could to the safety of her own rooms. She prayed every step of the way.

CHAPTER TWENTY-FOUR

Frank and Ann

Red Feather warned the braves to tell no one that One-Ear and Cochay were to die and Walk-Like-Willow would be his new squaw. Red Feather did not want his squaw to know she had been found out. He wanted One Eye and Cochay to watch as he took Walk-Like-Willow as his squaw. Then he would have great tortures for Cochay and One-Ear. She would pay for making him look weak in front of his people. Their deaths would be slow. Red Feather tried to console himself by thinking of what a great time it would be. He was glad he had Firewater left from last raid.

Fresh meat was needed for the celebration. The braves would go on a hunt. Only the two braves would stay to guard One-Ear. They were too lazy and fat to be good hunters anyway.

Before the hunters left, Chief Gray Wolf returned to his tent and told his squaw Blue Cloud, to keep an eye on Red Feather's squaw, Cochay. "See she not go near One- Ear!" Blue Cloud gave him a questioning look. He only said, "When we return with meat, all must be ready for great feast and celebration." Blue Cloud was even more curious when she came out of her tent and saw One-Ear had been moved and tied to a tree inside the camp. A brave sat on each side of him.

As soon as the Indians left for the hunt, the women started the preparations for the big celebration. No one seemed to know what it was all about. While Blue Cloud was readying for the celebration, she made a point of staying as close as she could to the Indians guarding Frank. She was hoping she would overhear something that would let her know what was transpiring. It was not long before she heard one of them say to the other, "I wonder if Cochay will have stars in her eyes for One-Ear when she die with him?" They both laughed.

Blue Cloud had a special place in her heart for Cochay. No one in the camp, including Chief Gray Wolf knew of their deep bond. Blue Cloud and her sister Little Fox had been stolen from the Caddo tribe many moons ago. Blue Cloud was twelve and her sister was fourteen. Blue Cloud was very pretty and Gray Wolf's father who was the reigning Chief at that time gave her to his son for his squaw. When Gray Wolf's father died, Gray Wolf took his place. Gray Wolf cared for Blue Cloud and most of the time treated her very well. She had borne his children and in her own way, she loved him.

Another brave had claimed her sister Little Fox as his squaw. Little Fox died while giving birth to her first child. The baby survived and Blue Cloud named her Cochay, after their mother. Some of the tribe knew Blue Cloud and Little Fox had been taken from another tribe, but none knew they were sisters and that Little Fox's child, Cochay was Blue Cloud's niece.

Blue Cloud had also noticed that Cochay had eyes for One-Ear. She could understand why. Red Feather had never been good or shown any kindness to Cochay. She did his every bidding. He was never pleased and looked for reasons to bash her about. One-Ear paid attention to her and even made her laugh. She also noticed this did not seem to bother Walk-Like-Willow. She did not realize as Ann did, that it was just a white man's way of being friendly.

She returned to her tent. She must think. There had to be some way she could save Cochay from humiliation and death. She sank to the floor, crossed her legs, put an elbow on her knee and cupped her hand under her chin. She did her best thinking, sitting like this. She came up with only one plan. She hoped the Great Spirit would be on her side and it would work.

Blue Cloud came out of her tent and looked about the camp for Cochay. She found her with other squaws preparing the paint for the celebration. She came and stood among them offering to help. Carefully she gave a signal with her eyes for Cochay to move out of hearing. She quickly told Cochay why the feast was being prepared and that she wanted to help Cochay escape. Cochay turned and looked at One Ear. She turned back to Blue Cloud and said, "Cochay will not go without One-Ear." Blue Cloud shrugged her shoulders. The two embraced and Blue Cloud went into her wickiup.

In the midst of Frank's ordeals since being in the Indian camp, the little girl they had treated so badly often came to his mind. Celeste had been dependent on their mercy just as he was now at the mercy of the Indians. He had not been merciful and now he was getting no mercy. He had mentioned his thoughts to Ann. He had expected her to chide him for his softness. He was surprised when she lowered her eyes and said, "We did wrong Frank and we are paying for it. I don't even care about being rich anymore. I just want to be free. If I had it to do over again, I would take Celeste right back to her mother. Sometimes I can't sleep at night for wondering what happened to her."

When the Indians brought Frank back into the camp and tied him to a tree, he knew he had little time left. Ann also knew. The Indians in the camp had a certain respect for Ann though none would admit it The Indians thought it was a sign of weakness to look up to a woman. Red Feather, in spite of himself, cared for her. They did not realize it was because she was beautiful, shapely and danced like a Spirit in the moonlight for them. Even so, the men guarding Frank would not let her get close enough to talk to him. After three tries, they grabbed Walk-Like-Willow and threw her brutally to the ground.

The Sleeping Camp

Blue Cloud had learned much about the power of herbs from her mother and grandmother before she had been taken from her own people. She had watched them use many of the herbs for sickness or poultices in their camp. Never before had she used the plants to put so many in a trance or asleep, but she had seen the herbs work. She would make sure the children ate last so she could dilute the potion. This plant would put you to sleep and it could also kill if too much was used.

Blue Cloud kept clay jars of the Pipe Plant, also known as Ghost-Flowers, She took the dried root and beat it to a powder. She kept a good supply for when Gray Wolf wanted to smoke the peace pipe. If the braves were drinking firewater and acting loco, she added some poppy seed or Hops to the powdered Ghost Flower and the Indians would fall fast asleep. Mixing these three together would put them all to sleep.

Blue Cloud joined the women cooking stew. Since there was no fresh meat, it was a watery vegetable stew. She checked each pot and stirred them carefully, adding the mixture she had put together. She did not know how long it would be before the hunters returned. She hoped they would have trouble finding any game so they would be delayed. She must get the Indians to eat as soon as she could. When she got close to Cochay, she whispered, "Do not eat stew!" Cochay nodded her head to show she understood. Blue Cloud would see to it that no one served Frank, even though she was certain the guards would not allow him to eat.

Not too long after eating, everyone became lethargic. Most lay down wherever they were and fell asleep. The Indian guards had been fed first and ate the most. They were first to roll over and fall into a deep sleep. Soon everyone was asleep except for Frank and Cochay. Blue Cloud had made sure she ate her share and fell into a slumber.

Cochay had provisions and water ready for their flight. She used a knife to cut Frank free. He had a hard time adjusting to the pain and weakness from being tied. Cochay gave him a drink of water and turned to leave, but Frank looked about for Ann. She too was sound asleep. He shook her and could not rouse her. He thought Cochay must have drugged the entire camp. Cochay pulled at him frantically and pointed to two horses, which belonged to the sleeping braves. It tore at his heart to leave Ann but he would get others to help and come back and free her too. Frank took the knife Cochay was holding, he was certain it would come in handy. They climbed on the horses and galloped away.

Cochay led, taking a well-used trail that Frank knew led to the river. When they came to a fork in the trail, just before the river, she drew the horse to a halt and turned the opposite direction of the river. Frank wanted to disagree; the river would be a much better way to go. She pointed to herself, then to the branch. She motioned for him to stay back. He watched as she grabbed the branch and swung from the horse. She swung herself into the tree and climbed onto the branch. She pointed at Frank and he did the same thing. Glad to be free of their riders, the horses ran up the trail, loving their new freedom.

They tried very hard not to knock leaves to the ground. When possible, they dropped from the limbs as close to the next tree as they could. When that was not feasible, they walked and covered their tracks. Finally they were at the river. Cochay knew exactly where Red Feather's dugout was hidden in the trees that overhung the river. They each took an oar and headed downstream.

When the squaws had come to this river to wash clothes, Blue Cloud had often pointed southwest and whispered, "Our people. Caddo." Cochay was going to try and make it across that mountain. The Caddos were her people and she was determined to find them.

CHAPTER TWENTY-FIVE

Reading Writing and White Sheets

Louise was very nervous and worried after she thought she may have seen a movement at the window that night, but when nothing came of it, she decided it had been her imagination. She often saw Marty and Mattie standing quietly just outside the yard and she knew they were hoping she would tell them she was ready to let them come for more lessons. On the third day, she relented and told them to tell Henry they could all come that night after darkness had set in. She would have liked to wait longer, but she was expecting Richard at any time and knew that her time would be spent with him. She thought about confessing to Richard that she had been teaching the children, but decided it might be an extra burden and he had enough on his mind already. Also, she needed to be planning their wedding. She had to admit there would not be time for classes for a long time. She couldn't help feeling relieved. The fright and worry she had experienced that night would be with her for a long time. Never again could she be in that cabin with the children without feeling that fear. The children had learned so much in such a short time and she was satisfied she had done her job. Tonight she would tell the children there would be no more classes. To soften their disappointment she would promise them that she would let them sit on her porch and read some of Michael's books. She would let them keep their pencils and paper. After her marriage she would be moving back to her own house. The thought brought tears to her eyes. If only Celeste was there to go home with them. She hadn't planned on staying with her parents this long and was ready to leave.

When Louise arrived at the cabin that evening, she found Henry waiting. He explained, "Marty and Mattie are both sick. They wanted to come anyway, but their mammy said they were burning with a fever and didn't need to be playing outside anymore after dark." Louise was doubly disappointed. She felt sad that the twins were sick and she had wanted to tell the three children at the same time. "Perhaps, Henry," she said, "It would be best to wait until the twins can come also." The look of disappointment on his face was too much for Louise. She relented and opened the door for him to come in.

Reading and basic arithmetic had been easy for Henry. Printing was difficult. She wanted him to practice printing. She told him to write a full page of some of his favorite words. Only then would she let him read. He loved to read aloud to her and set about quickly to fill his page. Louise walked by and smiled to herself as he saw him print, "Miss Louise." He looked up at her and said, "That is my most favorite of all words." Louise was touched and patted his shoulder.

Louise pretended to be walking around the room waiting for Henry; actually she was listening for any unusual sound. She heard none. When she first entered the room, she had checked the shades to make sure they were all the way down and there was no opening or slit where anyone could see in. If someone knocked at the door, she had everything out of sight except the paper Henry was working on. That would be easy enough to hide. She would dare anyone to come in that door without her permission. Henry finished his assignment and proudly showed it to her.

Each line showed an improvement in his printing. She smiled and said, "Henry, all you need is a little practice and you will be very good at this." Henry was obviously pleased, but anxious to start reading. She let him pick out a book from her drawer that he would especially like to read. While he was going through the books and not paying any attention to her, she decided take a peek outside.

Very carefully, with one finger, she pulled the shade slightly to the side. The moon was very pale and it was hard to see. Her eyes were drawn to a spot just a few feet from the door. White sheeted ghosts were standing in a small crowd. The door would have shielded the men when she pushed it open to leave. She would not have seen them until they were outside and she turned to close and lock the door. That would be too late. Terror filled her very being. Her heart began racing so fast she could hardly get her breath. She thought, "My body is trying to give me the resources to get me through this. I must think!" With great determination, she tried to think of a plan. Evidently, the men were waiting for Henry to come out. This might give her time to thwart their plan.

Louise hurried to the window on the opposite side of the room. Carefully she pulled the shade aside a little. No sign of anyone there.

Henry looked up and saw the terror in her eyes. His own eyes immediately bulged with fear. Louise motioned silently for him to come to her side. Louise grasped his shoulders, squeezing them firmly. She gave his shoulders a single shake, making sure he was listening to what she was about to tell him. Though he was terrified, his eyes met hers. Henry knew she was asking him to be brave.

Louise whispered, "Troublemakers are at the front door, <u>no one</u> is on this side. I am going to open the window. You must climb out of it without making <u>any</u> noise. As soon as you are a safe distance from here, run as fast as you can to my porch. The door will be open. Cleo is there. Tell her to hide you. I will come and help you as quickly as I can!" She shook his shoulders again and said, "Be brave! I know you can do it Henry." He nodded his head. He knew only too well that if he cried out or made any noise, he might lose his life.

Carefully, Louise lifted the shade, unlocked the window and slowly raised it. She was glad she had insisted Calvin make good locks and that the windows opened and slid easily. Henry straddled the ledge, dropped to the ground and moved cautiously away from the cabin. It took all of his grit to wait to run until he was out of their hearing.

Louise fought the urge to climb out of the window and run for her life. If Henry got far enough away, and she felt he was safe, that is exactly what she would do. She would leave the window open in case she was allowed that choice.

As it turned out, she was not left with any choices. The men outside had grown tired of waiting. Louise knew what they were up to as soon as she heard a soft tap at the door. They wanted her to think it was someone she knew that was tapping so softly. She moved to the door and in as innocent voice as she could muster, asked, "Who is it?" In response, there was another soft tap. When she didn't respond, they banged loudly on the door. A man's deep voice demanded she open the door. Louise refused. Then she could hear the men moving all around the cabin. She looked out the back window just in time to see a man pointing to the Master house. He yelled, "There he goes, I saw him running around the side of the house."

Louise had to get to the house now herself. She opened the door and two of the men brushed past her to check the inside of the cabin in case Henry was still inside and not the person they had seen running to the Morgan house. The others were running after Henry. This gave Louise the chance to run. She bolted out the door and ran as fast as she could to her fathers. If the men didn't stop her, she must get her father to help Henry.

She was certain the white ghosts would find him right away. There was no place to hide in her small living quarters.

As she neared the front of her parent's home, she saw two men in white sheets were already at the front door. An indignant, angry Dolores Morgan was facing them. Louise paused and heard her mother saying, "You better think twice before you come into my house uninvited." Louise turned, rushed past them and ran upstairs to her father's study. He looked up in alarm as she rushed in. "Father," she pleaded, "There is no time to explain. I need your help. Men are here after your stable boy, Henry. I am afraid he is in grave danger."

Mr. Morgan reached for his gun and started down the stairs. As soon as the men were in his sight, he pointed the gun directly at them. In a no nonsense voice, he ordered, "Put your guns down! Right now! No one comes in my home uninvited, I do not tolerate trespassers."

The men laid their guns on the floor. Mrs. Morgan picked them up and to Louise's surprise unloaded them. She walked up the stairs, carrying the guns with her. The men backed out the door and disappeared in the darkness.

Mr. Morgan asked, "Where is Henry"? Louise was already running out the door. Over her shoulder she called, "In my house." She prayed as she ran, "Don't let them find him."

Louise knew Cleo would be with Michael. She and her father ran to his bedroom. Cleo was standing by Michael's bed and three of the white 'ghosts' were also in the room. Cleo's entire body was shaking uncontrollably. Michael, ashen and visibly terrified was in his bed. He had his wooden replicas of animals, people and buggies in a heap on top of his blanket. He had evidently been playing with the toys his grandfather had carved for him when the shrouded men rushed in. There was no sign of Henry. Louise's fear turned to scorching anger. Straining to control her emotions, she demanded, "Get out! You are nothing but a pack of cowards!" Louise's father raised his gun and ordered, "Do as she says, <u>now</u>!" He added, "Stay one more second, and I will make you take your ridiculous shrouds off." The men couldn't get out of the house fast enough. Mr. Morgan followed them outside.

Louise picked Michael up and cradled him in her arms. She promised him that everything was all right now. She sat down with Michael and called Cleo to her side. Cleo sank to the floor and laid her head across Louise and Michael. Louise stroked Cleo as her Nanny had done for her in the past.

Mr. Morgan watched until he heard the men galloping away. He came into Michael's bedroom and told them the men were gone. He assured them, "They won't be back, at least not tonight."

He turned to Louise; "Whatever did Henry do to make these men come after him? By the way, where is Henry?"

At the mention of Henry, Louise was frightened all over again. She turned to Cleo, "Didn't Henry come here? I forgot all about poor Henry." Cleo looked at Michael and Michael looked at Cleo. They started laughing uncontrollably. They could not even answer. Michael managed to point to his bed. Louise walked to the big feather bed. She snatched the comforter back. Henry was almost even with the feather mattress as he lay there. His body was drenched in perspiration. Louise could not say a word. She burst into tears and sat down on the side of the bed. Mr. Morgan took Henry's hand and helped him to his feet. He reassured Henry over and over that he was safe. Louise regained her composure and started praising Henry for his courage. Finally Henry started talking, telling how fast he had run across the yards. "I ran like demons was after me and they was!"

It was a pitiful group that went into the Morgan's home that night. Mrs. Morgan, thoroughly offended by the smell of Henry's sweat did her best to hide her dislike of the situation. She knew this was one time she had to keep still.

Mr. Morgan told Henry to stay in the servant's quarters with Cleo and her mother. These quarters were attached to the main house and Henry was not to go outside at any time. He was still very frightened and was only too glad to stay inside. One of the servant's ran to tell Henry's mother and ask her to send him clean clothes. She insisted on bringing them herself. She wanted to make sure he was alright. Louise gave him some of Michael's books to read and he was off in another world.

Louise told Michael he could sleep with her in her parent's guest bedroom Michael sat on the edge of the bed, refusing to lie down.   Louise thought he was afraid the men might come back. She assured him they would not. Michael answered, "I know." He was silent for a moment, and then looked up at her, "I can't sleep. I don't want to sleep. There's something else!"

Louise begged him to tell her, she sensed it was not fear that was keeping him awake. It was more like he had been struck by an unbearable sadness. He started crying and his sobs turned into gulps of despair.

Louise's heart was breaking for him. She demanded, "Michael, I will not go to bed until you tell me. You cannot keep such a secret to yourself. Tell me and you can be sure I will be able to make you feel better about it." She nestled close to Michael and put her arm around him. They sat like this until he was able to speak.

"Mama, do you remember the day Grandpa let me paint the gate in the garden?" Louise said she remembered. Michael continued, "That was the day Mr. Richard came and wanted to help me paint. I was pouring some of my paint in a can for him and I tripped and spilled a little on one of his shoes. I felt bad about it but he said not to worry because they were old. Mr. Richard laughed and said, "These are my everyday shoes. It looks like someone painted a flag on my shoe. I rather like it and think I will just let it dry there. Everyone will think I am

146

very patriotic." Then he asked me if I thought it looked like a flag. He asked me, "Can you see it Michael?"

Michael took a deep breath, and exclaimed, "Mama, it did look just like someone had painted a small flag on his shoe." Michael started crying softly again.

Louise waited patiently, wondering, "What did any of this have to do with this night and his sadness?" Michael looked up at his mother as he said, "Mama, that same shoe was on one of the men that was in my bedroom tonight!"

It took Louise a minute to grasp the horror of it all. She tried to tell herself that perhaps he had given the shoes away. In her heart she knew better because she knew exactly which of the shrouded cowards was Richard. Anger rose inside her and gave her strength in spite of all that had been drained from her. She would deal with this later. Right now, she must help Michael.

She tried to explain that some people were weak. She told him she was glad that she had found out that Richard was one of these people and it was much better to know before they were married. She ended up by telling Michael, "We will tell your grandfather that we must go home. Henry is in great danger now, so we will ask your grandfather if we can take Henry with us. One day we will see that he is free. Perhaps we will even take Cleo with us also and free her from slavery." This really pleased Michael and he soon fell asleep.

Sleep did not come easily for Louise that night. She kept wondering how Richard had fooled her so completely. By the time she fall asleep, she had lost most of her respect for him. With the respect, went the love she had felt. She was amazed that she did not feel the need to ask if it was true, somehow she knew it was.

CHAPTER TWENTY-SIX

The Pact

The morning after the Blacks came for dinner, Bob left early so he could tell the adults something was wrong with Honey. He also wanted to question Tim about his time with Honey. The Blacks had just finished breakfast but were still at the table. Everyone was surprised to see Bob. When he explained what had happened with Honey, each responded with deep concern. Bob explained this was not the first time Honey had reacted like this and they had never found out why. He tried to reassure them by saying, "It probably had nothing to do with anything that happened during your visit, but I know you understand that I must ask." He questioned Tim, "Did anything unusual happen? Could something have frightened her?" Tim had no answers. He couldn't think of anything that had frightened or upset Honey. Now it seemed everyone started questioning poor Tim. Finally he said, "We did make a secret pact; but it wasn't about anything scary." All were at a loss. When Tim had gone outside, Lucy said, "We all know Tim is acutely sensitive to other peoples' feelings, I don't think he would ever say anything to hurt or scare Honey." The others all agreed.

When Bob left, Nat followed him outside. He explained, "I know your little girl was enjoying herself with us on the porch. She kept pulling on my sleeve, wanting to hear more. She did leave just as I was telling the last story. I can't remember which one it was. I figured she was just tired."

Bob's face had a stunned look as he said, "I thought you knew that Celeste does not belong to either of us."

Nat looked shocked and confessed that he had taken it for granted that Celeste belonged to one of them.

When Nat came back into the house, he announced, "No one told me that Honey was not Linda or Bob's child. You told me that she couldn't talk but that is about all I knew."

Lucy explained, "Most of the time we forget that she isn't theirs. They discovered her in the spring of the year and I would say she has been with them for about three months. Lucy then told Nat the full story of Honey. When she had finished, Nat exclaimed, "What a heartrending experience for a sweet little girl like Honey!" He sat quietly for a few moments and then said, "Now I am worried that I might have said something that frightened her." He called Tim in and asked, "Do you remember what I was talking about when Honey left the porch?" It took Tim only a minute to recall the last story. He answered, "It was about the time you were lost in the mountains Uncle Nat." A hurt look came over Nat's face. "Then that is it," he said, "Honey must have somehow got separated from her family and my story reminded her only too vividly of how terrible it is to be lost." He stopped and then went on, "I am going over there right now and try and fix it up with her, if I can."

Linda was surprised to find Nat at her door. He explained why he had come. Honey was still in bed and Linda led him to her bedside. Nat sat on the side of her bed. Honey turned away, her face toward the wall. Nat looked stricken. "Please Honey, I didn't mean to scare you. Even though I was lost, look, just look at me, here I am. I am all right and you might have been lost, but you are with people who love you. Was it because I was talking about being lost that you left before I even told you the rest of the story?"

Honey felt sorry for Nat and sad that she couldn't explain to him that it wasn't about being lost. She turned to look at him and shook her head back and forth. Thinking he might remind her of someone that had hurt her, he asked, "Do you like me Honey?" She shook her head vigorously up and down. Nat and Linda were both thrilled to see that little head nodding "Yes."

After that visit, Nat came over often. He could tell Honey was glad to see him, even though she always kept her distance. Nat tried his best to get her to take walks with him, or sit on his lap. She would always smile at him, but that was the most she would do.

It was soon obvious to Bob that it was no longer Honey that Nat was coming to see. He noticed how Linda and Nat's eyes lit up when they saw each other. There was no doubt; Linda and Nat had fallen in love with each other. Bob couldn't believe the change in Linda. Whatever Nat said or did was all right with her. She never tried to control him as she had all the other men that had courted her. Bob sensed it wouldn't be long before they would be married and he wondered and worried about losing Honey. In his heart he knew that Honey would not want to live with Linda and Nat. He couldn't raise a child by himself and he couldn't let her go. He needed her and he knew she needed him. He lay awake at night trying to come up with a plan.

CHAPTER TWENTY-SEVEN

Louise and Michael

Louise spent the next part of that horrible night wondering if she had ever really been in love with Richard. She finally came to the conclusion that she really knew nothing about his deepest feelings. She knew very little about his family. She went over that first day she had met him at the tea. Suddenly it became very clear to her. She remembered thinking; "He appeals to the mothering instinct in women. He seems so defenseless. He makes you want to reach out and help him like you would a child." Losing Celeste had made her very vulnerable. She had mistaken wanting to mother him, for love. Louise was relieved and felt it would not take her long to be free of her past ties to Richard. She closed her eyes and drifted off.

Michael was still asleep when Louise slipped out of bed. The events of the night before were like a nightmare. Her mother and father were waiting to have breakfast with her. She saw the worry, concern and questions on their faces.

Louise tried her best to eat and finally pushed her plate aside. She explained to her parents why the assailants were after Henry. She confessed it was all of her doing. She did not tell them that Richard had probably been one of them.

Mrs. Morgan looked shocked and bewildered. Mr. Morgan knew his daughter so well. None of it surprised him. He felt even more love and respect for her. Louise could see this in his eyes.

Next, Louise explained to her parents that she felt it would be safer for all and best if she and Michael would return to their own home. Her mother started to protest saying, "Louise, what about Richard? He deserves to know of your plans." She would have said more, but the look on Louise's face stopped her. Louise responded, "Richard will understand, he will not need any explanations." Her father looked perplexed, though he never questioned her.

Later, when Louise and her father were alone, she asked about taking Henry and Cleo with them. Mr. Morgan had been worried about Henry's safety and told her he thought it was a wonderful idea. He would sign both of them over to her. Louise explained that she did not want to accept his offer unless he understood she planned to eventually make them a free people. He thought for a moment and then said, "You can do what ever pleases you." Louise spoke again, "I do have one more thing that I feel you should know. I do not want anyone else to know what I am about to tell you." She told him about Richard. He said, "None of this surprises me Louise, he is not the man for you!" She hugged her father and thanked him for all his love and concern. She said, "We would like to leave as soon as possible." He was too sad to speak. Tears welled in his eyes as he nodded his head in agreement.

The carriage was packed and ready to leave. Louise's father offered to go with them but Louise insisted he stay with her mother in case there was trouble. Jonathon knew she was right. He would have one of his most trusted servants, Moses, drive the carriage and he would also send another along.

Jonathon realized the men who came in their sheets were probably friends of his. He was almost certain they would not come back, especially in the daylight. In any case, it would take them a while to organize and meanwhile Louise and Henry would be quite a distance away or home. He agreed with Louise that they should leave as soon as possible. It was decided they would leave at daylight the following morning. The slaves were all cautioned to keep their departure a secret.

Cleo had only her mother to leave. She confided to her mother that she dearly loved Michael and was thrilled beyond words to be going with them. Her mother was sad, but happy for her daughter.

That evening as Louise sat on her front steps, she heard someone approaching. She was shocked when she saw it was Richard. He reached out to hold her in his arms and acted bewildered when she stopped him. "Louise," he implored, "Whatever is wrong?"

In a detached tone, Louise explained that she knew he was one of the men who had terrified them so the night before.

Richard was visibly stunned. Louise could see he wanted to deny it and knew that avenue was useless. He tried to explain, "I had just gotten back from my trip and was anxious to come and see you. The men came and insisted I come here with them. They said it was a way that I could prove I was worthy of being a representative for this state. I felt if I was present, I could protect you and your family if things got out of hand. I would never have let them harm you or Michael. I tried to tell them it was too much to ask of me. Of course the men all like your father, so did not want their identity known. It was decided we would cover ourselves with sheets. In that way, I figured you would never know and I would never chastise you for trying to teach Henry. Louise, you surely knew what you were doing was wrong." Richard begged for her to understand. He pleaded with her to forgive him.

While he was pleading, Louise never voiced what she was thinking, "You look just like a little boy who was caught stealing and wants me to overlook it."

"I suppose," Louise, said, "It didn't matter what happened to Henry." Richard had no answer for that. He could think of nothing more to say.

Louise turned and walked up the steps. Before she entered her door she turned and said, "People like you will never understand people like me. It is all over between us. You will find someone else and I hope you will be happy. It would be best if you forgot about me, as I plan to forget about you." She went inside and closed the door. It had been easier than she had thought.

The Trip

The carriage was ready and waiting. The moon was still out and the sun had barely started to show itself when Mr. and Mrs. Morgan as well as most of the servants gathered around the carriage. It was a very sad assemblage. Two of the most forlorn faces were those of the twins. Louise put an arm around each and promised she and Michael would come back to see them. She gave each of them a gift tied with a bright red ribbon. Their eyes lit up, they knew it was their very own book.

Louise asked her father to tell Sydney goodbye. "Tell her everything that happened. Tell her I said that it was all worthwhile and I would do it all over again."

The carriage occupants were very quiet as they started their journey. The same thought was on all of their minds, "Would the men come after them? What would happen if they found them?"

When they stopped to camp for the night and saw no sign of danger, everyone felt more secure and lighthearted. They sat around their campfire and shared the baskets of food Mrs. Morgan had sent for their journey.

After their meal, Michael described the house and farm to Henry and Cleo. Henry asked, "Do you have any horses?"

Michael assured him they did. Henry said, "Then I'll be happy."
Cleo asked, "Do you have a cabin that I can live in? Who will I
be living with? Louise explained that there were no cabins. You
will have the extra bedroom in my house for now." Louise told
them both about Dan and Sarah. She said, "I know you will
really like them. Sarah is very quiet, but I have a feeling she will
take a liking to both of you." This pleased Henry and Cleo.

On the third morning, the house finally came into view.
Even though Louise's heart was burdened that Celeste was not
with them, she could not stop the warm, glowing feeling that
settled inside her. She felt as if she had found a long lost lover
and friend. The dream of Celeste came to her, as it had so many
times in her saddest moments. She could hear that sweet voice,
"Mama, I _am_ coming home." Aaron was in the picture too, that
reassuring smile on his face. Surely, the Lord had blessed her
with this vision.

Dan And Sarah

Sarah was in her cabin when she heard the carriage arrive.
It was very early in the morning and she wondered who would
be coming by so early. She hurried outside and watched as one
of the occupants climbed out. It was Michael! Sarah couldn't
believe her eyes and ran as fast as she could to tell Dan. He
was feeding the livestock, but dropped the pitchfork as soon as
he heard the news and ran to the carriage. Sarah ran behind
him, stopping at a distance when she saw the strangers that
were standing in the lane. Dan grabbed Michael, hugging him
till Michael could scarcely breathe. He then grabbed Louise's
hand and shook it up and down, over and over. "Are you here
to stay?" Louise assured him they were home for good. He
looked all around, hoping to see Celeste.

Louise ran to Sarah and embraced her warmly. She took
Sarah's hand and pulled her to the little group. Sarah was so

touched that Louise was holding her hand that she forgot to put the shawl across her face. No one seemed to notice the scars on her face. Michael hugged her and the others smiled broadly.

Meanwhile, Louise unlocked her door and invited the others inside. The house was just as neat as when she left it. Sarah had evidently kept it dusted and swept. There was fresh wood in the cook stove. Louise soon had a fire going. She put on some water for tea and asked Sarah if she could bring some food from her cabin.

Henry came back from putting the horses away and washed his hands at the sink. Dan, Henry and the servants did not want to sit at the table. Louise insisted. In no time, they were all sitting around drinking tea and talking. Louise put the food Sarah brought on the table. There was not much of a variety, but it tasted wonderful to the weary travelers.

Dan asked why they had decided to come home. Louise let Michael recount the events of that frightening night. Michael's eyes were big, his face full of excitement as he told of how the men had searched for Henry. Henry swelled with pride. It was the first time he had been the main subject of any conversation. When everyone laughed after finding out where Henry had been hidden, Henry laughed the loudest. He reveled in getting so much attention. Louise filled in what Michael didn't know. Dan and Sarah were completely spellbound. No one could have found a better audience.

Louise decided Henry could have Aaron's former office in the old furniture warehouse. It had its' own entrance and a fireplace. He could use the shelves for his belongings. She was glad she had made extra feather ticks in case she needed an extra place for someone to sleep. Later Dan could make him a bed frame for the tick. When she showed Henry his room, his eyes filled with tears. He turned his head to hide them from her and said, "You are just too good to me, Miss Louise."

As soon as Louise got a chance, she went to Aaron's graveside. Dan had kept it in perfect condition. He or Sarah had planted more flowers. "What wonderful people they are," she thought. Aaron had been so right when he promised her they would not be sorry for hiring Dan." She sank down in the grass and said a prayer. She rose to her feet and whispered, "I miss you dear Aaron and I miss Celeste." She walked away thinking; "I am going to keep trusting that Celeste will be found. I must find some special way to help others now that I am home. I promised Nanny I would."

Mr. Morgan's servant, Moses, planned on leaving early the next morning. He announced, "I promised we would get right back. Mastah don't need to be worrying. He gwine to be mighty pleased to hear about our fine trip."

CHAPTER TWENTY-EIGHT

The Hunt

When the Indians returned from their hunt, they knew something was terribly wrong even before they were close to the camp. No noises of the children playing came to their ears. In one accord the Indians dismounted. Each held a weapon and silently stole towards their camp. They all believed enemies had invaded the camp, stealing the young squaws and killing the rest. They were bewildered to find them all asleep. A few were rousing and when they were questioned had no idea why they had all been sleeping. They were as confused as the returning hunters.

Red Feather was the first to realize that One-Ear and Cochay were gone. He ran to Walk-Like-Willow's tent. He expected her to be gone also. Red Feather was surprised to find her sound asleep.

As soon as everyone was awake, Chief Gray Wolf summoned his people. All were questioned. No one could tell him anything that was out of the ordinary, not even the Chief's squaw, Blue Cloud.

Red Feather knew time was precious. He was going after One- Ear and Cochay. He would not be humiliated like this. One-Ear's guards complained loudly that their horses were missing and were anxious to join Red Feather in his hunt. Red

Feather also took the two braves that were with him when he had captured Frank and Ann.

Red Feather brought an extra horse and tossed Walk-Like-Willow on it. In an angry tone, he said, "You come with me." Ann would have fought going, but she wanted to be there if they caught Frank and Cochay. At least she would know what happened to them.

Ann was sure that Frank loved her. Cochay must have put something in the food to make them sleep. She was certain that Frank had tried to awaken her Ann consoled herself with the thought, "Frank will get help and come back for me."

The Trail

It was easy for Red Feather and the two braves to see where the ground was disturbed and the horses mounted. They followed the trail to the fork and saw where they evidently were trying to decide which trail to take. Red Feather could see they did not head for the river and this made him very happy. The river would take them further away in a much shorter time and it would be much harder to find where they disembarked. His face was filled with fury; he would find no rest until he captured them. They would pay dearly for humiliating him. How foolish One-Ear was to not choose the river.

Red Feather led, Walk-Like-Willow was next, and then the four braves. She had no way of escaping. The trail was narrow and had not been used for a while. Red Feather could see many signs that the horses were indeed on this trail. The droppings of the horses were still damp. Red Feather sensed they were closing in on his prey. They would be at his mercy very soon.

One thing puzzled Red Feather. There were places along the trail where he could see the horses had traveled at a very slow pace and even grazed. Perhaps One-Ear was so weak he could not ride very fast. He thought, "One-Ear not worthy to be called a man."

Red Feather and his group hadn't gone very far when they came to a clearing. Red Feather had often camped in this place because there was a spring near by. To his chagrin, he saw the two horses they had been trailing all day. They were grazing contentedly. The horses raised their heads and looked at the intruders. Unimpressed, they returned to their grazing.

It didn't take Red Feather long to realize he had been tricked. They had been following two horses that had no riders. He realized they must have taken the trail to the river. Cochay knew where his dugout was. He should have known they would take the fastest way out. The nerve of Cochay using his dugout as their means of escape.

The fat braves jumped on their own horses and forced the horses they had been riding back on the trail towards the Apache camp. They would send the horses the opposite way when they reached the fork in the trail. Red Feather turned his horse around and the others followed.

CHAPTER TWENTY NINE

Frank and Cochay

Frank had often wished he had a better sense of direction. His goal was to head for a fort or town where he could find help and rescue Ann. The truth was that he did not have the slightest idea which way to go. Instead, he had to follow Cochay and had no idea where she was going. He knew some of the language but not enough to ask her though he sensed she had a destination in mind. He had tried pointing to her, then to himself and shrugging his shoulders as he spread out his arms in a questioning manner. Each time she pointed to the mountain. He hoped she intended on crossing it. Once on the other side, he felt they would eventually come to a home or town. He knew they could not feel safe until they were at least across the mountain, and perhaps, not even then. He shuddered as he thought of Red Feather and how irate he would be when he returned to camp and found the two of them gone. He wondered how long they could survive on the food and water she had brought.

They finally reached the mountain and Cochay did not stop. They had climbed for some time and the air was getting much colder. Soon Frank saw tiny flakes of snow swirling around. Cochay stopped and looked around. She picked out a low mountain ledge, not as deep as a cave but it would afford them some protection. Cochay started breaking small trees and debris. She piled them around the ledge. As soon as Frank saw what she was doing, he helped her. When it was packed down enough to keep most of the snow and wind out they crawled inside. The wind sounded angry and Frank realized Cochay had just taken him out of a blinding snowstorm. They huddled together, shaking from the cold. They were both exhausted from their journey. Frank wondered if they would freeze to death if they fell asleep. He looked at Cochay, he could see she was exhausted but awake. He realized she too was worried that she might "sleep the sleep of death?"

Frank was not aware that he drifted off. It certainly was not a very restful sleep. His brain invaded his sleep with nightmares of Red Feather finding them and Ann burning at the stake because he had escaped.

When Frank awakened he was still tired, but some of his energy had returned. Cochay gave him a small piece of the beef jerky to chew on. He scooped some of the snow and let it melt in his mouth. Cochay pointed to her eyes and closed them as if asleep. She then held one of his eyes open with her fingers. He nodded his head showing he understood. It was his turn to stay awake while she slept. He must not let her sleep long enough to let the cold drain her life from her.

Luckily for them, the storm did not last long. It was one of those violent mountain storms that erupted suddenly and lasted only a short time. When daylight came, they crawled out of their shelter and started out again. The sun came out and though they were not warm enough, they were not miserable. The sun eventually melted the snow and it was easier to walk. Suddenly Cochay cried out. At first it frightened Frank and then he realized it was not a cry of fear. It was more like a cry of discovery. When he reached her, he saw that she had found a trail. Not wide enough for a wagon, probably one used by hunters and trappers who frequented the mountain. Frank had never been a spiritual man; but he fell to his knees and said, "Thank You God!" It had to be divine help that had brought them to this trail. The chances of finding someone to help them would be much greater now.

The Wilderness Man

Not too far from Cochay and Frank was another traveler. When someone asked him where his home was, he often replied, "The Wilderness." It was true. He had lived in wildernesses since he was a young man. He had hunted and trapped all those years and saved enough money to live on for the rest of his days. Sometimes he had traded with the Indians for gold. The gold meant nothing to them and he could tell they thought white men foolish for giving them a valuable fur for a piece of rock.

His wilderness days were almost over. He was tired of being alone and it was high time he found a wife and started a family of his own. He planned on selling his mule to the first buyer he came across. He would climb on his horse and ride as fast as he could towards the only family he had.

He was so busy thinking about leaving the wilderness he loved that he never noticed he had made a wrong turn. He had been lost many times, but never in this area. Getting lost in the wilderness is no problem when you don't have a home. You just move on. This time it was different. He had a destination and he was eager to get there.

The snowstorm erupted about the time he realized he was on the wrong trail. He had no choice. He set up his camp and hoped the storm would not last long.

The following morning he took his horse by the reins and his mule followed. It did not take him long to find the trail and once on it, he mounted his horse. The horse was limping and he dismounted and checked her hooves. He saw the problem right away. Something was lodged in the cleft of the hoof.

Taking his knife, he worked until he dislodged the rather large stone. He had just placed the horse's hoof on the ground when he heard the movement of something or someone on the trail behind him. He led the animals off the trail and out of sight.

It wasn't long before an Indian woman followed by a white man came into sight. They appeared tired and weary. They looked harmless enough. His curiosity was aroused and he called out, "Hey". He could not see the face of the Indian. The man turned ashen and fear seemed to freeze him where he stood.

The Mountain Man called out, "Sorry, I didn't mean to frighten you. I mean you no harm. Perhaps I can be of some help to you." He stepped forward, extending his hand, "Around here, they call me 'Bear.' The Indian's gave me that name." Frank clasped Bear's hand, and said, Frank." He then nodded in Cochay's direction. "This is Cochay. I don't know if she needs any help, but I sure could use some directions." Bear replied, "I will be glad to help in any way I can, but first let's have a little food and water. He could tell the two were very weary and possibly without food and water.

Bear took some food and water out that he had strapped on his mule. They all sat along the trail while they ate. Frank explained to the man how the Apache Indians had captured him and his wife. He told how he and Cochay had escaped and that he wanted to find someone to help him rescue his wife.

Bear asked, "Do you know the name of the Chief of that tribe?"

Frank responded, "I sure do! Chief Gray Wolf."

Bear said he had been in Gray Wolf's camp a few times. "They are a tribe that does not care for white people. I never really felt I could trust them. They would rather fight than learn new ways to do things. I did like to trade my furs to them as they usually paid with gold. The trouble is they were mostly interested in "Fire Water."

Frank explained that he did not know enough Apache to find out where Cochay was headed. Bear said, "I do know quite a bit of the Apache language. Do you want me to question her?" Frank replied, "Yes, I sure would like to know where she is headed. She seems to have a certain destination in mind. All she will say is caddo."

Bear spoke a few words in the Apache tongue. She answered and Bear explained to Frank, "She is going to her people. The Caddos."

Frank looked surprised and said, "I always thought she was an Apache." He turned to Cochay and pointed his finger at her, "You Apache?" Cochay did not want to admit she was part Apache. She despised Red Feather." She shook her head back and forth and said, "Caddo"

Frank had never heard of the Caddo tribe and asked Bear if he had. Bear said, "I have often traded with them when I have been on my way to visit my family. If you don't know anything about them, you will be surprised to know that Texas is a Caddoan name. It means 'those who are friends'. The Caddo Indians are the friendliest of all Indians that I have met. They also live the closest to the way we live and are quite civilized. They even use some furniture. They are a very progressive and colorful people. I have never felt uneasy in their camp."

"Well," Frank said, "I want to get to a fort or someplace where I can ask the soldiers to find my wife and free her. If you know where a fort is, could you tell me how to get there? If it is in a different direction then the Caddos, she can go her way and I will go mine."

Although Bear was in a hurry, he knew he had to help. The fort was not too far out of the way and he agreed to take him there.

Frank thanked him and asked him another question. "How do you think the Caddos will treat her if she finds their camp?"

Bear thought for a moment and replied, "The women are treated well. I think they will welcome her. I also think she will really like living with the Caddos."

Frank asked, "Then how about pointing her in the direction of her people?"

Bear touched Cochay on the shoulder. When she looked up at him, he pointed northeast and said, "Caddo."

Cochay started in that direction. After a few steps she stopped and looked at Frank. She beckoned for him to come. He shook his head negatively and motioned for her to go on. She came back and stood at his side.

Frank shrugged his shoulders and said, "Guess she doesn't want to go without me. I will see that she finds her people; but first I am going to see about finding my wife."

The further they traveled down the mountainside, the warmer the weather became. They were glad to see sunshine and it was good to feel warm and comfortable. As they came out of the mountains, Bear pointed to a cabin in the distance. The small log cabin and its' surroundings looked neat and inviting. Small threads of blue smoke curled lazily from the chimney. Frank pictured a pot of stew cooking over the coals.

Bear explained, "I am sure you will be glad to know that I have been friends with these wonderful people for years. They are always glad to see me and will make all of us welcome."

The man and his wife were indeed very happy to see them. Bear introduced everyone. Jared and Christina Anderson invited them inside. Frank had to suppress a smile. Indeed there was a black iron pot simmering over the hot coals. Christina set the table and put the food on. She showed each where to sit but Cochay held back. Christina set Cochay's food on the fireplace stone, smiled at Cochay and motioned for her to eat there. When Christina joined Bear and Frank, she said, "I am sure the woman will enjoy her food much better if she does not have to join us at the table." Frank told Christina that he could not remember eating anything that tasted so good." Bear agreed. After they ate, she prepared extra food for their journey. When they were outside, Bear and Jared moved off to the side and talked quietly. They headed for the corral and came back leading two horses. Bear paid him and turned to Frank and Cochay. "The horses are yours," he explained. When Frank tried to thank Bear for the horses, he waved him aside. "This will make our journey much quicker and easier." As they rode away, Bear called out to Jared, "Take care of my mule and take that stubborn streak out of her." Jared laughed and waved goodbye.

CHAPTER THIRTY

Closing In

Red Feather became angrier by the minute. To think that Cochay and One-Ear had tricked him into following horses that had no riders. . When they reached the fork, he whopped the last one across his hind-quarters and the horses ran towards the Apache camp. Red Feather and his group turned right and headed for the river. It was just as Red Feather suspected, his dugout was gone. He checked the areas where other Indians hid their dugouts. They were all in place. He had worked hard and long on his dugout and it beat all the others whenever he raced with other braves. On top of that, he hated to admit that his own squaw had outwitted him. He would make her suffer long for this. Death would come slowly. She had disgraced him in front of all his people. He must regain their respect. He would never come back to his people until he had righted the wrong Cochay and Frank had subjected him to.

Red Feather ordered three of the Indians to ride along one of the riverbanks. He crossed to the opposite bank with Walk-Like-Willow and the other brave. The first day they found no traces of anyone leaving the river. The following day they found an area where someone had tried very hard to hide their exit from the river. Tracks of a man and woman had been brushed over. It didn't take Red Feather long to find his very own dugout hidden in the cover of the low hanging brush. Just as he figured, they were headed for the mountain. Of course, his prey would take the straightest and most accessible approach to the mountain. His heart lifted and his spirit was renewed. He would find them, and he would teach them that slaves existed only for the pleasures of their master.

Because of many rocky areas, Red Feather and his small band did not find their tracking as easy as he thought. He could not find any clues as to which way they had traveled. Perhaps they did not go into the mountains. He believed that One-Ear would most likely head for the nearest settlement. He searched for days in that direction and then returned to the area where he had last tracked them and tried another direction to no avail. He knew Cochay had never been to this mountain and wondered if One-Ear had been. Maybe they were lost and wandering on the mountainside. At last he picked out an area that was covered with trees and started up the mountainside. After several hours of climbing, they came upon the tracks of someone traveling with a horse and mule. Red Feather knew that this would be one of the men who hunted and trapped in the Indian's territories. They followed his tracks. The Great Spirit had led him again. The man's tracks soon mingled with two more sets of footprints. He was positive they belonged to Cochay and One-Ear. Red Feather followed the tracks down the mountain and into a grassy area leading away from the mountain. Three people had followed the trail out of the mountains. Red Feather saw the cabin in the distance and knew someone inside that cabin could give him some information. .

Red Feather watched the house for a long time to see who lived there. At last he saw an older man leave the barn and in a little while, a woman left the house, walking towards the man. Red Feather ordered one of the braves to dismount and hold Ann's horse's reins to prevent her from trying to escape.

When the woman reached her husband, the Indians shouted and galloped towards them. Jared Anderson and his wife Christina had enjoyed their last visitors so much that the last thing that was on their mind was an attack from Indians. In all the years they had lived there, this had never happened before. The couple ran as fast as they could for their cabin. Their hearts were full of fear. Red Feather slid from his horse. He must show them right away that he meant business. He slapped the woman with such force that she hit the rocky ground and lay still. Then Red Feather walked over and kicked her. She never flinched. He was disappointed and thought, "She die too easily, if not she will die after we kill man."

The man used this chance to run again. As he ran, he prayed, "Please, let my Christina live." He knew he could not escape, but he was hoping to lead them away from his wife. He was afraid the blow had killed her, but if it hadn't perhaps they might not hurt her further."

Red Feather grunted to the braves telling them to surround the man, but not to injure him. He did not want the man to die until he had the information he wanted. The braves rode after him and formed a circle with their horses, preventing him from running further. Red Feather sauntered over to the man. He wanted his victim to have plenty of time to be completely terrified. A man in that situation would tell you anything you wanted to know.

Grabbing his shirt, Red Feather pulled him close and then propelled him to the ground. The fall knocked his breath from him. As soon as the man was able to breathe again, Red Feather yanked him to his feet and threw him down again. He was careful not to throw him so hard this time. He would be worthless to him if unconscious or dead.

As the man lay on the ground, Red Feather brandished his knife. He spoke, "White men and squaw? Where they go?"

The man was surprised this Apache spoke any English. Most Apaches hated the white man and would not speak their language even if they could. Bear was a good man and a friend of his. He wondered why they would be after him. He did not want to say anything that would endanger his friend. He was silent.

Red Feather had one of the braves pin the man's arms behind him. Red Feather took his knife and drew a circle around his head. He made sure it was only deep enough to cause a little bleeding across his forehead.

Jared Anderson knew he was going to die. He tried to gather up his courage. He thought, "Christina is gone, what does it matter? I will do my utmost to die bravely."

The Indian spoke again, "Squaw is mine. Where did squaw go?"

Jared thought, "Now that is a different matter, he is after his squaw. He just wants his squaw back"

Jared said, "Your squaw go to Caddo village."

It was Red Feather's turn to look surprised. He said, "You lie!"

The old man shook his head and said, "I am honest man. I speak truth."

Red Feather believed him, but he would take his scalp for knowing that his squaw was with another man.

It was time for another surprise for Red Feather and his braves. A shot rang out and one of the braves fell from his horse. Blood was running from his back and he lay very still. Red Feather jumped on his horse and rode for his life. The other braves were quick to follow. He had taken it for granted that the man and woman lived alone. Someone else was in that house and whoever it was, knew how to shoot a gun! He thought, "Oh well, I know now, where to find squaw and One-Ear."

Ann had watched the entire fiasco. She was glad when she heard the gunshot and saw the brave fall to the ground. She wished it had been Red Feather. She also wished he would leave without her, but she saw them riding towards her and her guard.

Jared scrambled to his feet and ran towards the house for his gun. Who had fired that shot? Had Bear came back? Standing outside the door of the cabin was his very own Christina. Pale as a ghost but still the prettiest little gal he had ever seen.

Jared laughed in spite of what they had been through when his usually kind and loving Christina greeted him with the words, "Now, we will have to bury that Indian!"

CHAPTER THIRTY ONE

Fort Mason

Frank was very glad that Bear had been kind enough to take them to Fort Mason. He could sense Bear was anxious to be on his way. The fort had been especially quiet for several weeks and the squadron of soldiers was ready for some kind of challenge. Bear, Frank and Cochay were escorted to the Captain. Frank explained how the Apache Red Feather had captured him and his wife. He said they were kept prisoners and endured much suffering because of them. He told how he and Cochay had escaped. He pleaded, "Would you and your men try to find and free my wife? I will go with you if you want but I must warn you, I have no idea which way to go after we are over the mountains. I have never been good at directions." Frank was relieved when the Captain told him they knew exactly where Red Feather's camp was and they would love an excuse to capture or kill him. The Captain asked Frank for a good description of Ann and advised him it would not be wise for him to travel with them, as he did not have the proper training.

Before Bear left, he drew a map for Frank showing the way to Caddo country. Bear explained, "The woods are full of pine trees, creeks and springs. A river also runs through their territory. You will find the trails well-used and wide enough for carriages. The Caddis camps are very close to the Texas Louisiana border." Bear was satisfied that he had done his part so he wished them luck and went on his way.

As the soldiers rode away, Frank pointed to them and told Cochay, "They find Walk-Like-Willow." She lowered her head and nodded ever so gently. Frank felt a pang of guilt. She had saved him and he knew she felt he was deserting her. With his hand, he lifted her chin until their eyes met, and promised, "When soldiers return, I will take you to Caddo's." He pointed in the direction Bear had showed them. He had never seen a smile on her face since their escape. She smiled now and Frank knew she understood.

One of the remaining soldiers showed them where they could wash up and sleep. It was nice to be clean and sleep in a bed again, even if it was a soldier's cot.

Before Frank could sleep, he had to settle some things in his mind. He thought back on his past life, wanting to understand himself and Ann better. There were too many things about their feelings and actions that he was finding that he did not like. He knew he had improved in some ways, but he wanted to be a better man.

Frank and Ann's Early Years

Frank was actually surprised to realize that he really cared about what happened to Cochay. In the past, he would have sent her on without a second thought. Until he had met Ann he had been not only 'Number One,' but also the only one he cared about. He had been orphaned at an early age and while growing up, no one had ever shown him any love. When Frank got older, he soon realized that the ladies thought him quite handsome. He also came to realize that he had a way with the ladies. When he worked, he spent most of his money for clothes and was always very dapper. A wealthy French lady who had been widowed took him into her home. He lived there under the pretense that he was a visiting cousin. She taught him how to dress and act. She introduced him as a Duke. She paid him to escort her about town and to be available when she needed him. She was an ugly woman and loved being escorted by a handsome young man. Frank saved every cent he could. As soon as he had saved enough for his fare, he left for America. He never told the woman, just disappeared out of her life. He arrived in America at an early age and though he had many different jobs, he was frugal and saved a good sum of money.

Frank was surprised to find such an attractive girl as Ann willing to marry him. He was also surprised to find out her life had also been an unhappy one. Her parents had divorced and when her mother remarried, she found out too late that her new husband was a cruel and selfish man. Her mother had not lived long and Ann always felt she died from the beatings he inflicted on her. When the mother was gone, he took to beating Ann. She was determined he was not going to have that pleasure very long. She ran away when she was thirteen. Living on the streets in England was better than the abuse she had received from her drunken stepfather.

Eventually she met a lonely English widow. Her husband had left her well off. She lived in the country and was confined to a wheelchair. She hired Ann to care for her. Ann hated living in the country but having a steady income was worth the sacrifice. Miss Helen, as Ann called her, was very kind to her. In spite of this, Ann often said unkind things and took her time in responding to her needs. It infuriated Ann that the woman never reacted to the mean things she said or did.

The only family the English woman had was a sister and a brother-in-law who lived in America. Eventually the sister invited Helen to live with them. She happily accepted. She asked Ann to escort her to America and promised she would continue to employ her at her sister's home. Her sister had agreed to this, but Ann did not even get inside the door before the woman said, "I am sorry we do not have room for you. From now on, I will see to the needs of my sister." Miss Helen was apologetic and begged her sister to relent. She would not. Finally Helen gave up and said, "Can't you tell her someone that might need her services?" The sister gave Ann a small amount of money and told her of a rooming house where she could get a room and that was the extent of her help. Miss Helen paid her an extra month's wages and Ann was on her own. Neither Ann nor Miss Helen knew that it was because the husband had a roaming eye and Ann was so beautiful. The sister was not going to provide someone as lovely as Ann for her husband to ogle.

Ann knocked on strange doors. She checked with the local businesses. They were all very sympathetic but did not have work for her. Those that could afford to hire help already had. Some had servants of their own.

Finally Ann was forced to resort to one of the saloons where a sign was on the door, "Dancer Wanted." She had never been in a saloon and her cheeks blushed red when she walked in. She had never danced, however the man was only too happy to hire Ann. The other girls were very friendly and in no time they had her doing all the kicks and flounces. That is where she met Frank.

Frank's reverie brought him back to the present. As bad as his past may have been, the Indians had been the worst tormentors and caused the most pain. He did have to admit to himself that he was a better man now than before he had been captured. The experience had put something in his heart that he never had before, concern for other people. The entire time they were captured, he had worried about Ann. He marveled at the way Cochay had saved him from a sure death. It would have been much easier for her to slip away by herself. He thought of Celeste again. "We caused her so much suffering. Just because we had an unhappy childhood, we wanted an innocent child to be miserable." He promised himself, "As soon as I can, I will do my best to find her and take her back to her mother." This thought comforted him and he fell asleep. He would not have slept so well if he had known Red Feather would 'own' him again.

Frank and Cochay

Almost two weeks passed before Frank saw the squadron of soldiers returning to the fort. He looked in vain hoping to see Ann ride in with them. When one of the officers approached him, Frank knew by the look on his face that they had not found her or else she was dead.

The officer explained that the Apache camp was deserted. The squadron looked for miles around with no results. The officer promised they would continue to search.

Frank was depressed by the news but thanked him for looking for Ann. He explained to the officer, "I am taking Cochay to the Caddo village. I will stay there until I hear from you. If I must leave, I will try and leave word where you can find me.

The Officer in charge gave them provisions and water for their journey. Frank thanked them for their help and he and Cochay left for the Caddo village.

CHAPTER THIRTY-TWO

Louise-Home Again

Louise hadn't realized how much she missed being in her own home until she was back. Of course, Celeste was constantly on her mind and her heart leaped at the slightest noise. If someone came up the lane she ran to meet him or her, hoping against hope that it was someone bringing Celeste home or someone with news of her whereabouts. During the day she managed to stay busy. Evenings were the worst. Those were the times when Michael seemed to miss Celeste the most also. He might be reading a book and suddenly look up and say, "Remember the time Celeste saw a picture of a zebra and thought it was a pony." Often Louise had forgotten things he mentioned about Celeste and they would laugh or cry together.

Sarah had blossomed since their return. She and Cleo had become great friends. When Cleo finished helping Louise in the house, she often went with Sarah and they helped Dan with his work. Sometimes they would sew together or go for walks.

One day Sarah confided to Cleo, "I think Celeste was stolen by the Indians. Sometimes I can't sleep at night thinking of that sweet little girl and how she might be treated." She started shaking as if she were having a severe chill. Cleo put her arms around her and soothed her hand across her back. Sarah wept and sobbed as if her heart was broken. She didn't realize that she was also weeping for herself and the atrocities she had suffered.

After that, she never wore her shawl again. Some of her lost spirit had returned. She was happier then she had been for years. Dan noticed and this made his own heart joyous. He wished so much that Celeste would be found and Miss Louise could also have joy in her heart again.

Henry took over the care of the horses. He helped milk the cows and did other chores. Michael was probably almost five years younger than Henry and he followed Henry wherever he went. Henry loved it and never tired of having him around. Michael was impressed with the way Henry handled the horses and told him so. Henry beamed, he never imagined a slave person could be so happy.

Henry showed his appreciation by working hard. Miss Louise gave him a small wage. She explained that when he was old enough, she was going to make him a free man. At first the very thought frightened him. He pleaded, "Oh no, Miss Louise, I am as happy as I can be stayin right here." So Louise told him a little of what being free could mean. She said he might want to go north. There, he could get a 'real' job and have a family of his own. A family no one could separate by selling him, his wife or children.

After that, he dreamed of being free and making his own choices. He saved his pittance of a wage. Cleo made his clothes for him and the only thing he ever bought was a book. He was afraid to be seen in town, so asked Dan to get him one when he went for the groceries. Since Dan could not read, he asked the clerk to pick one out for him.

Dan came home with Oliver Twist by Charles Dickens. Henry loved the story. He kept thanking Dan for getting it until Dan was embarrassed and said, "I didn't do nothin but bring it home to you Henry." Henry retorted, "You just don't

179

understand Dan because you are a white man. They wouldn't even let me buy a book." He wanted to show Dan just how glad he was for the book. He came up with a way. He asked Dan, "How would you like it if I came over every night and read it to you and Sarah? Then you could see why I like this story so much." Dan thought that was about the best idea he had ever heard and told Henry so.

Henry asked Miss Louise if Michael could join them. She said he could but must be home by eight. She suggested he ask Cleo if she would like to come, of course, she was thrilled to accept the invitation. It was a good thing Henry had to leave each night to bring Michael home or the listeners would have begged him to read it straight through.

The next time Dan was going to town, he asked Henry, "If I buy a book, will you read it to us Henry?" Henry was quite flattered and quickly promised that he would.

Louise was happy Henry had thought of reading the book to them. She never let on that being alone those nights was almost unbearable.

Once again Michael came to her aid. He said, "It's a shame that everyone can't read. I think you ought to teach them all to read like you did Henry and the twins."

Louise had tears in her eyes as she hugged Michael and said, "What would I do without you Michael. You are such a dear son. I will ask them tomorrow. Why didn't I think of it right away?"

The next day she sent Michael to ask Dan, Sarah and Henry to come to the house. She also asked Cleo to join them. When she explained her plan, they were overjoyed, but leery. Dan voiced their uncertainty for them all when he said, "Miss Louise, Don't you think we are too old to learn to read?" Louise assured them, "You can all learn to read, I promise."

Henry said, "If I could learn to read, you can too. I never even dared to dream about reading. I know lots of words now and I even talk plainer unless I get scared or nervous. I can sit out there under a tree and go to all kinds of other places and lands. I can fly on a magic carpet or watch those girls scratch and tear each others' hair out and never leave my seat out there in the grass under a tree."

Louise smiled at him and said, "I plan on you helping me teach them Henry." Henry was so proud that he could hardly contain himself.

Louise couldn't wait to get out the flash cards and primers.

The Morgans

Jonathon Morgan was relieved to see his servants and carriage coming up the lane. Moses told him that Louise, Michael, Cleo and Henry had arrived safely. They wanted to tell him every detail of their trip. Jonathon hid the smile playing on his lips. They sounded like they had been on a holiday. He chuckled to himself as he walked away. He knew Louise would try to see that they all enjoyed themselves. He was amazed at her faith and strength. He had never heard her complain about Celeste being taken away from her. She only said, "I know that someday I will have her back if I believe." Jonathon hurried in the house to tell Dolores that Louise, Michael and the rest had arrived safely.

It was obvious by the look on her face that Dolores was relieved they were safely home, still she could not help but say, "I think Louise made a big mistake by not marrying Richard. I will never understand that girl. I was so sure she really cared for him."

Jonathon shook his head slowly, "Poor Dolores, she will never understand." He started to blurt out the truth, changed his mind and walked out of the house. He knew she would always believe Louise was the one who was out of line.

The fact was that Louise had no sooner left than Dolores penned a letter to Richard, telling him how sorry she was that Louise had broken their engagement. She invited him to come for a visit. Richard wrote back immediately and told her he would love to come. "Perhaps," he wrote, "Louise may change her mind after she has time to think things over." Dolores was thrilled with his response.

Richard came for a brief visit, Jonathon made sure he was not home that day.

During his visit, Richard asked Mrs. Morgan if she could possibly help him entertain some visiting dignitaries who would be coming to Natchitoches in a week. Richard explained, "One of the guests will be a House Representative of the state of Illinois, Mark Austin. Some of his aides will be with him. They will be doing a study of our political groups in Louisiana. This is one of their stops." Dolores was elated and told him she would be happy to entertain as many as he wanted to bring along.

As soon as Jonathon came home, Dolores told him about the dinner she would be planning. Her face was animated as she read the names from the list Richard gave her. She begged Jonathon to join them. She pleaded, "It just wouldn't look right if you weren't in your place at the head of the table." Jonathon knew how important this was to Dolores and agreed to join them. He said," I have one favor to ask, do not sit Richard anywhere near me. I have heard some good things about Mark Austin. Please seat him to my right." Dolores was only too happy to grant his request.

For Dolores, the time seemed to fly by and it was the evening of the dinner. Everything was planned. Two wonderful violinists would entertain them after dinner.

Jonathon was anxious to meet Mark Austin. He turned out to be a middle-aged man, perhaps in his late forties. He was rather tall with premature gray hair and probing blue eyes. He stood very erect and Jonathon noticed that whomever he was speaking with, he was comfortable looking straight into their eyes. A trait that Jonathon thought spoke well of a man regarding his integrity and confidence.

As Jonathon had requested, Mark was seated to his right. He had never met a man he enjoyed visiting with as much as he did Mark Austin. When Jonathon's plate was whisked away, the food had scarcely been touched. It was not so much that he had been talking, but that he had been listening. Mark told him that he was a very good friend of a man named Abraham Lincoln. He said, "I feel he is a great man and someday this nation will all have heard of him. The slave states will not like him because he is against slavery. He feels slavery separates our states and causes much conflict. I think he is right, but I am against slavery for a deeper reason. I think no man or woman should be a slave for another man or woman. Many people like myself, are against slavery. I feel that one day there will be an uprising that could turn into something very serious. Perhaps an all out war."

When the dinner music started and the guests had been moved to the parlor, Jonathan asked Mark if he would join him in his study for a short visit.

In the study, Jonathon encouraged Mark to tell him more of his thoughts on slavery. Mark asked, "Do you know how slavery started in America?" Jonathon admitted he did not. Mark explained, "Slavery actually started in Virginia. The men who came here from England were not used to rough and hard labor and were not about to make it a part of their lifestyle." Mark raised his eyebrows, his face registering contempt, and said, " For my part, I think any man worth his salt is not afraid of hard work. Of course, with their attitudes, the new settlements did not have a chance to make it. When Sir Thomas Dale became governor of the Jamestown colony, he gave each of the settlers some free land. They did show an interest in growing tobacco. It was a very good incentive, but of course this meant hard work. There were many men in England who wanted to come to America, but could not afford the fare. The colonists' agreed to pay their fare if they would agree to work a certain number of years to pay them back. This made them indentured servants, but after serving the years they signed for, they were free to leave. One of the ships that came to Virginia in 1619 had the first load of colored people. These people were able to tolerate the hot sun and work long hours in the tobacco fields. There became a great demand for them. At first they were treated the same as the indentured servants, but eventually became full slaves and the colonists actually came to own them. We can be certain that slavery is a dangerous subject and will become more so." Mark took a sip from his coffee cup, looked Jonathon straight in the eyes and asked, "I have told you my stand on slavery, may I ask you yours?"

Jonathon looked very surprised, then his expression changed to a perplexed look and he finally answered, "Mark would you believe I have never been asked that question? All I can tell you is the relationship I have with my servants. I do not like or use the word slaves when I refer or think of them. Servants, yes, but not slaves. My very best man Moses is a highly intelligent and valuable servant. I let him know I appreciate him and he is very loyal to me. I would imagine that if you offered him his freedom, he would tell you he is happy where he is. He might say, "'The Mastah is very good to me. He provides me with everything I need, food, clothes, a decent place to live and I ain't got no worries. I don want no worries in this world cause it is just a short stop here till I get to my real home" Jonathon continued, "There are also some who would be lost if they were on their own. There are some who have no ambition. I guess if I had a man or woman whose heart cried out to be free, I would set him or her free. My daughter took two of my servants when she went home and she plans to set them free. I signed them over to her and gave her my blessing to do so."

Mark laughed and said, "I was all set to have a little debate with you, Mr. Morgan, but I am afraid I can't at this moment, find a reasonable argument for your thoughts."

Jonathon responded, "Then let's get on with the real reason I asked you to join me in my study. I was quite pleased when you admired the painting in the parlor and said you have a great love for art. I decided I would like to show you an oil painting that I cherish. I have not been able to share this with anyone I have come in contact with. You will understand why when you see the picture. I am anxious to see what you think of it."

Jonathon took the painting from the closet. He unwrapped the cloth that covered the picture and handed it to Mark.

Mark's facial expression showed that he was very impressed. He held the picture and studied it. He raised his eyes twice to look at Jonathon, as if to say, "How did you get this! Where did it come from?"

Jonathon said, "My daughter Louise painted this." It was the picture Louise had painted of Mattie and Marty. They were both looking at a book they were sharing. Their faces were alive with happiness and excitement. Louise had captured all that reading meant to them in the picture. Jonathon had found it under another painting on her easel in the cabin. It was signed at the bottom, "Louise Morgan Lorell."

Mark asked, "I don't suppose you would.....no, I know you wouldn't sell it to me, no matter how much I offered. Someday this painting will be worth a fortune. Thank you for sharing it with me." Mark paused a moment and then said, "Would you ask your daughter if she would do a painting for me? I would pay her a good price for it."

Jonathon said, "I will give you her address right now and you can write and ask her yourself. I have a feeling she would feel honored to paint one for you. I will tell her to be expecting a note from you." He wrote the address down, handed it to

Mark, who said he couldn't wait to write her. Jonathon put his arm across Mark's shoulders and they returned to the parlor.

When Mark left that evening, he promised Jonathon if he ever came this way again, he would make sure he visited the Morgan's.

CHAPTER THIRTY-THREE

Tim

Bob was on his way to the Blacks. He dreaded plying Tim with more questions, but something Tim had said, kept coming to Bob's mind. It was about the secret pact. Bob felt he should try at least one more time. He confessed to Tim's mom, "I feel guilty in pursuing this. I don't want Tim to feel he did anything wrong, but this could possibly be a clue to her fears and perhaps even her very identity." His heart ached as he said this. The thought of losing Honey was almost more then he could bear.

Lucy called Tim in from the yard. He gave Bob an inquisitive look when he saw him. He knew Mr. Bob was there to question him again. He looked up at him and waited expectantly. Bob felt miserable, only the thought of helping Honey made him continue.

In a soft voice, he said, "Tim, we are trying to help Honey. Can you just give us an idea of what your pact was about? Was it something that she would be afraid to keep to herself?"

Tim finally said, "We were just making up our own sign language. Honey was very good at it and she loved it. She never acted like she was afraid. Not once!"

"Well Tim," Bob said, "I am certain that would be exciting and not the least bit scary. I don't think you will mind answering my next question since it has nothing to do with your promise.

I know that Honey liked your Uncle Nat very much. She sat by him on the porch that day but now she keeps her distance from him. I believe she actually really enjoys his teasing ways and would like being near him. I think it was something he was talking about that scared her. Perhaps you could ask Honey some questions about this with your sign language."

Tim was actually very hurt that Honey avoided his Uncle Nat. He wanted everyone to like him, especially Honey. It suddenly came to him that he had actually made it possible for either of them to break their promise. He said, "Mr. Bob, there is a way I can break our promise. I told Honey we could break it if we dug up the bones we buried in the moonlight. I will try and find out why she won't go near my Uncle Nat, but someone must take me to dig up the bones."

Bob shook Tim's hands and said, "I myself will take you to dig up the bones when the moon is out. We will keep this to ourselves Tim." Tim breathed a sigh of relief. Nat laughed to himself, "I would just as soon no one knew that I was out helping dig up bones in the moonlight."

As Tim lay in bed that night, he came to the conclusion that helping Honey was more important than anything else. First, he would have to dig up the bones in the moonlight, because a promise is a promise. He fell asleep thinking, "Honey will be glad if it helps find her family." It was his best sleep since all of this began.

By The Light of the Moon

A few days later, Bob told Linda before he left for work, that he had invited Nat and Tim for supper and to spend the night. She knew how excited Honey would be, so wanted to surprise her. Honey was sitting on the back porch, her arm around Mitzi, when Linda called her in. She asked Honey to set the table for their evening meal. While Honey was getting

188

the plates, Linda said, "Put on two extra plates Honey, we are having company tonight." Honey looked up, a question on her face. Linda smiled and said, "It's a surprise for you."

As soon as Honey finished, she sat on the front porch with Mitzi. She usually waited there for Bob to come home. They had established a little ritual. He would pull up and she and Mitzi would get in the carriage with him and he would take them for a fast ride before putting the horses away. She was wondering if Bob would bring their guests. It was the most excited she had been since that first day when she met Tim's Uncle Nat. At last she saw Bob coming but he had no surprise visitors with him. She waved and she and Mitzi ran to climb into the carriage for their ride. When they came back, she and Mitzi sat on the porch again. Soon she saw Nat ride up on his horse. This was no surprise as he often came for meals. Not too far behind him another rider was approaching. Celeste was thrilled to see that it was Tim. He was no sooner off his horse when he called, "I'm staying overnight!" Nat could see the joy on Honey's face.

Tim and Honey played outside until Linda called them in. Tim begged the adults to play, "Hide the Button" with them. Honey loved playing the game. Tim insisted Honey be first. Everyone would put their head on the table with their eyes closed while one person hid the button. When someone got closest to the button, the one who hid the button would shout, "You are warm," If they got even closer, they would call, "You are getting HOT." If they moved further away from it, they would call, "You are getting cold." Since Honey couldn't speak, she would wave frantically smiling or showing disapproval. Bob was thrilled to see Honey so happy. He thought of her as his little angel. He didn't believe he would ever again see a child so vulnerable and lovable as Honey. He couldn't have loved her more if she had been his very own.

After Celeste was in bed and darkness was settling in, Bob went with Tim to the woods as he had promised. They carried a lantern to the place where the bones were buried. With the moon shining down upon them, Tim uncovered the bones he and Honey had buried. He was free from his promise. Tomorrow he must try to learn as much as he could about who Honey was and where she came from.

Questions and Answers

Bob and Nat had previously explained to the best of their ability what Tim needed to find out. They told him to ask her questions such as, "Do you have a family? Did someone steal you from your family? Was it Indians? Was it something that Uncle Nat said that day on the porch that upset and scared you? Just anything that might provide a clue."

Bob had stayed home from the store the next day. He wanted to be there in case Honey became upset again. It was all planned out. Tim and Honey would play as they usually did. Perhaps they could make some new signs, but Tim was not to question her until after lunch. Bob would sit on the porch rocker pretending to read a book and they could sit on the steps.

Time went by too fast for Tim. He had been dreading questioning Honey about her identity. He was nervous and yet hoped his questions would please Mr. Bob.

Tim's first question was, "Do you like Indians?" Honey looked perplexed and then shrugged her shoulders as if to say she didn't really know. Bob thought, "The Indians must not have had anything to do with her plight."

Next Tim asked, "Do you have a mother and father?" Bob seemed to be engrossed in his book; but he knew Celeste had turned to look at him. When Honey turned back to face Tim, she looked perplexed. She nodded yes and then she shook

190

her head no. Tim said, "I don't know what you mean." She thought awhile and then pointed to Bob and shook her head back and forth. Tim thought for a while and said, "Are you saying Mr. Bob isn't your father?" Now Honey shook her head harder showing she did not mean that. Tim thought again and finally, much to Bob's relief, asked, "Do you mean you do not have a father?" Celeste nodded, looking sad. Tim inquired, "Did he die?" Again she gave him a positive nod. Tim felt a great sadness for Honey. The sadness showed in his face and Honey forgot her own sadness. She wanted to make Tim feel better. She pointed to herself and then to Tim. Tim couldn't understand. She went in the house and came out with one of the books that Bob had often read to her. It had a picture of a family. She pointed to the mother in the picture, and then to the boy. Tim's eyes lit up, "You have a mother and a brother," he exclaimed. She nodded emphatically. Bob stole a glance. She seemed so happy to have someone to tell about her family. Bob's first emotion was one of happiness for her and he wasn't prepared for the next feeling that surged through him. It was a mixture of fear and jealousy. Could he love this little girl so much, that he would consider depriving her of her own family? He listened with mixed emotions as Tim continued.

"Did you live a long way from here?" Honey nodded her head in a very solemn way. "Did someone steal you?" he asked. Honey did not know how to answer that question. She shrugged her shoulders slightly, a perplexed look on her face. "Were you with your mother and brother and just couldn't find them?" Honey didn't know how to answer that either.

Tim did not know what to ask next. It wasn't going very well. It was confusing to him. He tried to think of what the grownups had suggested he ask. When he pictured his Uncle Nat, he remembered. Now he asked, "When Uncle Nat was telling stories that day, did he say something that scared you?" Bob glanced at Honey; he could see the strained look on her face. Perhaps he should interfere and let Tim continue the questions another day.

Just as he was going to stand to his feet, Honey nodded slowly. "Was it because he talked about being lost?" She gave a negative response. "He was talking about Indians," he offered. Again, she shook her head negatively. Tim knew the story so well. He tried to think of what else could have affected her. Then he remembered someone else that was in the story, and he said, "There was another man and an Indian woman in the story, was it something about one of them?" Bob saw Honey quiver and her face turn pale. Bob jumped to his feet. This was enough for a day. They would have to continue another time. "Tim, why don't you and Honey bring Mitzi and I will take you all for a ride?"

Tim also noticed the question frightened Honey. He wasn't about to quit. He grabbed Honey's hand and asked, "Do you think you know the man?" Before Bob scooped her into his arms, Honey nodded her head. Honey clung to Bob with all of her might. Her heart was crying out for some assurance from this man she loved and trusted. He did not disappoint her. He sat back in the rocker; and cradled her in his arms. "I will never let anyone take you from me Honey, unless it is your very own mother." He felt her body relax. She lay there, feeling content and safe in his arms.

Over Honey's head, Bob smiled at Tim. He said, "You are one fine boy Tim. Now why don't you bring that book over here and I will read it to the two of you?" He looked down at his precious cargo and asked, "Would you like that Honey?"

When Bob had finished the story, Honey climbed down from his lap. She was ready to play again. She remembered Bob's offer of a ride and pointed to the horses. He took them and Mitzi for a ride though he couldn't wait to go in the house and question Nat. He also knew Nat and Linda were waiting in anticipation.

CHAPTER THIRTY-FOUR

Help Me Make It Through The Day

It was three a.m., October fifth, 1853, and Louise was wide-awake. In two more days, it would be Celeste's date of birth. Louise was remembering what her life had been like in those years. Such wonderful days, she had a husband she loved with all of her heart and a son she loved so much she would have died for him. They had plenty of whatever they wanted and although that made life easier, she had known the material things were not what brought real happiness and contentment. It was the love that filled their home. It was waking up in the morning with a husband who adored you, it was Michael crawling into bed with them, it was looking out the window and whispering "Thank You God for the beautiful sunrise, last night's sunset and the love in this household."

She remembered that the day before Celeste was born; she had been awakened by pain. She welcomed the pain because it meant the arrival of another little one that would bring more love into their lives. The pain had lasted all that day and the following night. It wasn't until the following day that Celeste was born.

Her prayer was very different this time. Over and over she pleaded, "Help me to keep the faith you have instilled in me thus far. Help me through this day and most of all help me through tomorrow. It has been six months and I have always hoped that Celeste would be home by her birth date. I don't believe you have that in your plans; so I beg you to help me through this hard to bear time. I know Your Will is best. Amen."

Louise felt better after her prayers but she still couldn't sleep. She got up and sat at the kitchen table. She was surprised to see Cleo walk into the kitchen. Cleo said, "I heard you stirrin' round. Don't you feel well? Is there something I can do to help?"

Louise's lips were trembling and it took her a moment to answer. She told Cleo, "The day after tomorrow is Celeste's birthday." She didn't have to say more. Cleo sat down next to her and put her hand over Louise's. "I know your heart is broken Miss Louise. I wish I could help you." Louise looked up and saw tears streaming down Cleo's cheeks. She was deeply touched; she had not shared her vulnerability with anyone for a long, long time. She laid her head and hands on the table and sobbed. Cleo put her arm around Louise's back and they cried together. When Louise arose, she was totally exhausted and ready to crawl back into bed. She slept until almost noon. She had never done that in her life.

The next morning, Cleo cautioned Dan, Sarah and Henry, "Be careful what you say around Miss Louise tomorrow, it is Celeste's birthday." Sadness enveloped them all. Everyone walked around with a heavy heart.

That morning Louise received a letter from Aaron's mother. She wrote, "These are very sad days, especially knowing that out little Celeste has a birthday now and we still have no news. We remember all of you each morning at our breakfast table and pray it will be the day we hear she is home. She wished she was well enough to make the trip to visit them and begged Louise and Michael to come and see them. She thanked Louise for writing her often and enclosed a note for Michael and a bright shiny silver dollar. Louise couldn't bring herself to visit them without Celeste. Meanwhile, she kept her promise to write often.

Later that afternoon, Dan was going for groceries and Louise asked him to take Michael along. She added, "I think it is time Henry goes with you. No one is going to bother him, tell him that I insist he go along. This will be good for Michael as well as Henry."

Dan was excited because he wanted to buy a book. He told Louise, "If Michael goes along, he can help me pick out a good book. I'm sure Henry will read it to us. The next book I buy after this one, Miss Louise, ain't nobody goin to read that book to me. By then, Sarah and I will be reading ourselves."

Louise smiled and said, "At the rate you two are learning, I think you will be buying another book before very long."

Henry was thrilled Miss Louise had insisted he ride to town with Dan and Michael. He knew he would be safe with Dan around. He believed and often bragged to Michael, "I bet Dan could whup up on anybody."

Michael and Henry were buying themselves a small bag of horehound candy when Michael felt someone punch him. He turned around in surprise. There stood his old friend Lance grinning as big as could be. They were so glad to see each other. Lance called to his mother, "Look Mama, its Michael." Sharon was surprised too. She asked Michael all kinds of questions, beginning with, "When did you and your mother get back? Michael answered all of her questions and Sharon went looking for Dan. She wanted to ask him about Louise. When she found Dan, she first asked him why Michael had not been in school. Dan said Miss Louise had been teaching him for the present time, but planned to have him back in school the following Monday. Dan told her that Louise was having an extra hard time right now. He explained, "Tomorrow is Celeste's birthday."

Sharon was silent for a moment and then said, "We can't let her have a quiet day tomorrow. We must do something to keep her busy. I will tell the neighbors that there will be a picnic tomorrow at Louise's. We will all bring the food. Don't tell her or Michael. We'll surprise them. A surprise is just what they need." Dan thought it was a wonderful idea. He thanked her profusely and told her how they had all been dreading the day.

Sharon and her family were the first to arrive the next day. Louise was overjoyed to see them. One by one all the neighbors came. The children had a marvelous time. Henry thought he was too big to play with the others, but he had fun watching them. When they ran out of their games, he taught them how to play "Red Rover, Red Rover." The boys thought it was a great game and laughed when it was a girl's turn and she rarely broke through when two boys were clasping their hands together. After the game, they told Henry, "That is a great game Henry." Henry felt like he had just won a million dollars. .

The men played horseshoe and visited. The women told Louise all that had happened during the time she was gone. They laughed when Louise told them she came very close to marrying and came to her senses just before tying the knot. Of course they wanted to know every detail and Louise wished she could have shared all of it with them. She might tell Sharon later, the others wouldn't have understood at all.

The neighbors who had thought Sarah might have been responsible for Celeste's disappearance felt ashamed of themselves after they met her. They could tell she had the heart of a 'doe'.

Everyone had a wonderful time and decided they would do this at least once every month. Louise was thankful the day had been shared with so many caring people.

The Morgans

Mrs. Morgan was writing a letter to Louise. She wanted to mention Richard had been kind enough to come for a visit and show he had no ill feelings. She wrote, "I know he still cares for you." She said she was pleased to tell her there had been no more trouble from anyone about Louise's bad decision to teach the colored children. She added, "I am certain it is only because of the great respect the people have for your father and I." She wrote, "Your father wanted to come for a visit at Christmas but I would rather you and Michael came to see us." She started to suggest that perhaps Richard could come for dinner while Louise was there but decided that could wait. It would be better if he just 'happened' to drop by. She signed the letter and then added a PostScript. "The election is coming up, I am quite certain Richard will be our new Senator."

CHAPTER THIRTY-FIVE

Celeste

Linda and Nat gave Bob their full attention as he repeated all that had unfolded as Tim questioned Honey. They listened, completely overwhelmed by it all. Tim had done a wonderful job. Thanks to him, they knew Honey's father was dead, she had a mother and a brother and the man in Nat's story had been the cause of her panic.

Nat was silent, obviously deep in thought. Finally he spoke, "It is almost impossible to imagine, but it sounds as if the last story I told her and Tim which was about the time I got lost and met a man and an Indian squaw in the mountains, had something to do with Celeste's disappearance. The man must have been responsible for Celeste's suffering. I wish I had found out more about him. I can't even remember his name and I don't remember if he mentioned his wife's name. I thought I would never see either of them again and if I remember right, I only told him the nick-name everyone calls me in that part of the country. In fact, I don't think he even told me his last name. It was all quite casual. In a deeply reproachful voice, he added, "If only I had asked him where he was from."

Linda said, "Don't blame yourself for that Nat. You were trying to help them. None of us would have inquired about his personal life."

Bob spoke again, "Nat, tell us everything that happened when you were with that man and perhaps we might notice something that would help."

Nat told everything that took place and Linda and Bob started asking more questions. Nat answered Bob's first, "What did he look like?" Nat described him. Bob was beside himself as he said; "Your description fits the man who came through here about the time we found Celeste. The French accent and all, though I am quite sure he was not missing an ear. Perhaps the Indians did that." He turned to Linda; "Do you agree that it sounds like the same man, Linda?"

Linda assured him that she did. In a positive voice, she said," I remember now, his name was Frank and his wife's name was Ann. They were going to California in the hopes of finding gold."

Now Bob was really excited, "The woman said where she was from but I was not interested in any of her conversation, so there is no way I would remember. You were quite interested Linda, where did she say they were from?"

Linda thought a moment and said, "I did not hear where she said, Bob. I do remember why I didn't hear her and why you didn't either. It was at that moment that little Diane Johnson fell down and cried. It frightened us all. You remember Bob, you ran to pick her up. I do remember she talked a lot about being in New Orleans, but she was definitely from somewhere else."

Nat said, "I am certain the man's name was Frank. They could have picked Honey up anywhere along their travels." Now they all were silent, sadness enveloping their faces.

After some time, Bob lamented, "Every time we think we have something to go on, it goes nowhere." He continued, "Linda, make a list of everyone who was here that evening. We must call on all of them and see if anyone remembers where she said they were from. He turned to Nat, "I am going to post a message to Fort Mason and see if they will give me his full name. He may still be there or they may know where he went. I know you said he was going to take the Indian woman to the Caddo tribe.   Maybe his wife was returned and they started west again."

Bob penned the letter that night. He explained why they needed the information and asked them to reply at once. Bob posted it the next morning. Linda and Nat took Celeste and visited each of the families who had been at their picnic. Celeste had no idea why they were visiting so many people. She thought it was wonderful. She was especially glad to see Tim.

Bob was disappointed that none of their friends could remember where the couple had lived. All of the women remembered she often visited New Orleans.

A Change of Plans

Nat and Linda planned on getting married in the spring. Linda wanted to have a big wedding. She started designing and then sewing on her wedding dress. When Nat told Linda he would prefer living in the country, she said it did not matter to her. They picked out some land about five miles from Linda's present home. Nat hired some men and started building the house. When Nat approached Linda with the suggestion they marry right away, Linda did not find his suggestion favorable. "Nat," she pleaded, "You know I want a big wedding. You promised me!"

Nat explained, "I think we both know that your brother will go looking for that man, Frank. If and when he does, I want to be free to go with him and help in any way I can. If it happens soon, we will have to postpone our wedding and I don't think either of us wants that. I will not let him go alone."

Linda was aghast. She did not like the idea of Nat ever being far away from her. Never could she love a man as she did him. In a firm voice, she announced, "Then I will go with you!"

Nat took her in his arms and said softly, "Now you know why we must get married right away."

Linda asked Nat what he thought about taking Honey to live with them after the wedding. He explained, "I would love to have her live with us and we will, but only if Bob suggests it. I am not going to be responsible for taking his greatest joy from him. Only her own family should be allowed to do that. I am sure Bob will make some arrangements for her care."

They need not have worried. As soon as Bob heard of the wedding plans, he asked an elderly widow to live with them temporarily. Bob explained that they were trying to find Celeste's family. If they did not find them, he would like to have her on a permanent basis. Patricia O'Connor accepted. She missed having someone to cook and clean for. Happiness shone on her face.

The O'Connors and their only child came to America from Ireland. After her husband died, she moved in with her daughter Shelby and her husband Miles. She was a natural born homemaker. She had always loved cooking and baking and was glad that she would have a man as well as a child to cook for. She started packing as soon as Bob left. He had always been one of her favorite people.

CHAPTER THIRTY-SIX

Frank And Cochay find Caddo village

Cochay was nervous about approaching the Caddo Indians. Some tribes never accepted the women back, once they were captured and taken away. Since Cochay was part Apache, this decreased her chances of being accepted.

When they camped for the night, Cochay tossed and turned in her sleep, sometimes moaning. Frank hoped they could find the Caddo tribe. If not, he didn't know where he would take her.

Frank recognized the Caddo area when they approached. It was just as Nat had described it. There were several trails and Frank decided on the one that appeared the most traveled. He knew they would eventually come to one of the camps. He hoped it would be one where the Chief of the tribes lived.

At last they came to an area where many of the Caddos lived. Frank was surprised to see they lived in mud houses. They were thatched and looked like large beehives. They were covered with cut cane and grasses. They slowed their horses to a walk, rode into the camp and dismounted.

The Indians looked surprised and curious. They came toward them from all directions. The Indian women wore cotton clothing of various colors. The men all had unusual hairstyles. Frank raised his hand in greeting. No one responded. Some of the Indians aimed their bows and arrows at them. One of the men approached them, his hair was shaved on both sides and the shaved areas were painted red. The hair that ran down the middle of his head and the back of his neck was long and reached his waist. He folded his arm across his chest and stood as if he were waiting for them to explain why they were there. Frank decided he must be the chief.

Cochay stood with her head down. Frank pointed at her and said, "Caddo." The Indian looked her over and said, "She no Caddo." He turned and walked away motioning for the others to do the same. Only the men with the bows and arrows stayed. Frank motioned for Cochay to sit on the ground. He sat down beside her. The man approached them again and the people came back to stare. This time the Indian said, "I speak English. Why you point to her and say Caddo?"

Frank said, "She told me she is Caddo Indian." Before the man could say more, Frank asked, "Are you the Chief?"

The Indian replied, "Chief in our tribe called Caddi. Me Caddi of our people. He pointed to one of the Indians who had stayed close to his side the entire time. This brave, my Canahac. Frank realized he must be one of the Sub Chiefs of the tribe.

The Caddi approached Cochay, reached for her hand and pulled her to her feet. He spoke in the Caddo tongue to her. She did not respond and he said, "She does not know our tongue. I only ask her name."

Frank answered for her. "She is called Cochay and she speak Apache tongue."

The Caddi now turned to the throng surrounding them and spoke. Frank heard the word "Cochay" and knew he was probably telling them her name and asking if anyone knew her. All the Indians that Frank glanced at were shaking their heads negatively. Then one of the older squaws walked towards them. She spoke to Cochay. Frank again heard "Cochay." Sadly this is the only word Cochay understood also.

The Caddi explained to Frank, "She says her name is also Cochay and asks the name of squaw's mother."

Frank wondered how he could make Cochay understand. He knew many of the names of the little Apache girls and their mother's names. He extended his hand in front of him about two feet from the ground and said, "Moon Beam." He raised his hand to his shoulder and said, "Still Water." He repeated this using the names of little girls in the Apache camp and their mother. He lowered his hand and said, "Cochay," then raised his hand and looked at Cochay, hoping for an answer. Cochay's eyes lit up; she understood and answered, "Little Fox."

Frank watched in amazement as the old Indian squaw cried out. Her cry made him think of the cry of a wounded animal. Chills went through him and he thought, "I will never forget the anguish in that cry." Tears streamed down her face as she carried on a dialog with the Chief.

The Chief explained to Frank, "This Cochay say when I, the Caddi was only papoose, Apaches attack and kill many of our people. Take young girls away. Take her Little Fox and Blue Cloud. Her heart break like bird's egg that fall to the ground. She think Cochay is great daughter belonging to her. She wants to know where Little Fox and Blue Cloud are."

Cochay heard "Blue Cloud" in the conversation and looked up in surprise.

Frank answered, "There is a Blue Cloud, she is Chief Gray Wolf's squaw. I remember no Little Fox."

Frank turned to Cochay and said "Little Fox?" He shrugged his shoulders. Cochay understood that gesture. She pointed to the ground and to the sky.

Frank told the Chief that Little Fox no longer lived.

The Chief replied, "Too bad she die. We know of Chief Gray Wolf. Does he treat Blue Cloud good?"

When the Chief had learned all that he could, he explained it to the Cochay of his village. At the same time Frank went through the measurements with his hands but this time he added a third dimension to show Cochay that this old woman was her grandmother.

Tears of grief and happiness poured down the old squaws' cheeks. The two Cochay's embraced and clung to each other. The old squaw took Cochay by the hand and led her to her home.

Frank was invited to join the Caddi and some of the braves in smoking the peace pipe. As Frank took his turn at the pipe, his heart felt heavy. It was as if he had witnessed something sad instead of a joyful reunion and wondered why he should feel such sadness. Once again he realized how much he had missed in his life. He had seen an example this day of the love of a family. So many years had passed since this woman's daughters had been taken but the love had never left her heart. He felt a sense of gladness knowing that he had helped bring about and witness such happiness.

As usual, at times like this, Celeste came into his thoughts. He wished he had it to do over again. He would take that little girl right back to her mother. When he found Ann or what had happened to her, he would look for Celeste. He would return her to her family and witness the joy of a family being together again. Perhaps they would forgive him and he in turn could forgive himself.

After smoking the peace pipe, Frank explained to the Caddi about Ann. He asked if he could stay in their village until he heard from the soldiers. The Caddi said, "Our village welcomes you. You may stay there with Caddo families," he pointed to a large hut and said, "Your home." He smiled. You teach me more English and I teach you Caddo language."

Frank placed his hand on the Caddi's shoulder and said, "Thank you. I will do my best to help your village in any way I can. The Apache who held us prisoners made our lives very bad. It is a great prize to be with good people." Frank could see the Caddi appreciated the tribute he had made to him and his people.

Frank did not like the idea of living surrounded by Indian families but found out it was not such a bad idea. He was surprised to see upon entering the communal that a wooden frame formed the roof. It was covered with cut cane and long grasses. He was even more surprised to see beds and chairs made out of wood. The floor was covered with cane that had been split and made into mats. Large cane mats also formed partitions between each family's spaces. The Caddi gave him one of his buffalo skins with the hair still on it for a blanket and showed Frank his partition.

The hut was made with an area in the center left open. Frank found this was where the women prepared and cooked the meals. The squaws almost fought over who would give Frank his food. He found the people to be clean and easy to get along with.

The next time Frank saw Cochay he was amazed. She had on a very pretty dress. Her hair was parted in the middle and braided on each side. She had a lovely beaded necklace on and all in all she looked quite fetching.

Frank and Cochay did their best to learn the Caddoan language. The Caddi taught Frank the most and Frank would pass on what he learned to Cochay.

Frank found out that if a brave wanted a particular maiden to be his, he would take her a gift. If she accepted, she would go and live with him. If another brave brought a better gift that the woman wanted, she was not obligated to stay with the original man. Frank was very careful not to take a gift to Cochay's house. He still enjoyed teasing her and she loved giggling at him. He knew it wouldn't be long before one of the braves would be bringing a gift to Cochay's house.

Caddo or some of the other braves often took Frank with them when they went to hunt squirrels, raccoons and deer.

The Caddi showed Frank a particular tree and said, "Tree called Bois de arc. Everyone say they never see this tree till they come to our village. This must be only place this tree grows. Wood strong and bend best of all into good bows. I good bow maker. Will show you how to make good bow." Frank thanked him and laughed as he said, "I have never shot bow and arrow. You will teach me that too?" The Caddi smiled and agreed he would.

Soon Frank had his own bow and arrow. He found out he was actually a very good shot with the bow and arrow. The Caddos, unlike the Apaches ate fish.   Sometimes they caught turtles. The Caddo had large areas they cleared in the forest. They raised cotton, grew squash, corn, beans and pumpkins. All in all, they ate very well.

Frank tried to keep busy so he would not focus on worrying about Ann. He helped with whatever work he could. Time passed and he began thinking the soldiers were never coming and perhaps he should go back to the fort and check on her. Eventually, he even made the mistake of thinking Red Feather was no longer looking for him.

CHAPTER THIRTY-SEVEN

The Change

Nat and Linda assured Bob that they understood when he told them, "Linda, since you and Bob will soon have your own house, I would like Honey to stay with me. I don't feel like I am being completely selfish because I think the least Honey experiences in changes, the better it will be for her. They both agreed with him. Secretly, Linda was glad to have her new home and husband all to herself. Besides, she knew Bob was Honey's favorite and would prefer to stay with him.

Bob held Honey on his lap as he explained to her that Mrs. O'Connor would be living with them and caring for her. He questioned her, "You do like Mrs. O'Connor, don't you?" Honey smiled. She liked Mrs. O'Connor; she always hugged little children. She never held on to them though. She just hugged them and let them go. She smiled at Bob again and he knew she thoroughly approved. Her smile melted his heart all over again. Relieved, he laughed and said, "I bet she will even let you go barefoot!" Honey gave him a bigger smile and crawled down from his lap. She thrust her bonnet on her head and took Bob's hand. Bob whistled for Mitzi and the three of them piled in the carriage. They were on their way to fetch Mrs. O'Connor.

The Wedding

Linda finished her lovely white wedding dress. She made Celeste one that matched, except she added little pink flowers and pink trim on the collar and sleeve hems. She added pink ribbons to match One for the waist and one for her hair. Linda had Bob order white patent leather shoes for both of them.

After the wedding, Nat and Bob went on and on about how beautiful they both were. All of the neighbors and friends came for the wedding. All of the ladies brought the food. After the ceremony and lunch, Mrs. O'Connor played some Irish songs on the piano. Linda talked Bob into doing an Irish jig with her. Honey clapped her hands in glee. Tim tried to get Celeste to try an Irish jig, but she was too shy. Bob and Celeste were both a little sad when it came time to tell the newly weds goodbye. It helped to have Mrs. O'Connor's smiling face and twinkling eyes with them after Linda left.

Mrs. O'Connor fit right in as if she had always been there. Bob had explained to her about Honey's past and how she sometimes withdrew from everyone. Mrs. O'Connor's tender heart almost broke. She let her go barefooted and often took her and Mitzi to romp in the woods. She loved the woods herself. She would point to the different flowers and tell Celeste their names.

When Bob came home, he would usually find them both on the front porch waiting for him. Sometimes Honey would be sound asleep, her head on Mrs. O'Connor's ample lap. Bob often thought, "Surely the Lord himself sent this woman" She was like a voice for Honey. Often at the supper table, Mrs. O'Connor would tell Bob about their day. Things that he knew Honey would love to tell him if she could speak. She would include Honey with words, such as, "Didn't you Honey," and "Honey was the one who found a flower that I had never seen before. Didn't you Honey?" Honey would nod and look from

209

Bob's face to Mrs. O'Connor's, her face registering joy, sadness or whatever the dialogue called for.

One evening when Honey had been tucked away for the night, Mrs. O'Connor asked Bob if he had noticed that Honey seemed sad and withdrawn. Bob said he had noticed and thought she may be coming down with a cold or needed to go to bed early.

Mrs. O'Connor confided, "Something quite unusual happened today. My daughter Shelby came for a visit. I saw her approaching the house and hurried to tell Honey. She was coloring at the kitchen table and smiled at me when I told her we had a visitor. My daughter sat down next to her. I said, "Honey, this is my daughter, Miss Shelby." Honey looked up and started to smile. When her eyes met Shelby's, the smile disappeared and right before my eyes, she turned pale. Mrs. O'Connor shuddered and then continued. "Shelby always relates well to children and she did her best to make Honey happy again. She told Honey how nice her coloring was, but Honey went to the other side of the table and just stood there, staring at her. Shelby and I were both uncomfortable. We tried to visit, hoping she would go back to her coloring, but she continued to stare. Finally, my Shelby could stand it no longer. She went over and scooped Honey right into her arms and sat down, all the time holding her close. Honey buried her face in Shelby's hair and though she never made a sound, tears ran down her face. It looked like it was extremely hard for her to cry, because she couldn't sob aloud. It broke both of our hearts. I tried to think of something that was different about Shelby and the only thing is her hair. It is long and a lovely deep red. Honey kept her face against it. I knew then what it had to be. I said, 'Honey, does your mama have red hair?" She nodded and Shelby held her even tighter and just rocked her back and forth. She fell asleep that way. Shelby didn't want to leave; she was so hurt for Honey. I told her I thought it would be better if she did. When Honey awakened, I told her that Miss Shelby had to go home. I explained that she would come and see us another day. She has been quiet and listless ever since. Do you think I did right Bob?"

Bob assured her that he thought she handled it perfectly. He said, "'It is almost more than I can bear, however I do have something to tell her in the morning that I think will help her get through this. I talked to the teacher today and told her about Honey and also that I didn't know how old she really is. She thinks it would be a good idea to let her attend school, regardless of her age. She teaches first through fifth in one classroom. That means Tim will be in her room. He will watch out for her. We can always let her stay home if she doesn't adjust. I thought you could go with me each morning, take the carriage, drop Celeste at school and pick her up after school. I don't need it during the day. You could wait at your daughters, or whatever you might like to do. The two of you can come to the store and we can all go home together. I will start closing the store early so the two of you won't have such a wait."

Mrs. O'Connor would have waited in the school room if she thought it would make Honey and Bob happy.

The next morning, Bob told Honey that he had arranged for her to attend school. He explained that Tim and some of the other children she knew would be in the same room. "Do you want to go to school?" he asked. Honey nodded her head vigorously. "Then it is settled, Mrs. O'Connor and I will take you in the morning.

After several days at school, Bob visited the teacher and asked how she was doing. The teacher said, "She is adjusting very well. I don't think she could be happier. It is amazing what she has already absorbed. You can stop worrying. She is where she belongs.

CHAPTER THIRTY-EIGHT

The Red Feather Hunt

Red Feather often wondered who had warned Cochay and Frank they were going to die. He wished he knew who it was. They would not survive to be a traitor again. He did finally recall that Cochay's mother had been taken from the Caddo tribe. Cochay must be hoping the Caddo's would take her in. If the Caddo tribe accepted her, they would not allow him to take her against her will, even if she was his squaw. He may have to find a way to seize Cochay as well as One-Ear without the Caddo's realizing. Red Feather also knew the Caddo Indians would not welcome any Apaches.

There was a time he had respected the Caddos. They were great horse thieves. They had the finest bows of any of the tribes and they were good at using them. Now, some of the Caddo's sent their children to school and lived too much like the white man. They were traitors. The Caddos were a peace-loving tribe and very friendly with pale faces. He and his braves would be vastly outnumbered. He had patience when he wanted something bad enough. He would wait for many moons if he had to. His time would come. If Red Feather had not had so much malice on his mind, he may have been able to jump to safety when his horse suddenly reared and fell backwards. This was prairie land and snakes were plentiful. A large rattler coiled and sprung in the horse's path. The horse landed on Red Feather. The horse rolled over and stood, apparently unharmed. Red Feather was not so lucky. Excruciating pain shot through his leg and Red Feather could see the bone piercing his skin. The braves washed the area with water from their drinking pouches. They extended his leg and put the bone in place as best they could. There was nothing on the prairie to use to keep it in place. The best the braves could come up with was their arrows. They took off the points of four of their arrows and placed the shafts along the break. They secured this with the buffalo leather thongs. It was too dangerous to camp in the open space of prairie land. They must return to the protection of the wooded area and set up camp until Red Feather could travel again. It meant weeks of delay. The thought that he may never walk again or that he may die crossed Red Feather's mind. Surely the Great Spirit Ussen would let him right the wrong his squaw had heaped upon him before his time to die.

Red Feather's leg hung from the side of the horse and he suffered in silence as he rode along. They set up camp among the trees. The braves cut splints from tree branches and reset Red Feather's broken bone. They found herbs and applied to the exposed area to help the wound heal. Red Feather pleaded with Ussen to let him heal quickly.

Ann hated being with the Indians, but she was thankful that a stream and spring were nearby where she could bathe and wash the food before she was forced to cook it. She hoped that somehow she could escape. She was not to be that lucky. The braves knew that if she got away, Red Feather would put an arrow through the heart of the man who was supposed to be guarding her.

Turkeys were plentiful in the nearby prairie and Red Feather could only watch as the braves scared them into flight. Since turkeys can only fly a short distance and only a few feet off the ground, the braves raced on their horses and swept them up as the birds came in for a landing. Rabbits were also plentiful; but

Red Feather would have gladly forfeited the good supply of food for the capture of Cochay and One-Ear.

Ann tried to keep track of the days they spent at the makeshift camp while Red Feather was waiting for his broken leg to heal. She was bored almost to tears. She had tried scratching a line in the dirt for each day but the braves always rubbed them out. The weeks of lying around were also very hard on Red Feather, who was always on the move. He planned and re-planned how he would find One-Ear and Cochay and what he would do with them. He hoped they were living with the Caddos. He would hate it if he arrived at the camp and they had already been killed or were gone.

Finally Red Feather could stand it no longer and he hobbled to his horse. It was time to continue their journey. After only two days of travel, his leg became so swollen and red they had to stop and set up camp again.

This campsite wasn't near as nice or as handy. There was no spring for drinking water nearby and no creek. Their water vessels were too small to hold enough water for cooking. They had to ride several miles to get water and food. Ann wished the braves would get weary and leave Red Feather to his own demise. No such luck, they were too anxious to capture Cochay and One-Ear. They wanted to see what Red Feather would do to them. Apaches could only have one wife so they figured Cochay must die before Red Feather took Ann as his new squaw. They wanted to watch One-Ear as he saw Ann become Red Feather's squaw.

Red Feather overheard one of the brave's say, "Cochay must die before Red Feather can take new squaw." Red Feather became very angry and retorted, "Great Spirit Ussen know Cochay did bad thing, and Great Spirit will not mind when I take Walk-Like-Willow for my squaw." He wanted Cochay to know he would not be one minute without his own squaw.

Finally Red Feather could ride again. He was able to walk much better too. They had been at this camp for four weeks.

CHAPTER THIRTY-NINE

The Soldier

On school days, Mrs. O'Connor, Celeste and Bob came home together. Mitzi was always waiting. They were surprised one night that Mitzi was lying on the porch next to a stranger. Mitzi heard the carriage coming and ran to greet them as usual. When the stranger rose to his feet, they saw that he was a soldier. He walked to the carriage, shook hands with Bob and nodded to Mrs. O'Connor and Celeste. The man said, "Sergeant Baxter at your service." Bob introduced Mrs. O'Connor, Honey and himself.

The stranger spoke to Mrs. O'Connor, "Do not be alarmed, I am not the bearer of bad news, but I would like to talk to Mr. Edwards alone."

He then turned his full attention to Bob. The man explained, "Not too long ago, we received a letter from this address, inquiring about a certain man. I believe the letter was from you. Is that correct?" Bob said he had written the letter. "Due to the expediency of the letter, I was sent immediately to deliver a message."

Bob was alert now and said, "Yes, I have been waiting for an answer. I appreciate you making a special trip to deliver it. The little girl mentioned in the letter is the one you just met."

The soldier glanced at Celeste and remarked, "A lovely child." He turned his attention back to Bob and said, "The man you inquired about is Frank DuBois. According to Mr. Dubois, he and his wife had been captured by one of the Apache tribes. He had escaped, but not his wife. He wanted us to find the tribe and free her. We were sorry to return from our search and tell him that Chief Gray Wolf and all of his tribe had disappeared. We checked for miles around. They were not to be found. We surmised that the Chief knew there would be trouble if Mr. Dubois made it back to his people. We promised Mr. Dubois we would be on the lookout for the Apache band. An Indian woman accompanied him. He was adamant about taking this woman to the Caddo people. We promised him that if we found his wife Ann, we would send scouts to inform him. I am sure you will find him there. He seemed very concerned about his wife so I don't think he will be moving on for some time. We told him it might be months before we discover her whereabouts, if ever. The Caddo people are very friendly and treat white people well, so I feel it is safe for you to go there. The man Frank seemed like a decent enough chap. If going there is a problem for you, I would be at your disposal to travel with you. I must warn you that traveling with a soldier might make your journey more dangerous. Rebel Indians who hate white people hate us the most."

Bob thanked the man and told him that his brother–in–law would go with him. "He is as wily as any Indian and has lived in the wilderness among them for years. He told us he has been in the Caddo camp."

The soldier was more than happy to accept Bob's invitation to spend the night. He explained to Bob, "I rode hard to get here. I am weary and my horse is too. I hope you don't mind, I took it upon myself to rub her down and leave her in your barn. A good night's rest is just what we both need. My orders were to return to the fort as soon as possible."

True to his word, the soldier left right after breakfast. Bob set off in the other direction to tell Nat and Linda the news. He knew Nat would gladly go with him to look for Frank. If there was trouble, there was no one he would rather have on his side.

Honey

Bob did not like the idea of Linda going with them to search for Frank but Linda insisted she was going whether Bob liked it or not. She told him, "Nat and I married so we could be together!" Nat assured Bob that it would be all right. He explained, "The Caddo Indians are a very civilized tribe. They live very much like we do. I would never take Linda if I thought they might cause her any harm." Bob relented and the trip was planned.

The time came when Bob knew he had to tell Honey that he had to go on a trip. He explained to Mrs. O'Connor, "I dread telling Honey that I will be leaving her. I only hope she will trust that I will be back and she will be happy and safe with you." When supper was over that evening Bob sat Honey on his lap. He explained to her that he had to go on a trip. Honey shook her head vigorously. She pounded her little fists on his chest. Bob had known it would be hard, but he had never seen her react so strongly. He explained again that Mrs. O'Connor would be with her while he was gone. She threw her arms around his neck and sobbed though she never made a sound. Bob thought, "If only I could tell her I am going in the hopes of locating her mother and brother." He considered telling her and decided, "If I didn't find out who or where her mother is, it would be devastating to her. It would be the same as dashing her hopes forever."

Honey cried herself to sleep and Bob carried her to bed. He stood looking down at her, trying to think of something to ease the parting. He could think of nothing. He wished he had a

217

wife. She would help him handle this and Honey would have probably been content to stay with her.

The ordeal exhausted Bob. He fell asleep almost as soon as his head touched the pillow. He awakened in the middle of the night with a strange feeling. He opened his eyes to look around the room. Someone was standing by his bed. The moonlight was just bright enough to see that it was Honey. He wondered how long she had been there. He got out of bed and carried her back to her bed again. He said, "Honey, you will get sick if you don't get your rest. Go to sleep and you will feel better about this in the morning."

Bob awakened the next morning to find Honey lying by his side. She was wide-awake. He asked, "Honey, didn't you stay in your bed and sleep?" She shook her head, "No." He was beside himself. He wondered if she had slept any. He took her by the hand and went to look for Mrs. O'Connor.

They found her in the kitchen preparing breakfast. Bob said, "Mrs. O'Connor, I need your help. I have told Honey that I would be leaving her for a while. She doesn't want me to go. She was up most of the night. Tell her that you are going to stay with her. Tell her it is all right. You must help me."

Mrs. O'Connor told Honey they would have a wonderful time while he was gone. She said Tim could come and play with her and even spend the night. She promised her everything she could think of that Honey loved to do. She told her that Mitzi would miss her. Honey only shook her head slowly, "No, No, No."

Bob could tell that Honey tried to eat her breakfast and couldn't. She stayed by his side constantly while he finished his packing. She followed him everywhere he went. She would not leave him, even when she had to go to the toilet. The wetness finally ran down her legs and formed a little puddle. This was too much for Bob. He swooped her up in his arms and said, "I give up! I will take you along. I can't bear to leave you anyway." He stood Honey on her feet and explained, "This will be a very long trip. Are you sure you want to go?" She gave him a big smile and nodded positively. "In that case," Bob said, "We must find Mrs. O'Connor and let her pack your clothes."

Mrs. O'Connor offered to go with them also. Bob assured her that it wasn't necessary. "Honey is used to Linda and she can care for her. Just keep the home fires burning until Honey and I come home." They left early the following morning.

Bob's Quest

Nat figured the trip would take them about a week. He knew the area well, where the settlements were and many of the people who lived along the way. They would spend the nights in the settled areas if possible, making the trip safer.

When they were riding through a small town or settlement, Bob sometimes let Honey sit on the driver's seat beside him. He could see that she loved that. She would wave to the people who called out to them. He thought everything she did was special, even the way she waved. Not up and down like most children he had seen, her fingers stayed straight and only her hand moved back and forth.

The settler's were very gracious about inviting them for meals and to spend the night. In most cases they sent them away with extra food and water. Bob or Nat insisted on paying for their meals. No one wanted to accept the money but if they did not take it, they would find it later on the bed or dresser. Sometimes Linda and Nat would stay at a different home than Bob and Honey. The people were starved for company and conversation. They all begged them to stop if they came that way on their way home.

Linda had brought books for Honey to look at and sometimes she read to her. She also brought little surprises for Honey to open on the way. Each day when she saw Honey was tiring from the trip, she would give her a present to open. Nothing could top the first gift she gave her. Linda had taken clay and made an exact duplicate of Mitzi. She fired it and then she painted it. She knew Honey was terribly lonesome for Mitzi. When she wasn't holding her cherished gift, she had it in her pocket.

When Honey fell asleep, Linda cradled her head in her lap. Usually when Honey slept, Linda soon drifted off with her. When the roads were not too rough, Honey would stand and look out the carriage window. She never gave any indication that the trip was hard or boring to her. She remembered too well the terrible trip that had brought her to these people. She tried not to think of her mother or brother as she rode along. She did not want to appear unhappy. She was too thankful that she was with Mister Bob, her protector and someone she loved so very much.

When Honey was in some strange bed or camping along the way, she would close her eyes and try to picture her mother and Michael. Their faces were fading and this frightened her. "What if she saw them someday and didn't recognize them?" She wondered if mothers ever forgot what their little girls looked like. She wanted to ask and wished over and over that she could talk again, even just long enough to ask that question. When she was alone or in bed at night, she often tried very hard to make sounds.

She had learned her alphabet at school and knew which sounds went with each letter of the alphabet. She had not learned yet how to put the sounds together to say the word. When she learned this and how to write, she often planned how she would write her name down and show Bob. She could not remember her last name anymore. She would write her mother's name in very large print, 'Louise,' and next to it, write, 'My Mother,' in very large print. She would do her Daddy and Michael in the same way. She would color over the printing in her favorite color, red. In smaller print, she would add Sarah and Dan and color their names in blue. She would picture doing this and smile or if she was in bed, drift off to sleep.

CHAPTER FORTY

Red Feather Reaches Caddo Village

When they came to the forest of pines and the river, Red Feather knew they were close to the Caddoan's village. He took a wide strip of deerskin that he had cut and saved for a certain purpose. It was time to use the strip; he laid it across Ann's eyes and tied it behind her head. She would not be able to see to give any calls of alarm to anyone. He threw her on his horse and mounted in front of her. Ann refused to hold on to Red Feather until she fell off. She was sore and bruised and finally forced herself to put her arms around Red Feather's torso. He thought she was trying to prove that she was a very good rider and did not need to hold on. He secretly admired how well she could ride.

At last they were as close as they could go on horseback. They dismounted and one of the braves guarded Ann while the others crept close to the village. It didn't take them long to pick out One-Ear. He seemed to be great friends of the Caddos. This angered Red Feather all the more. Such traitors these Caddos were. They watched the camp each day and were surprised to learn that One-Ear and Cochay lived in separate places. Cochay was rarely seen outside unless she was with a very old woman.

Red Feather began to wonder if One-Ear ever left the camp. His leg still throbbed with pain, but he would wait.

Red Feather and the braves had been watching for several days when One-Ear finally took his bow and arrow and mounted his horse. He rode out of camp without the slightest thought of danger. The Apaches followed him at a safe distance on foot. They watched as One-Ear caught a turtle. When he knelt at the riverside to wash the meat he had taken out of the shell, Red Feather came up behind him. There was no noise, no warning. Red Feather hit him on the back of the head with a club. One-Ear pitched forward, falling headlong into the river.

The braves yanked him face down out of the water. Red Feather tied One-Ear's hands so tight the blood could barely circulate. One-Ear gasped and coughed until he could breathe again. Red Feather tied a band over One-Ear's mouth. Now, Red Feather took great pleasure in rolling him over so he could see the face of his captor. Frank's eyes widened in disbelief and fear as he met Red Feathers eyes. Red Feather said, "You mine, One-Ear. Not get away this time!

Frank heard a familiar voice say, "Take this off my eyes. Take this off my eyes! What is going on?" He recognized the voice as Ann's. It was almost impossible to bear all of this. It would have been better if he had never seen Ann again than to see her in the hands of cruel Red Feather.

Red Feather whipped the deer hide from Ann's eyes. He wanted her to see what a pitiful example of a man One-Ear was. Ann shook her head sadly and cried out, "Oh Frank!" She had never felt like giving up; but weariness overcame her and she cried softly.

Before he had the braves throw One-Ear over his horse he wanted to torment him some more. He walked over to where One-Ear was lying on the ground. In a triumphant voice, he said, "Walk-Like-Willow will soon be my squaw."

A scream of sadness and loathing tore from Ann's lips. She cried out, "NO, NEVER!" Red Feather was shocked. Why would this squaw not want him? He had always treated her better than he had treated any squaw he had ever known. She did not deserve him, she must die also.

Red Feather turned to Walk-Like-Willow and announced, "Then you will die too." Red Feather too, was suddenly weary of it all. He decided, "I will kill them now. There will be no great celebration in front of Chief Gray Wolf and the tribe. He spoke to Walk- Like-Willow again, "You will both die before moon leaves sky this night." Red Feather would never admit he was actually very hurt that Ann was willing to die rather than be his squaw.

Red Feather put the band over Ann's mouth again. He was trying to decide how he wanted the two pale faces to die when he heard a noise. It was the beating of horse's hooves. He peered out at the nearby trail. His heart was aching from Ann's rejection He didn't care if an entire pale face squadron was following this carriage, he wanted to hurt everyone in sight. He placed the arrow in his bow, aimed and released the arrow.

CHAPTER FORTY-ONE

Complete Shock

Bob had been driving the horses and when Nat said they were in Caddo country, he halted the team and handed the reins to Nat. He called out, "I am going to tell Honey we are soon going to see Indians and she should not be afraid. Bob climbed down and got in the carriage with Linda and Honey. He sat Honey on his lap and said, "Honey, we will soon be seeing Indians. Nat knows the Indians that live here. He has spent many nights with them and says they are friendly. He even knows the chief over all of them. You do not have to be afraid of them. They will not harm us; in fact I think you will enjoy seeing their camp. We don't plan to be here long and perhaps we will soon be on our way home. If we leave right away, you won't even have to get out of the carriage unless you want to. Do you think you will be afraid to be around Indians, Honey?"

Honey smiled and shook her head back and forth. Bob was relieved. She cuddled up against him and Bob could not resist holding her a little longer. She fell fast asleep in no time. Bob had just laid her down in the seat and was ready to call to Nat when the carriage came to an abrupt halt. Out of the corner of his eye, he saw Nat fall headlong from the driver's seat. He rolled and then lay still. Linda saw it too and they both hurried out the carriage door. Linda rushed to Nat's side. Bob was the first to see the arrow, which was partially hidden by his body.

Watching

Red Feather shot the arrow just as the carriage rounded the bend. The arrow hit the man in his forearm knocking him sideways. He jerked the reins, and the horses came to a sudden stop. The man tumbled over the side of the carriage and landed on the ground. The Apaches watched as a paleface woman and man scrambled out of the carriage door. Neither noticed Red Feather or his men standing in the shelter of the trees. The woman turned the man on the ground over and saw the arrow. She looked up, her eyes full of terror.

Meanwhile, the man who was in the carriage was scrambling to the driver seat. He was reaching for his gun when Red Feather said in a chilling voice, "No!" Bob turned to face the direction the voice came from. There was no fear in Bob's eyes as he stared at the band of Indians. All had their arrows in place, aimed directly at him.

Bob's first thought was of Honey. He glanced sideways checking to see if the carriage door was closed so the Indians would not discover her. He hoped Nat was still alive and not seriously hurt. After all, Nat was the one he had depended on to know the Indians and be able to talk with them.

Linda was crying and stroking Nat's face. She pleaded, "Nat, Nat, Don't die." Bob raised his voice and said, "Linda." When he had her attention he said, "Honey." Linda understood. She held Nat close and cried softly.

Red Feather lowered his bow and limped to the unconscious man. The braves had moved forward and had their arrows still aimed at Bob. Red Feather leaned over and peered into Nat's face. He was surprised to see that he knew the man. He was a trader that had been in his camp. He could not remember if he was one who brought firewater to trade. After he killed these

225

people, he would check the wagon for firewater. He knew this man to be of great strength, he must be killed. He turned and went back to the clearing in the trees. He lowered the bands from One-Ear and Walk-Like-Willow's eyes. He wanted them to see the ensuing bloodshed.

Red Feather stood in front of his braves and spoke in Apache tongue, "We see who is best arrow shooter of white man. Aim for heart. I shoot man on ground. His heart will be hardest to shoot for. When I raise bow, I will give signal."

Red Feather turned around and put the arrow back in the bow. He was ready to raise the bow when the carriage door came open. Bob and Linda were horrified. Red Feather lowered his bow again and watched to see who was coming out.

Honey managed to reach the step and then climbed down. The sun shone on her hair and lit it up like a halo. Bob thought his heart would break. The little angel he loved more than anything in the world. He started towards her but one of the braves grunted and waved him back with his bow.

When Celeste's eyes adjusted, the first thing she saw was Red Feather. She remembered Bob telling her not to fear the Indians. She wanted very much to show Mr. Bob how brave she was. Her heart was racing but she must not let Mr. Bob know.

Red Feather dropped his bow and arrow to the ground and limped closer to get a better view of her. She thought, "Poor Indian! He is hurting."

The Indians lowered their bows; there was not a sound to be heard.

Red Feather was trembling. Standing before him was the little girl who had freed him so many years ago. She had not grown or changed in all these years. She not only freed him from being a slave but she fed him and provided a way of escape. If Red Feather was right, she was one of Ussen's spirits. He fell to his knees and leaned forward until his forehead touched the ground. The Indians were very unsure as to what they should do.

Red Feather would never lower himself like this unless it was before a Spirit. One by one, they also knelt in obeisance.

A little girl from Red Feather's past who had once saved him was now responsible for sparing more lives. They would never know, at least in this life; that their lives had been spared because of her.

Honey thought the man had fallen because of his bad knee. She felt even sadder. She reached out and tenderly laid her hand on top of his head.

Never in his lifetime had Red Feather felt such shame and degradation. It was worse than when he had been a slave. Ussen had sent this beautiful little Spirit again. He knew she came because he had made Walk-Like-Willow and One-Ear slaves. She was telling him to free his captives as he had once been freed.

Honey tugged at Red Feather's shoulder for him to get up. He leaned back on his knees. Honey reached in her pocket and gave Red Feather her most cherished possession. The replica of her beloved Mitzi.

Linda thought Honey might have known this Indian. In a quivering voice, she asked, "Honey, do you know this Indian?" Honey threw her hands out in a half circle and shrugged her shoulders to show she did not know him. Red Feather thought she was showing him, as she had done so many years ago, that he was free and he should go. He backed away from her until he came to his horse. He mounted and motioned his band to do the same. They led their horses out and started up the trail. After a short distance Red Feather turned and raised his hand in a farewell gesture. Honey smiled and held her arm high as she waved. Red Feather fingered the gift she had given him as he rode along. He thought, "Me great brave, have gift from Spirit sent by Ussen. He did not have to return to his people in shame. His braves could attest to that!"

Linda and Bob watched the scene before them. It was like a drama from some great opera. When it was over, Linda was half crying and half laughing. Bob felt light headed and it was hard to clear his mind and take charge of the immediate situation.

Frank and Ann had also been watching. Never had they witnessed such an incredulous scene. They both had recognized Celeste and now hung their heads in shame. Bob recovered, ran to Linda and said, "Linda, you must calm down. Take Honey for a walk. I'll take care of Nat." She knew Bob did not want Honey to see the arrow. She ran to Honey, took her by the hand and led her up the trail in front of the carriage.

Nat was breathing and Bob could see that the arrow had only passed through the fleshy part of Nat's right arm. The fall to the ground must have been what rendered him unconscious. He was afraid the tip of the arrow might have poison on it so he broke the protruding arrow off and pulled the shaft out. He tore part of his shirt off and wrapped it tightly around the injury. If the arrow was not poisoned, the wound was not severe at all.

When Bob stood again, he was shocked to see a man and woman among the trees. They were evidently prisoners of the Indians. He untied them and realized it was the man and woman they were searching for. The man he had promised Honey he would never allow near her again. Hiding all of his emotion, Bob asked, "Were those Caddo Indians?" Frank answered, "No, they were Apaches."

Frank and Ann would have liked to ride away. The last people they wanted to see was this couple who had offered them hospitality that night so long ago. Frank and Ann were so ashamed they could not meet Bob's eyes. In the old days, they would have looked for a quick route of escape but they needed to right some terrible wrongs. They were both ready to confess and help in any way they could.

Bob had Frank and Ann help him get Nat into the carriage. Bob watched while they mounted their horses and ordered them to follow behind the carriage. He warned them, "Stay far away from that little girl. I do not want her to recognize you. Do not leave." He picked up his gun and in an unemotional voice said, "I will shoot you myself if you try. I have a lot of questions to ask you when my friend gets help."

Frank spoke, "We remember you and your sister. You do not have to use a gun. We give our word we will follow you and tell you everything we know." Bob could tell by the look on the man's face that he meant it.

When Linda and Celeste came back, Bob told Linda what had transpired and said, "Honey will have to sit with me."

When they reached the Caddo camp, Frank was the one who came forward and told the Caddi they needed help for Nat. Two of the squaws tended to the wound. Frank translated for the squaws. He repeated, "The squaws said he must lie quietly for a few days, he will soon be fine. They have special herbs on the wound." Bob hurried to tell Linda what the squaws had said and that he was taking the couple to another part of the camp to question them.

The Caddo camp was much different than anything Honey had ever seen and she was content to sit with Linda and look around. Many of the Indians, especially the children chattered and stared at Linda and Honey. The children gradually came closer to the carriage to get a better view of the girl with yellow corn silk hair. Linda let Honey open the carriage and climb down. The children withdrew and then came closer again. One time Honey waved at the children. They acted embarrassed and giggled. She waved again and this time one of the very young children attempted to wave back. Now the Indian children laughed and rolled on the ground. Honey jumped as high as she could. All of the Indian children did the same. Now she hopped on one foot and they did the same. Finally the children were laughing so hard, they had to sit down on the grass. So Honey also sat down and now the children laughed even harder. It was sheer entertainment for Honey.

CHAPTER FORTY-TWO

Confession Time

Bob led Frank and Ann away from the carriage. They sat under some of the trees. Frank spoke, "Now the three of us will talk." Frank kept his arm around Ann as he told about finding Celeste in their covered wagon, and all that had transpired since. He did not hold anything back. There were tears in both of their eyes as Frank finished and said, "I know we don't deserve to do so, but we beg you to let us ask Celeste if she can forgive us."

As the story unfolded, Bob's chest tightened until he was worried his heart might stop. He had to realize that each time they referred to Celeste, it really was Honey. He felt as if he was in some kind of nightmare. When the confession was complete, Ann begged Bob to let them ask Celeste to forgive them. Bob replied, "I think it is necessary that you ask her forgiveness but I must ask Celeste first. I will do that right now."

Bob laughed as he approached Honey and saw the fun she and the Indian children were having. He hated to interrupt them. He explained to her that they had found Frank and Ann. He said, "They are very, very sorry for the way they treated you Honey. They have been having a very hard time themselves. Some very mean Indians captured them and treated them very badly. They were lost from each other for a long time and just this very day found each other. I can tell they are truly sorry and they want to tell you how sorry they are. Would that be all right with you? You can sit on my lap while they talk to you." Honey reached for his hand and he lifted and held her in his arms.

Linda had been yearning to run to Nat's side. Now she was so taken in by it all that she followed Bob as he carried Honey to face the people who were most responsible for much of the horror Honey had been through.

At the sight of Celeste, Frank and Ann started crying and neither could stop. It seemed all of the past events were closing in on them. At last, they regained enough composure to tell Celeste how sorry they were. They finished by saying, "We will take you home Celeste, if you will let us."

Celeste shook her head "No" and touched Bob several times on his chest with her forefinger. Ann said, "She wants you to take her home. I don't blame her. We will go with you or we will tell you exactly where she lives."

Bob said he had a lot more questions to ask them. He explained, "I know all of us are exhausted. We need a good nights' rest and we can decide a lot of things after that"

Linda spoke, "I guess we will never know why the Indians bowed before Honey and let all of us live."

Ann said, "Red Feather is a very cruel man but once in a while I did see a tiny bit of compassion in him. Never enough though to believe what happened if I had not witnessed it."

Everyone was silent for a moment and then Frank said, "You will all need a place to sleep. I am friends with the leader of this tribe and I know he will have mats prepared for all of you to sleep on."

As Bob and Linda walked away, Linda shook her head slowly. Her voice was sad and faraway as she said, "Well Bob, their selfishness has affected a lot of lives. Of course, the people who have suffered the most have been Honey and her family. Frank and Ann have paid a big price for their part and seem to have come out better people. Red Feather must have been in

Celeste's life at some point for him to act the way he did. We have all grown to love her, especially you Bob. Now we will have to part with her." She paused and then asked, "Do you think we should call her Honey or her real name?"

Bob's voice was barely audible as he said, "I will ask her tomorrow."

Linda hurried to Nat's side.

Decisions

Linda sat at Nat's bedside through the night. Sheer exhaustion finally took over and she fell asleep. She awakened with a start, berating herself for sleeping. Nat had not moved. The sun was shining and she was glad to see daylight. She picked up Nat's hand and squeezed it softly. She whispered, "Dear Nat." To her surprise, he opened his eyes. He looked confused and said, "What happened?" He started to sit up and Linda cautioned him to lie still. She explained how he had been injured. He insisted she tell him everything that happened. He was amazed by it all.

When Linda finished, Nat slid his feet out of the bed and said, "We must get Honey home as soon as we can." Linda was all set to be the perfect 'nurse' for him. In a firm voice she said, "Nat, you can't go anywhere until you are well." He assured her that he would move slowly and not overdo. He said, "You can stay by my side and keep an eye on me. I do believe this old wilderness man is going to enjoy being coddled by the likes of you." Linda's heart melted as if it was butter and she waited as Nat slowly rose to his feet.

Everyone was delighted when Nat walked out with Linda. Other then being a little pale and a bandage on his arm, no one would have guessed anything was wrong with him. "I am used to the wilderness and getting knocked around," he explained.

"When do we leave to take Honey home?" They all agreed Honey should be returned to her mother as soon as possible.

Bob said, "I have one more question to ask Honey and I think all of you will want to hear this."

He asked Celeste, "Now that we know your real name is Celeste, what do you want us to call you?"

She looked around at each person and then at Bob. She waited. He inquired, "Shall we call you Celeste?" She nodded her head, and then pointed to each person present, except for Bob. Bob didn't know if that included him or not. He said, "Do you want all of us to call you Celeste?" She shook her head "No" as she pointed at him. "Do you want me to still call you Honey?" She nodded positively. He lifted her up and swung her round and round, as he called out, "Then you will be my Honey forever!"

Bob asked Linda to take Celeste with her so he could finish talking to Frank and Ann. He asked them if they wanted to go along when they took Celeste home. Ann felt they should go and tell Celeste's mother and brother how sorry they were.

Then Frank said, "I actually think we would put a blight on the happiness of everyone if we returned with Celeste. Perhaps it would be wiser if we wrote her and the family after she has some time to heal. Actually it terrifies me to think of facing her." Bob agreed with Frank.

Ann said, "We still plan to go to California but we no longer care about getting rich. I do know something I haven't even told Frank. I hid a gold nugget that is big enough to give us a new start somewhere. I am sure we can find it." Frank smiled and said, "Leave it to you, Ann."

Frank continued, "If I could have one wish right now, I would wish that I could be a mouse in the corner just long enough to see that reunion." "That is how I feel," Ann agreed, "but that is part of the penalty we will pay for the grief we have caused."

Bob spoke again, "Now that we have that settled. Let's get down to business. Frank, I want you to draw a map of the quickest way to Honey's home. When you are through, I want both of you to tell me everything you know about Celeste and her family. I want to know everything you can tell me. What is Celeste's mother like? Did you know her father? How old is her brother? Do they live close to Shreve Landing? Does anyone else live with them? Everything you can think of. Most of all, I want to know about her mother. I want to know any and everything you can tell me about her. It will help me know the best way to break the news to her.

CHAPTER FORTY-TWO

Long Days and Lonesome Nights

November had turned into December. The days were shorter; darkness with its gloom came too soon. It had been easier for Louise when the days were longer. Nights were so much harder to endure. Last night had been a very restless night and she had to make herself get up to meet the day.

After breakfast Louise wandered outside. She had to admit it was a beautiful day. The Louisiana sun was shining in full array. No need for even a sweater. She saw Dan approaching. He was waving a letter that had arrived for her. With every letter, she wished it would be something about Celeste. So far she had been disappointed. She called out, "Who is it from Dan?"

Dan stopped in his tracks. He was so proud he could read. He sounded out the words. Mmm-or-gan. He called, "It is from your mother."

Louise tried to hide her disappointment. She sat on the porch and read the letter. Her mother sounded overjoyed because Richard had been elected Senator. She begged Louise and Michael to come for the holidays. A note was included from her father also asking her to come. Louise thought, "Poor father, he doesn't know that mother wants me to come in the hopes she can rekindle the relationship between Richard and me. I imagine we had better go for father's sake." Louise smiled to herself as she thought of her mother's relationship with Michael. She paid more attention to him in a week then she had to her in a year's time. She often hugged him and joked with him. She seemed to just adore him. Louise decided it was because her mother felt no responsibility or obligations as far as his upbringing was concerned.

Louise sat for a while and tried to think of something she could do to keep herself busy. She called out to Dan, "I think I'll take a ride to Sharon's. Would you have Henry bring my horse to me? I should be home before Michael gets in from school."

Dan and Henry watched as Louise trotted down the lane. When she reached the road, she brought the horse to a full gallop, her auburn hair looked like a red banner in the bright sun. Dan said, "Miss Louise is one strong lady. She does her best to keep her suffering to herself. She is always trying to make life happier for someone else."

Henry admitted, "I never knew what happy was till I knew Miss Louise. She has made me happy and that's for sure!" Dan chuckled all the way to the barn over that remark."

Henry was cleaning out the horse's stalls and Dan planned on helping him. He was heading for the barn when he saw someone riding up the lane. He did not recognize the man and stood waiting for him to approach.

The visitor swung himself down from the saddle, extended his hand and said, "My name is Bob Edwards; you must be Dan." Dan looked surprised and said, "That's me alright, how did you know?"

Bob laughed, "Dan, I have to tell you, <u>that</u> is a long story in itself. Right now I would just like to know if Louise Lorell is home."

Dan told him she was not home. Bob looked disappointed. He thought a moment and then asked, "Do you think she will be gone long?"

Dan inquired, "Do you know Miss Louise?"

Bob sensed that Dan was leery of his questions. He replied, "I have never met her; but I am looking forward to doing so." Bob stood quietly pondering in his mind how he should handle the situation. He decided he would tell Dan why he was here. He asked, "Is there a quiet place we could talk?"

Dan motioned to his porch and Bob followed him. They sat down on the steps and Bob explained, "We are bringing her little girl home to her." As soon as Bob said this, Dan leaped from the step and yelled "Praise God! Praise God!" Bob wasn't expecting this and his head snapped up in surprise.

When Dan settled down he asked, "Is she all right?" Bob explained that she had lost her voice.

Disbelief and pain spread across Dan's face. "Mr. Edwards, that little girl had a voice that was as sweet as could be. It hurts me to hear that."

Bob said, "I took her to a doctor who is a good friend of mine. After examining her, he could find no physical reason for her loss of speech. He told me that trauma can cause a person to lose their voice; but many do recover. I have always felt that she will."

Now Dan asked. "Would you tell me how you found Celeste? Could my wife Sarah hear also? We feel we are just like family and it has been hard on us too. I even had one man ask me if I thought poor Sarah had anything to do with Celeste being gone. I never even told Sarah about that. It would have broken her heart more. Her heart has been broken enough already." Frank and Ann had told Bob that Sarah was badly scarred and Bob understood. He felt good about sharing the happy news with her. Bob said, "I would love for Sarah to hear. In fact, I need a woman's view in all of this."

Dan called Sarah and she joined them on the porch. Bob told a story that he knew he would tell many times in his lifetime. Dan and Sarah were both crying when he finished. Dan asked, "When will Celeste be coming home?"

Bob answered, "I figure they should be here in two days. I rode ahead to let Mrs. Lorell know her daughter is coming. Now I am wondering if I should tell her or wait until she sees her daughter with her own eyes. She has been through enough days, weeks and months of not knowing and I am not sure how she should be told. Sarah rarely spoke, but this time she said, "If I were the mother, I would rather wait until I saw her with my very own eyes. I know how things go sometimes. Something could happen to detain them and then she would be afraid that something happened again." Dan agreed.

"In that case," Bob said, "We have to think of a reason for my being here."

Dan had the answer, "Miss Louise just ain't a snoopy lady. She won't ask a lot of questions. If I say you are a friend, she will make you welcome." Bob liked the sound of that.

Few would ever know how happy Bob was to hear they wanted to wait to tell the mother that Honey had been found. He wanted to get to know the woman who was the mother of a child that he himself loved so very much. So far, no one had said anything negative about her, but he wanted to see for himself. He wanted this woman to understand how hard it would be for him to part with Honey. If only he could think of a way to stay in Honey's life.

Dan spent the afternoon showing Bob around the farm. He introduced him to Henry and he immediately wanted to show Bob that he had his very own room. He explained to Bob, "This is my very own room, nobody sleeps in this room but me. Nobody even comes in here less I bring them."

When Dan and Henry left to pick up Michael from school Bob waited on Dan's porch. He was lost in thought.

Dan and Henry were not gone long. The boy, Bob knew must be Michael, jumped down from the carriage. Just then, another lone rider came up the lane. Bob was about to get his first glimpse of Louise Lorell. She slid down from the saddle and Michael ran to greet her.

Bob could wait no longer. He rose to his feet and called Sarah. "Would you walk with me to meet Mrs. Lorell and her son?" he asked.

CHAPTER FORTY-FOUR

Getting To Know You

Louise was surprised to see Sarah approaching with a stranger. She was tired from her long ride and in a hurry to start the evening meal. She hoped this didn't mean a long wait before she could get into the house.

Dan said, "Miss Louise, I want you to meet Bob Edwards. He is a friend of ours. He will be staying a couple of days, then he'll be on his way back to Dallas."

Louise was surprised to hear he was a friend of Dan and Sarah's. She looked at the man, her curiosity aroused. She extended her hand and he took it. She never liked it when she shook hands with someone and they continued to hold her hand after the handshake, it made her uncomfortable. This man held on to her hand, almost too tightly, as if she had some deep secret that he wanted to glean from her. She could tell he was certainly not being flirtatious. She was sure that he wasn't even aware that he was holding her hand. Never had she felt like someone was trying to look into the depth of her heart. He was not smiling and she wondered if he was always so serious.

It was Sarah who came to her rescue. "Miss Louise, I hope you don't mind. Cleo and I have both been cooking today. We thought it would be nice if we all ate together tonight"

Bob released her hand and Louise assured Sarah, "That is a wonderful idea. Why don't all of you come inside now?" Bob turned to Michael, "And what is your name young man?"

Everyone always enjoyed being together. The supper was delicious and Louise praised Cleo and Sarah's flair for cooking.

Bob watched in amazement at this unusual gathering. They all joined in the conversation. Each had something to offer of interest. They were careful to include their guest. The part that really got him was when they started talking about books. Each was reading a different book. They said things like, "Wait until I finish reading this book, I just know you will love it when we trade. It is almost as good as *Oliver Twist.* Then Michael asked, "What books have you read lately Mr. Bob?"

Without thinking Bob replied, "About the most exciting book I have read lately is Red Riding Hood. I read a story almost every night to my ------. Bob stopped in the middle of the sentence. He felt foolish." Michael finished for him, "Your little girl, huh?" Bob just smiled at Michael.

Louise thought, "Well at least I know he is a family man."

Cleo spoke, "Mr. Edwards, are you surprised to hear about colored folks reading?" Dan added, "And a country bumpkin like me?"

Bob said, "To tell you the truth I have been more impressed than surprised. Many people learn to read; but few enjoy the results of reading as much as all of you evidently do. For instance, I can tell by what Dan is reading that he would really like my brother-in-law Nat. He lived in the wilderness for years. He can tell you true stories that would make your hair raise."

In a serious voice, Henry said, "If I ever meet him, I will ask him to tell me every story he can think of and I will write a book about them."

Bob replied, "I have a feeling you will meet him Henry."

Cleo said, "Mr. Bob, do you know how we all learned to read?" She never waited for an answer and went on. "It was this lady right here, Miss Louise. She taught us to read." Louise's face flushed. She knew they were all going to start singing her praises and it embarrassed her. Bob gave her an admiring glance.

They were all trying to tell Bob about it. Louise interrupted, "Let's put these dishes away and then talk." Henry wasn't to be shushed, he said, "Mr. Bob, if you will stay in my room tonight, I will tell you a real story. How I almost got shot or strung up and Miss Louise was in terrible trouble for it. She and Michael took me here to save us all."

Louise started to say it wasn't quite like that when Bob said, "Henry, I would rather hear your story than to spend the night in a king's palace."

To himself, he wondered, "What kind of a woman is this? No wonder Honey is such a brave little girl."

When everyone left that evening, Louise brought Bob a stack of quilts so he could fix a pallet to sleep on in Henry's room. She admonished Henry, "Now don't get too carried away with your story."

Henry had found some new words to use in telling 'his' story. He no longer said, "The Mastah, he lived in a great big house." He now said, "The Morgan's lived in an elegant house," Henry could tell Mr. Bob was thoroughly enjoying every word. He loved telling it and wished he could have made the story last a little longer.

Henry was thrilled when Mr. Bob started asking him all kinds of questions such as, "Who was the man that Michael recognized by the paint on his shoes?" Henry answered, "Why it was none other then Mr. Jenner himself." Bob pushed on, "Was Mr. Jenner a relative of the family?" In a complacent tone, Henry said, "No, Mr. Jenner was just wanting to marry Miss Louise and probably boss her around." He wanted people to vote for him. Miss Louise was going to marry him until she found out he was in those shoes, hidden under a sheet and going to help string me up."

When Henry and Bob had finished their conversation, Bob said, "Henry that is the most interesting story I have heard for a long time. Grasping for something to keep Bob's attention longer, Henry came up with something he knew would hold Mr. Bob's attention. "You know," he said confidentially, "Miss Louise don't believe in slavery. She gwine' to give me my 'free' papers when I gets old enough." When Henry was excited, he reverted back to his old way of talking. He added, "She want Cleo to be free too, but Cleo don wanna be free."

Bob's last thought as he drifted off was of Louise. "What a magnificent person, full of surprises and to think she looks so vulnerable and feminine!"

Getting To Know More About You

The next morning Louise asked Dan to take her to town for some extra provisions. Henry had just told Dan that one of the cows was trying to have her calf, so Louise was ready to give up the idea of any shopping until at least tomorrow.

Bob spoke up, "Dan, if you don't need me, I would be glad to take Miss Louise. I want to see the town and I need a few things myself." Dan thought that was a good idea and so did Louise.

Bob was surprised to see the 'Trading Post' was a rather large building and well constructed. A long porch extended the length of the building with various merchandise displayed here and there. The inside of the store was bigger than Bob's own store, but many of the shelves were empty. A few chairs and a bench were visible at the far end of the room where several men were congregated, visiting and evidently passing the time of day. One area had a sign, "Post Office," Another area had a homemade sign that said, 'Fresh Meat.' A man behind that counter had a white apron on and was slicing a pork loin. An open door on one side of the room had a sign overhead that read, 'Stage Stop.' Several people were choosing their groceries from shelves that were also only partially stocked. Another shelf held a display of yard goods. The owner was quite elderly and looked as if he was overtaxed and weary. Bob paid for his groceries and then talked with the owner until Louise was ready to go.

Louise had a questioning look on her face when she saw how many groceries Bob had purchased. He explained, "These are for Sarah." Actually he knew Nat and Linda would need to spend a night or two before starting back and he wanted to do his part. Louise showed Bob around the town and then they headed for home.

On the ride back, Louise asked Bob about his family. He told her he was not married, had one sister Linda and a new brother-in-law named Nat. He told her what he did for a living and described where he lived. He made a point of telling her about Mitzi. He wanted her familiar with everything when she found out where Honey had been and why. He told her about his housekeeper, Mrs. O'Connor. He told her about Nat's family and his nephew Tim. She may have wondered why he was telling her all of this, but if she did, she was polite and never let on.

Louise was perplexed. Bob had admitted he had a child he read bedtime stories to. Had his wife died? Why didn't he mention his offspring? Perhaps all of this had something to do with the sadness he spoke of in his life. Perhaps he had lost both of them in some horrible accident or sickness. She wouldn't pry, but she did ask him how he came up with a name like Mitzi for a collie. Bob explained that a German family by the name of Saltzman had settled next to them when he was a little boy. He and the man's son, Reid, had become good friends. The boy's father wanted to be called Herr Mitz. He was a very humorous

man and made us laugh a lot. I named our dog in memory of Herr Mitz and his family. Since our dog is a Fraulein and not a Herr, I just added an 'i,' and that is how our collie got the name of Mitzi. I have often laughed to myself wondering what Herr Mitz would say about our dog's name. I have a feeling he would say something like, ""If you name your dog, 'Herr Mitzi,' the poor dog will run to you every time you say her name."
"Herr Mitzi, Herr Mitzi."

Louise laughed. Bob smiled slightly and Louise said, "You are so serious, do you ever really laugh? I have seen nothing more then a half smile on your face." She expected him to smile and perhaps even laugh when she said this to him. Instead he looked at her more serious than ever. "Louise, I left home on a very special mission. I needed some answers and found them in a most unusual way. I still have to finish my mission before I return home. It is one of the most wonderful experiences a man could be involved in, but it will also leave me with a broken heart. Can you understand now why you haven't seen me smiling or laughing?"

Louise wanted to tell him about Celeste. She wondered if his heartbreak was as deep as hers. She watched his eyes as he spoke, tears were gathering and she decided that he was indeed experiencing great suffering. She reached out and laid her hand across his. In a soft voice she said, "Can you tell me about it? I too have a broken heart and I will share that with you."

Bob looked directly into her eyes as he said, "I promise you that before I leave I will pour out my heart to you."

When they were home, he hurried to take his groceries to Sarah. He simply handed them to her and ran back to help Louise. Henry came to put the team away and asked if he could help Louise carry the groceries in. Bob was quick to tell Henry he would help her.

When Louise had finished putting the groceries away, she brewed a pot of tea. Bob sat across from her as they drank their tea. During the ensuing conversation, Bob took both of Louise's hands in his. Louise started to pull her hands away, but forgot when he asked, "Louise, do you think you could share with me what happened to your husband? She started to say that she could not, but was so touched by the look in his eyes that she could not refuse. Instead she said, "It's a long story." Bob squeezed her hands and said, "I have all night and all day and… Louise interrupted. As she told Bob about meeting Aaron, she found herself wanting to tell him more and more. She told about the day she cried so hard in the garden and now she just had to tell him about the children. She told how happy they were when Michael came into their lives, but when she started to tell him about Celeste, she started crying and couldn't go on. Bob came around the table and put his arms around her shoulders. He said, "I am sorry I asked Louise. It was inconsiderate of me. Don't say another word. There are plenty of other things to talk about."

Louise went to the sink and dipped some water out of the basin and washed the tears away. She said, "The trouble is that I want to tell you." They sat quietly for a moment and then Louise finished her story."

Bob stood up. He was gripping the back of the chair so hard that his knuckles were white. He walked back and forth in the kitchen, and then went out the kitchen door. She could see him standing completely still, as if deep in thought.

Bob was indeed deep in thought. He wanted so much to tell her that Celeste was on her way home. He wanted to confess everything and it took all of his will power not to do so. When he felt stronger, he went back inside. Louise asked, "Do you want to tell me about your sorrow now?" Bob took her hands and pulled her to him. Like a father comforting his little girl, he held her ever so gently.

He said, "I will tell you later. For right now, I think there is enough sadness in this room." Bob figured Nat should be able to make the trip by late afternoon the following day and Louise would know the truth. He opened the kitchen door and said, "Meanwhile, let's take a walk and see if you have a new calf in your barn."

Before Louise fell asleep that night, she realized he still had not told her about his troubles." She didn't wonder for long, the day had worn her out. She fell into a deep sleep.

As for Bob, he did not sleep well. He could not get Louise off his mind. He had never felt so strongly about anyone. Was he falling in love? Perhaps he just felt sorry for Louise? Was his mind tricking him because he didn't want to lose Honey?" His heart answered, "I don't want to lose Honey or Louise either."

CHAPTER FORTY-FIVE

Waiting

The next morning the sun was shining and it was a beautiful warm Louisiana day as it sometimes is in December. Everything was arranged for Celeste's homecoming. Dan had asked Sarah and Cleo to plan a picnic dinner in Louise's back yard, weather permitting. Bob wanted those who loved Honey best to share in her homecoming. Dan and Bob would sit where they could see the carriage turn into the lane. Bob explained to Dan, "When you see the carriage coming, hurry down and stop them. Make sure Honey is with them and that she is okay. Ask Nat to wait until you motion for him to come. When I know everything is all right, I will call the rest to join us in the front yard."

Bob, Dan, and Sarah were so excited and nervous that Bob wondered how the others didn't notice something was wrong. Sarah kept dropping things. Dan jumped at every noise and kept running to the side of the yard and looking toward the road. One time Cleo did say, "Well, I swan Dan, is the law after you or something? I never saw you so fidgety." Dan gave Bob a "Whew" look and settled down a little.

Dan left to pick Michael up from school. When they were back, he helped the ladies carry the food to the back yard. Bob stayed in his chair, thinking over all that had happened in the last few days. There was a lot to think about.

Everyone enjoyed the meal and helped carry the dishes inside. The ladies finished the dishes and sat on the back porch. Bob had asked Michael and Henry to stay in the back yard and they were throwing a baseball back and forth.

Bob had just said in a low tone to Dan, "I hope they come before it starts to get chilly and everyone wants to move inside," when he saw the carriage turn in. Dan started down the lane to meet it. Bob felt like his heart was trying to beat its' way out of his chest.

Mission Completed-December 15, 1851

Dan hurried down the lane motioning them to stop. When Dan came back, he nodded to Bob that everything was okay. Bob hurried to ask the ladies to join them. He called Michael and Henry. They all gathered around Bob, thinking he had something to tell them. Dan moved to stand by Sarah and took her hand in his. No one noticed as he motioned for the carriage to come.

Bob faced Louise and Michael. He said, "Louise, this morning I told you that I was on a mission. I am about to finish my part in it. I hope I have handled this last part of it with wisdom. You and Michael are about to have the happiest moment of your lives." He then stepped to the side and away from the group.

Louise was listening with all of her heart. "What could he mean!" Nothing could be the happiest moment of her life except, except----she never got any further. She heard the horses and carriage, and turned in that direction. Everyone turned with her. The carriage came to a stop, the door opened and a woman stepped down. She reached up and lifted a little girl to the ground. The little girl wore a pink ribbon in her blonde hair; she had on an adorable white dress with pink trim, long, white leg stockings and white patent leather shoes. The little girl looked at each one of them until her eyes found Louise.

Louise thought her heart would burst with joy. She tried to run to her, but her feet would not move. Instead Celeste ran and threw her arms around Louise's legs. Louise dropped to her knees and she and Michael hugged and kissed her. They cried and laughed and then laughed and cried. Tears of joy ran down everyone's faces. Louise held Celeste at arms length and cried, "Celeste, Celeste, Is it really you?" Celeste reached for Michael's hand and nodded her head up and down.

Louise wanted to make sure Celeste was not harmed in any way. She looked her over. It truly was her very own little Celeste. She saw no injuries. She noticed her clothing and shoes. The dress was lovely, painstakingly put together. The shoes were store bought. She looked like a well taken care of little princess.

Louise lifted Celeste and cradled her in her arms. She looked down and smiled at Michael. She stood Celeste on the ground again. There was something she wanted Celeste to say. She longed to hear it, her heart cried out to hear it. She wanted Celeste to say "Mama." Instead Celeste looked all around, smiling at each one. She continued looking into the crowd as if someone was missing. Then she looked to the side and saw Bob. She released her mother and Michael's hands. She ran to Bob and raised her arms to him. He lifted her up and held her close to his heart.

Louise stared in disbelief. She thought, "What is this all about?" Then, she remembered what Bob had said that he was on a mission and how it would make some very happy but would break his heart. He had found Celeste somehow and anyone could see he loved her with all his heart.

Bob set Celeste back on her feet. She took his hand and led him to her mother and brother. She stood there waiting as if he would know what to do next. They all stood as if suspended in time. Now Celeste pulled on Bob's hands and pointed to her lips. She wanted Bob to tell them that she could not speak.

Bob found his voice and through his tears said, "Celeste wants me to tell you that she can not speak. Quickly he added, "I took her to a very good doctor, he said her voice will come back when she is home again." He had exaggerated slightly, but he hadn't intended to tell Louise in this way.

Louise did not disappoint Bob and faint like some mother's might do. Instead she lifted Celeste again and said, "That's all right Celeste. We will all help you and one of these days you will be talking again."

Nat and Linda had been standing in the background and Bob introduced them to everyone.

Louise asked, "Now will you all please come inside? I am sure Cleo will fix us some tea and then you can tell us the story we have been waiting so long to hear."

Cleo hurried to the house to brew the tea. Michael took Celeste by the hand and they followed. Louise beckoned to Dan and said, "Take my arm, please Dan, my knees are not going to hold me up much longer. I must hear everything these dear people can tell me about our Celeste."

Dan lifted Louise easily into his arms. Tenderly he carried her to the sofa. Michael and Celeste sat next to her. She put an arm around each of them. By now, all the others had come into the room.

Everyone sat quietly, each lost in his own thoughts. When Cleo and Sarah had served the tea, Bob looked at Louise and said, "Have you had enough for one day or do you want to hear how Honey came into our lives?"

Louise looked perplexed and inquired, "Honey?" Bob said, "I am afraid you will have to tolerate me calling her Honey for a while. When you hear my story, you will understand why." Louise said, "I must admit, all of this has taken a lot out of me but, there is no way I could close my eyes until I hear every word you have to tell me."

Bob continued," It might be hardest for Honey as I will be telling things that are very, very painful and distressing to her. Usually, when I have something I am not sure about that involves Honey, I ask her. She lets me know what I should do. Louise, you will have to make the decision this time." Louise answered, "I must admit that it gives me a little twinge of jealousy to think you know my daughter so well. I have always handled situations such as this in the same manner. I ask the child involved. It is your story, you have my permission to ask Celeste."

Bob turned his full attention to Celeste and said, "Honey, your mother and Michael and all that love you need to know where you have been and the things that have happened to you. I know how you were treated (Louise cringed), before we found you. I will tell some of what I know and all that happened afterward. Would you rather I told it tomorrow or another day when you are not around?

Celeste stood to her feet; she pointed to Bob and made a big circle with her hand. Bob said, "She wants me to tell it all!" Celeste nodded and sat back down, snuggling as close as she could to her mother.

Bob said, "Michael, I want you to know that some parts of this will be hard for a brother to hear. Those bad times are over, but we don't want to tell this if it will be too hard for you."

Louise spoke up, "Michael has been through a lot himself, he has handled all of it in an extraordinary manner; but we will let Michael decide for himself."

Michael confided, "While my sister was gone, I imagined many things that might be happening to her. I thought we might never see her again. She still looks and acts like my sister. If Celeste can hear about the bad things she went through, then I want to be with her while she hears."

CHAPTER FORTY-SIX

The Story

Bob started the story by telling how Frank and Ann had first
found Celeste. He tried to remember to call her Celeste, but
finally gave up and just referred to her as Honey.'

The hardest part to tell was how Frank and Ann admitted
they mistreated Honey. They did not let her bathe, shook her,
sometimes slapped her, never gave her enough to eat and had
finally lost track of her in a strange town.

Then Bob explained how he and Linda found Honey in
their doghouse. He told how Honey loved their dog, Mitzi.
He told of her friend Tim and how he helped his Uncle Nat
realize he had met the man who could possibly tell them who
Honey really was. He told of the Indian who spared all of their
lives, including Frank and Ann, who were also his prisoners.
He told how Frank and Ann cried and confessed all. Bob tried
to soften the picture of Frank and Ann by telling of how they
had suffered and came to realize the suffering they had caused
to Honey and her family. He told how they had almost been
burned at the stake and how the Indians had cut Frank's ear off.
They confessed all, because, as they explained, they wanted to
be forgiven for all the heartbreak they had caused.

Bob told it so thoroughly that there were not many questions
to ask when he finished. Celeste had fallen asleep in her

mother's arms. Michael was wide-eyed and very proud of his little sister.

After everyone had asked their questions and settled down, Linda said, "It is hard to believe but it is after midnight."

Louise said, "I can believe it. I am happy to say that I am utterly exhausted, but so happy that if I weren't exhausted, I'm afraid I wouldn't be able to sleep for days. I am sorry but I am going to have to go to bed and think about all of this tomorrow. Celeste can sleep with me. She had never allowed anyone to sleep in Celeste's bed. Now she said, "Bob you may sleep in Celeste's bed, if you like, and perhaps Henry would let your sister and husband have his bed for the time being. Cleo will give clean linens to any who need them. Henry, would you mind taking Bob's pallet and perhaps you could sleep at Dan and Sarah's. Dan interjected, "We would be glad to let you stay as long as you want Henry."

Louise continued, "I am sorry but I must say goodnight. Linda and Nat, I will look forward to visiting with you tomorrow. I owe all of you so very much. I will never be able to thank you enough. Bob, I especially want to thank you. I couldn't have hoped to find Celeste in better hands. I am sure God picked you to take care of her. As for Frank and Ann, I will just have to pray about that."

Bob lifted Celeste from her mother's arms and followed Louise to her bedroom. He laid Celeste on the bed. As he turned to go, he said, "You know I usually read to her every night when I tuck her in" He laughed his wonderful laugh, "<u>You know</u>", he said, "Red Riding Hood or something like that." She remembered how he had said the latest book he read was 'Red Riding Hood' and now she understood. She laughed too. She walked over and put her arms around him and gave him a brief embrace. He held on to her just like he had held on to her hand. He turned at the door and said, I am going to Michael's room now, I want to make sure he is all right. He may need someone to talk to and perhaps listen a little, about what his sister has been through." Louise was so exhausted; her voice was barely audible as she said, "Thank you for thinking of that, you can be sure Michael needs someone right now. I'm sorry I didn't think of that myself."

CHAPTER FORTY-SIX

Getting To Feel Free and Easy

Nat and Linda wanted to leave the next day, but realized how hard it would be for Bob to say goodbye to Celeste. They also knew waiting would not make it any easier for him. They finally told him they would stay one more night. They could tell he was hoping they would stay longer though he never said a word. Although Celeste was across the room and sitting next to her mother, she evidently heard what they said. Celeste had shaken her head slowly, slipped off her mother's lap and crawled onto Bob's lap. After that she stayed as close to him as she could. Louise did not know what to do.

Anyone watching could see that Bob loved Celeste as his own and it was easy to see that Celeste loved and trusted Bob completely. Louise was afraid another traumatic experience, such as Bob leaving, would be too much for her to handle. She might never be able to speak again. She could not ask the man to give up his place in life even though she had considered this. She had a feeling Bob might even marry her just to keep Celeste in his life. Not that he would do that on purpose, but people can believe all kinds of things with the proper motive. That kind of a marriage would not be fair to any of them and she needed to be careful. Her final decision was to beg Bob, if need be, to stay for as long as he possibly could. When Bob had to leave she would take the children to visit both sets of grandparents. That would give Celeste something to look forward to and more time to adjust.

Louise realized she needed to talk with Michael. It would be a good time while Celeste was with Bob. Michael must not feel like he was or would be excluded in any way. She found him in the barnyard with Henry. She called and he came running. She put her arm around him and guided him to the garden bench swing. They both sat down and swung back and forth. Louise kept her arm around Michael and both were content to swing in silence. At last Michael said, "Mama, I don't think I will ever be as happy again, as I was when Celeste came home." Louise agreed, "Nor I, Michael." Louise spoke again, "Michael, you have already seen that Celeste is going to get a lot of attention, but in time, it will be like it used to be. Right now, it is just a mother and two happy children that she loves equally. I am sure you have also noticed that Celeste has come to need Mister Bob in her life. I am going to ask him to stay for a while, at least until she is better adjusted."

Michael assured Louise, "I just don't like a lot of attention Mama. I know you love me and I just kind of like to watch other people and listen to them. I like Mister Bob. I know he is not a man who pretends all the time, like Mr. Jenner did."

Louise did not know whether to laugh or cry. Where did this child get all of this wisdom? She decided laughing would be better for both of them. So she laughed and said, "I think I am the luckiest mother in the entire world to have a son like you."

After lunch that day, Celeste, held her hand up to Louise with only four fingers showing, then she closed her hand and held up five fingers. Louise realized she was asking her if she was four or five. She said, "You had your birthday October seventh, so you are five now. Michael and I have been waiting to celebrate your birthday when you got home. We saved your presents. This Saturday all of the neighbors are planning a picnic at Miss Sharon's, if the weather is nice. That will be a good time to celebrate your homecoming as well as your birthday. How would you like that?" Celeste gave her a big smile.

Celeste went outside and Louise watched as she went up to Bob. He was working in the flowerbed. Celeste ran and patted his arm. When he looked down, she held up five fingers. He laughed and swung her around. Louise knew he understood what she was telling him.

Watching the two, gave Louise an idea, she would ask Bob to come to the party. He couldn't refuse such a request! His sister and husband were in such a hurry; they would probably leave right away. She would tell Bob he could take the stagecoach home later. Day by day, she would try to talk him into staying longer.

That evening, Bob told Louise that his family wanted to leave the next day. He watched her reaction. It wasn't good. He could see the concern on her face. She said, "But you mustn't leave. There is a birthday party planned for Celeste Saturday."

Bob said, "I wouldn't miss the party for anything and I am glad you want me to stay longer, but I have a better plan. I started working on it the other day when we were in town. I asked the man who owns the Trading Post if he could use an extra man. He said that what he needed was someone to buy his place. He and his wife both came here from England. He has done very well but none of his children ever came as he thought they would. They are old and tired of working. They want to return to England and see their children before they die. He continued, "I offered to buy the store. The man was thrilled. He offered it to me for an amount I consider a very fair price. We shook hands and if you have no objections, I would like to rent the extra space you have in your building. I could make living quarters in it. Henry could continue to have his own place and privacy and I could live on the opposite side. That way I could still be here for Honey and I would not have to part with her. I hope you will not think that I have taken too much for granted."

Louise shook her head. She said, "Honestly Bob, I think you are the most unselfish man I have ever met. I know you have a big store where you are and a nice home."

Bob said, "I would sacrifice all of that and more. As for the store, mine started out as a trading post and grew because I worked hard. I can do the same here and you have to admit Shreves Landing is growing too"

Bob told Nat and Linda his plans. He asked Nat if he would close his store and put up a "For Sale" sign. Nat told Bob, "I will do better than that, I will run the store for you until you decide what you are going to do. If you want to stay here, I will find a buyer or buy it myself. I have been looking for something to do and though running a store doesn't sound like my cup of tea, I will never know if I don't try it."

Nat could see Bob was pleased. His voice sounded deeply touched as he said, "I hope you will enjoy it Nat. I can't think of anyone I would rather have take it over. Did Linda tell you she started out helping me in the store? She is very good at it and can be a big help."

He added, "There are two more favors that I need to ask. Would you tell Mrs. O'Connor what has happened and that I won't be coming home. Please tell her I would appreciate it if she would just stay in my home. I know she loves it there and an empty house is no good. I will send her what I owe her, plus a bonus. I think she needs the money. I have a man hired to feed the horses, as well as Celeste's pony. Tell her that as soon as it is possible, I will come and see everyone and take care of all my business. Ask her to tell Tim that if I can persuade Honey's mother and brother, Honey and I will bring them and show them where she lived and the people she knew."

Bob turned to Linda and asked, "Linda, if I make a list, would you and Nat put it all in my carriage. Hopefully you can hire someone to drive my team and bring it all to me. If not, just send this list of things on the stage coach. Linda and Nat were ready to promise him anything in order to leave and start their new life together.

Louise got busy as soon as everyone left and posted a letter to her family and to Aaron's. She told them the story in great detail. Louise asked her father to visit Sydney and tell her all that had transpired. She also told her mother they would not be there for Christmas. She invited them to come to her home. In her heart she knew they would come at once to see their granddaughter. She promised the Lorells she and the children would come as soon as she thought it was safe for Celeste to travel. She added, "If Mrs. Lorell is up to it, we would love it if the whole family came."

When all of this was settled, she visited Aaron's graveside. Before she left, she raised her eyes heavenward and whispered; "Your memory helped me through this Aaron."

Celeste's Party

Louise asked Henry to ride to Sharon's and tell her the wonderful news. She also sent a note explaining about Celeste's birthday.

Sharon was only too happy to tell all the neighbors about Celeste's return and invite them to the belated birthday party. When Saturday came, wagons and carriages were all over the Thompson plantation. When Celeste stepped out of the carriage, everyone cheered. Many had brought her a present. What a birthday party she had!

While the children were playing, the grown ups begged Bob to tell them about Celeste and how she had ended up at his house. Bob did not tell them just how badly Frank and

Ann had treated her. He did tell them most of the story. No one uttered a sound as he talked. When he finished, everyone talked at once. So many were asking questions that he had to ask them to raise their hands. Finally everyone ran out of questions and wandered off to do their own thing. When it was time to go home, it seemed all felt a special bond with each other. Louise hoped it would last.

Dan and Henry offered to help Bob build the bedroom and kitchenette in the furniture warehouse where Bob could live. Bob moved in as soon as they finished. .

Louise and Bob were together every moment they were free. Louise went shopping in his store one day and a local young lady was visiting with Bob. She was smiling and talking very sweetly to him although Bob did not seem aware of it. Louise felt pangs of jealousy and told herself she had no right to be jealous. She didn't want him out of her sight but she still didn't know if she could trust her feelings. Bob asked her to wait and ride home from the store with him so Louise sent Dan on with the carriage and groceries.

When Louise and Bob came home, she invited him in for tea. The children had spent the afternoon with Sarah and Dan and were eating supper with them. Bob sat down at the kitchen table. Louise had her back to him and was dipping the water to make the tea. Bob said, "Louise?" She answered "Yes", but did not turn to face him. He said, "Will you marry me?" She started to giggle at the humor of it all. She turned to look at him, ready to engage in a bit of banter. When she turned, a grin spread across his face and then he laughed. His face came alive and she thought she had never seen a more wonderful smile in her life. Her amusement faded. She had taken it all as a joke and was prepared to say "No" in such a way that he would laugh with her. Now, she felt like a silly schoolgirl. Her heart melted. She wondered what he would do if she flung herself into his arms? Could a person fall in love because of a smile?" She managed a nervous little laugh and said, "Oh Bob, you <u>can</u> be funny, can't you?

Bob said, "Right now, I feel very serious Louise. I realize now that you would never ask me to leave Celeste so I can't fool myself anymore that I only think I am in love with you to keep her. The real truth is that I love you with all my heart."

Louise decided it would be outrageously unlike her and very exciting to fling herself into his arms. So she did! Bob loved it. They talked until the children came in. They realized they had everything it took for a good marriage. They were hopelessly in love, respected each other, felt the same way about important things, especially in their faith. Celeste loved Bob and needed him in her life. Michael and Bob sincerely liked each other. Louise had noticed Michael as well as Celeste waited at the gate when it was time for Bob to come home from work. In his time off, Bob spent much of his time doing things with the children, as well as with Louise. When bedtime came, Bob never wanted to leave for his lonely bedroom and Louise never wanted him to leave. They had to admit it was time to say their vows. Of course, no one was surprised. Dan laughed and said, "Cleo and Sarah have been wondering how long it would take you two to admit it!"

Louise and Bob had a very simple wedding. Louise's parents came. Sydney sent a note with them, saying how happy she was that Celeste was home safely and she and her husband were very anxious to meet Bob. Dan and Sara dressed in their finest and stood with them. Cleo served tea and lunch.

Henry had read about people making a toast to the bride and groom. Tears were in his eyes as he raised his glass and said, "Love brought you together. Love will keep you together. We all want you to know Miss Louise, you not only taught us to read, you taught us how to love. We all thank you." Henry looked about, wondering if he had said the right things. There was complete silence, then Cleo said, "Amen," and everyone started clapping. The louder everyone clapped, the straighter Henry stood. He seemed to grow taller before their very eyes. Henry thought to himself, "That clapping sure makes me feel good, but no one can make me feel as good as I feel inside myself, because I have found out that I have the makings of an upright and honest man and I intend to carry myself in that direction cause it feels mighty good when I like myself."

Bob and Louise took Celeste to the local doctor and he also said he could find nothing physically wrong. He gave Louise exercises for Celeste to do that would strengthen her vocal chords. Louise did the exercises with Celeste faithfully, every night and morning, just as the doctor had prescribed. After several weeks, she could only make faint intermittent sounds. Louise began to wonder if she would ever be able to speak again.

Bob's Belongings Arrive

Linda wrote that they had found a very reliable man to personally deliver all the things Bob's carriage would hold. The young man's name was Gene Gregory. Gene was single and looking for adventure. Bob's team of horses would pull the carriage. Gene tied his own horse to the rear of the wagon. Nat would pay part of the fee when he left and Bob would pay the rest when he arrived. It cost quite a large sum but Bob didn't mind.

The letter also included a note from Mrs. O'Connor. She said how much she missed Bob and Celeste and that she would love to live in Bob's home until he made other plans.

Bob used the store's address and when Gene made the delivery, Bob asked him if he would follow him home. He had been using Louise's carriage and horses to go back and forth. He was happy to have his own carriage and horses again.

Gene helped Dan and Henry unload the crates and put the horses away. Bob invited the young man to stay for supper and spend the night. He was only too glad to accept.

Bob had kept his favorite delivery of all on the seat beside him. He carried it in the house and when Louise saw his treasure, she knew it was for Celeste. She smiled knowingly at him and ran to call the children in. Bob waited in another room until Michael and Celeste were seated on the sofa. Louise told Celeste that Bob had a surprise for her and said, "Close your eyes until we tell you to open them."

When Bob stood the treasure at her feet and told Celeste she could open her eyes, she scrambled from the couch and in a voice as plain as could be, cried out, "Mitzi" She threw her arms around her beloved dog. Mitzi whined and barked and then barked and whined. She ran in circles and then ran back to Celeste and ran circles around Celeste. There was no doubt; Celeste and Mitzi both cried tears of joy. Mitzi barked and Celeste laughed aloud. Mitzi followed Celeste as she threw her arms around Bob's pant legs. Tears of love glistened in Celeste's eyes as she looked up at him.

Mitzi followed again as Celeste ran to the couch and hugged her mother. Turning to Mitzi, she explained, "This is my Mama." She hugged Michael and said, "This is my brother Michael."

She went back to Mitzi, threw her arms around her and explained, "This is my best friend in all the world. She took care of me when I was all alone and afraid."

Everyone in the room had tears of happiness and love in their eyes. Louise said, "I don't think I need to remind anyone to say a special prayer of thanks tonight..

The End

SPECIAL NOTE
ADDED BY AUTHOR

When my first granddaughter Sallie Louise, was three years old, I made up stories on tapes for her. Louise, in the story is named after this granddaughter. Through the years, I continued to do this for each grandchild. Later, in order to encourage them to enjoy reading, I made up a story about gifts I bought for them. They could not open the gift until they read the story. When I bought a small doll for my granddaughter Julie (Celeste), I started this story for her and just kept writing.

Doll that inspired the story.

ABOUT THE AUTHOR

Norma Nelson has thrilled and entertained her family and friends for years with her stories and poems. You might find one of her poems in many households, *My Children*, which was sold by the Hallmark Shop in Alexandria, Louisiana. She was born on a farm in Illinois. Norma received her Registered Nurse Degree at St.Joseph Hospital in Joliet, Ill. She and her husband raised four sons. Norma began her writing career by telling stories to her four young sons to keep them entertained. Many times, the neighborhood children joined the audience. Norma followed her husband Joe up the career ladder from Joliet and Aurora, Illinois to Cedar Rapids, Iowa to Alexandria, Louisiana. The couple retired to Fairfield Bay, Arkansas for seven years and then moved to Oak Ridge, North Carolina. They now reside in Mission, Texas. Other than writing, her favorite pastime is playing golf. Celeste is one of the many stories she has written.

Printed in the United States
72761LV00005B/1-108